Cherished
Refrain

Love's Cherished Refrain

As heartache settles upon Chloe Celeste's home, will the fulfillment of her mother's dream help rekindle the love she once knew?

Kay D. Rizzo

Pacific Press Publishing Association
Boise, Idaho
Oshawa, Ontario, Canada

Edited by Bonnie Tyson-Flyn
Designed by Tim Larson
Cover photo © Sinclair Studios
Typeset in 10/12 New Century Schoolbook

Copyright © 1994 by
Pacific Press Publishing Association
Printed in the United States of America
All Rights Reserved

Library of Congress Cataloging-in-Publication Data

Rizzo, Kay D., 1943-
   Love's cherished refrain / Kay D. Rizzo.
       p.   cm. —(Chloe Celeste chronicles : bk. 4)
   ISBN 0-8163-1222-2
   1. Spouses of clergy—United States. 2. Married women—
United States. 3. Missionaries—China. 4. Americans—China.
I. Title.   II. Series: Rizzo, Kay D., 1943- Chloe Celeste
chronicles : 4.
PS3568.I836L675 1994
813'.54—dc20   94-27523
                                    CIP

94 95 96 97 98 • 5 4 3 2 1

Contents

Books by Kay D. Rizzo

The Chloe Celeste Chronicles
Love's Tender Prelude
Winter's Silent Song
Sweet Strings of Love
Love's Cherished Refrain

The Chloe Mae Chronicles
Flee My Father's House
Silence of My Love
Claims Upon My Heart
Still My Aching Heart

For His Honor
I Will Die Free
Never a Dull Moment
She Said No

Dedication

To a gentle daughter in Israel
and a fellow "free spirit,"
Sharon Krueger

Characters

From the rigorous high desert of Oregon to the teeming cities of the Orient, the family saga continues. Passion and politics, vows and vengeance, romance and reality, circles within circles intertwine and blend as God works out His will in the lives of the Chamberlain clan.

CHLOE CELESTE (CEECEE) CHAMBERLAIN—Adventure calls the high-spirited, compassionate young woman to step out in faith, to settle lingering doubts regarding the man she loves and the God she serves.

THADDEUS (THAD) ADAMS—A call to arms challenges the strong, committed young man far beyond the sirens of war and his ideals. Following his heart's desire may cost him his wife, his home, and possibly his very life.

CYRUS AND CHLOE MAE CHAMBERLAIN—A steady, constant source of strength for one another and for their children—will their love survive the reality of the dreams of their youth?

ELIZABETH MASTERS—The sultry Southern belle schemes to ensnare a man of God. Will she destroy the work of the Lord in the little southwestern community as well?

DR. MORTON RAYBURN—Fascinating, witty, and charming, the urbane university professor flatters a lonely, grief-stricken young woman onto dangerous ground, challenging her morals and her loyalty toward the man to whom she vowed her love.

MANDARIN HO FENG—Ruthless to his enemies, inscrutable to his subjects, the imperial overlord searches for the wis-

dom to bend to the winds of change and for the power to with-
stand the forces of evil threatening his world.

CHIN SHUI—To what lengths will the rugged bodyguard go
to protect the life of the mandarin's son, Dao Lin, and the lives
of the foreign devils in his charge?

DR. GEORGE GIBSON—The blustering, autocratic Scots-
man, who wrestles against disease, principalities, and tradi-
tion on the Chinese frontier, must combat the green-eyed
enemy within to win his biggest battle.

The Crazy Quilt

"I've changed my mind!" I pounded my fist in the palm of my hand and paced to the far side of the small room, paused for a moment, then whirled about to challenge my imaginary confidante. "That's it! I've changed my mind—I can't go through with the wedding. Don't try to talk me out of it." I tapped my toe to the pounding of my heart. "It's for the best, really. How could I even consider getting married? I'm still just a kid."

I waited for her to speak. "Chloe Celeste Chamberlain, don't be foolish. You can't back out from marrying Thaddeus now, less than three weeks from the wedding! Be reasonable."

"I can, and I will!"

"Tsk! Tsk! Think of all the money your parents have spent on the wedding."

"Money? I don't care about the money. I-I-I'll work the next ten years to pay them back."

"Well, you should! And what about all your relatives who are traveling across the United States to witness your marriage?"

"W-e-l-l, we'll have a big reunion picnic, then send them home!"

The imaginary confidante shook her head slowly. "What's the real problem, CeeCee? Are you afraid Thad doesn't love you?"

I didn't hesitate. "No, I know he loves me."

"Do you love him?"

Again I answered quickly. "Yes!"

"Can you think of any reason you shouldn't marry him?" Her direct gaze penetrated my defenses.

11

"No."

"What about God?"

"What about Him?" I sauntered toward the open window.

"Do you believe God guided the two of you together?"

"Oh yes. I don't doubt it for a minute."

"Then what's the problem?"

"W-e-l-l, it's been so long since I've seen him."

"Excuses! CeeCee, you know that love is a decision, not an emotion."

"Y-e-s."

"You realize that you're acting like a seventeen-year-old kid instead of an adult of twenty-three."

"I know," I wailed and threw myself on the bed. "Oh, what shall I do?"

A knock sounded on the bedroom door. "CeeCee, are you all right?"

I lifted my face from the pillow. "I'm fine, Aunt Faith."

"May I come in?"

"Of course." I hopped off the bed and ran to open the door. Aunt Faith stepped into the room and glanced about, her face wreathed with questions. "I thought I heard you talking to someone."

I plopped back onto the bed and fell backward, gazing at the ceiling over my head. "No, Aunt Faith. There's no one here but me, I'm afraid—just me."

"I could have sworn— well, no matter. I hate to bother you, but Fred Winstock just came to the door to ask if you could go sit with his wife, Myrtle, until he could find the doctor. She's gone into labor too early."

I leapt from the bed and ran to the mirror to straighten my hair. "Sure, where does she live?"

Aunt Faith cast a wry little smile my way. "A mile or two east of town. I'll drive you there."

"Is this her first baby?" I drew my tortoise shell combs up from my hairline to the base of my tightly wound chignon, catching the curls that had escaped during my tirade.

"Yes, she's barely seventeen."

"It could be a while, no matter which way things go for her."

"Meet you out front," Aunt Faith called on her way out of the bedroom. During the two years I'd been in Oregon working as a government nurse at the Klamath Indian reservation, I'd come to appreciate my aunt's quiet wisdom. Though not a blood relative, her husband, Indian Pete, had been my real father's best friend. He had saved the lives of my mother, my older brother, and me after my father had died in a mining disaster. While we didn't see them much once he set up his law practice in southern Oregon, I grew up calling them Uncle Pete and Aunt Faith.

I placed my diary and fountain pen inside my black leather medical case, then grabbed the small travel Bible my mother had given me before I left New York City. I considered taking along my pad of stationery but changed my mind when I heard my aunt and uncle's Oldsmobile idling outside the bedroom window.

We'd barely cleared the edge of town when my aunt, a wise and gentle woman of very few words, said, "It's natural to be nervous anticipating one's wedding day, you know."

My face reddened. "You heard."

She smiled. "I'm sorry, but I couldn't help it."

I sank back in the leather seat.

The woman stared straight ahead as she guided the automobile over the rutted gravel road. "Before I married your Uncle Pete, I, too, was apprehensive. I was marrying a man of thirty who'd spent several years living with white people, who'd graduated from the white man's university, and who talked and acted more like a white man than a red man."

"It must have been terrifying for you."

She glanced my way and smiled. "It was until I realized that the thought of living the rest of my life without him was even more frightening."

I frowned and pushed back a cuticle. "A woman gives up so much for a man."

"Yes, she does."

"Thad expects me to traipse after him across the Southwest while he preaches the gospel. And just what does he expect me to do? I had dreams and goals too, you know."

"That is the way it's done. Someday, maybe our daughters

will marry men who consider their wives' goals and desires as well."

"Well, Thad does, kind of—and it's not that I don't want to go. It's just that I would have liked to have my opinions considered as well. My mother had to sell her women's clinic when my father uprooted the entire family to move us from San Francisco to New York, then to London. And Cy's one of the most considerate men I've ever known."

Aunt Faith chuckled. "Honey, you have put into words the lament of thousands of women throughout history."

"I vowed that it wouldn't happen to me. And here I am, planning the week after my wedding to go trotting after my husband to Texas, of all places!"

Aunt Faith looked serious. "It sounds to me as if this issue is important enough for you to discuss with Thad before the wedding. You're wearing a heavy mantel of anger, my dear."

I didn't reply, for I knew the woman didn't really understand. This was no ordinary case. *How can I confront Thad with my objections when he believes that God is leading us into this ministry? And what if He is? I've prayed and prayed during the last few days, but He's been silent.*

Aunt Faith eased the Oldsmobile to a stop in front of the Winstock cabin. And cabin it was—no paint, listing toward the east, a roof that needed new shakes, a porch with railings missing, chickens pecking for sustenance in the weed-choked yard.

My aunt placed her hand atop mine as I reached for the case on the seat between us. "God be with you."

I grinned. "Thanks. I'm sure everything will be all right in there."

"I don't mean in there. I mean with Thad."

"Oh." I averted my eyes. A scream from inside the cabin spurred me to grab my case and race to the front door.

I did what I could to make the frightened young woman comfortable, but the closeness of her contractions disturbed me. After I quieted her down, I suggested she rest to conserve her strength. Then, with nothing to do but wait, I wandered into the main room of the cabin, sat down at the rough oak table, and took out my diary.

Beginnings and endings, birthing and dying, goodbyes and hellos, cotton threads stitching together the lights and darks in life's crazy quilt. I tapped my fountain pen on the partially filled page of my diary and gazed across the room. The cloudy day's diffused light muted the reds, yellows, and oranges in the quilt covering my dozing patient.

Occasionally I get lucky and catch a lost stitch or tie off a loose thread and begin again. But for now, all I can do is pray and wait.

I wandered across the silent room and peered between the faded yellow-and-white gingham curtains at the bleak gray world beyond the windowpane. The chill seeping through the cracks around the windowpanes raised goose bumps on my arms despite my heavy wool sweater. *Sure is cold for the end of May.*

Snatching a threadbare towel from the washstand beneath the window, I stuffed the towel around the base of the window's rotting frame. Despite my effort, the cold air continued to seep into the cabin. *Oh, well, I tried.* I pressed my forehead against the cold glass and shivered.

Thaddeus Adams, where are you today? Studying for final tests? Walking along the shore of Lake Michigan? Sorting and packing your belongings for the journey west? Wherever you are, I sure do wish I were with you. Three weeks— I tried to bring a vision of my future into focus. *Three weeks, and we'll be Mr. and Mrs. Thaddeus Adams, together forever and ever and ever! Chloe Celeste Adams. How many times during the previous six months have I written those words? Fifty times? A hundred? Five hundred?* A low moan plunged me back into reality.

"Nurse Chamberlain?" A note of panic filled my patient's voice. "Nurse Chamberlain!"

"Coming, Myrtle." The curtain fluttered into place as I hurried into my patient's bedroom.

"I hurt! I hurt bad!" Creases of pain wreathed the young woman's face. "Is Doc Jenkins here yet?"

"No, not yet, but don't worry." I doused a faded rose face cloth in the water basin, wrung it out, and smoothed it across her sweaty brow. "This baby's kicking up a fuss, letting you know he's there. He'll settle down in a while."

"It's not time, Miss Chamberlain." Myrtle rolled her head from side to side on the pillow, her eyes squeezed closed. "I can't give birth today; it's too soon!"

"I know, honey. I know." I massaged the mother-to-be's pain-furrowed brow.

The young woman's eyes blinked open in fear. "My baby won't make it, will he, if he's born tonight?"

"One step at a time, OK? As the Good Book says, don't anticipate trouble before it arrives."

"Where does it say that, Miss Chamberlain?"

"You got me." I laughed and poured a fresh cup of chamomile tea into Myrtle's chipped Wedgwood china cup. "I don't know. Probably somewhere in Ecclesiastes, I'd guess. Here, take another sip of tea. It will help calm your nerves."

"Did I tell you that my grandmother brought this cup with her from England, by ship, then by covered wagon?" A tear trickled down her cheek. "It's the only one left from a china service for twenty. I had two, but Fred broke the other—" She turned her face to the wall. "—in a fit of anger. He was drunk. Are you sure he isn't back yet? I think I hear the wagon."

"I don't think so, but I'll go check if you wish."

"No!" She grabbed my hand. "I don't want to be alone. I appreciate your coming to be with me."

"I'm glad I was staying the night with Uncle Pete and Aunt Faith so that I could be here to help."

Without warning, the woman gasped, then cried out, "Help! Help me! Oh no, it's too late. It's too late!"

I dashed to the foot of the bed and lifted the top sheet. One glance, and I knew there was little I or anyone else could do. *Oh, dear God, if it's in Your plan, save the life of this tiny baby.* I grabbed a clean towel from the top of the stack that I'd earlier placed on the foot of the bed and smoothed it beneath the woman. *And this poor young girl. She's just begun to live.*

"I want my mama," the girl wailed.

I could agree with that. *I wish my mother were here to help also. Birthings are her specialty, not mine.* I never helped deliver a baby without remembering the stories my mother used to tell about the babies she had delivered on the Kansas frontier. Another cry, another push from my young patient, and I held in my hands the tiny oblong head of a newborn. "There, there, Myrtle. You're doing fine. We're almost there. Just a little longer."

After I guided the infant from the birth canal into my hands, the tiny, perfectly formed body lay quiet and limp, a bluish tone to its skin. I did everything I could to force the baby's lungs to expand, to inhale its first breath.

"My baby, give me my baby!" the woman screamed when I wrapped a blue flannel receiving blanket around the dead child and placed the body in the homemade wooden cradle beside the bed.

With heavy heart, I cared for the whimpering young mother. "What is it?"

"A boy," I whispered.

"A boy, my baby boy."

I didn't like Myrtle's pallor as I rinsed her face. She'd lost a lot of blood, and I hoped the herbal tea I'd insisted she drink immediately after the delivery would stop the hemorrhaging. Otherwise, all I could do was wait.

"I-I-I'm very tired," Myrtle whispered. "I feel so very tired."

"You should, sweetie. You worked hard. Close your eyes and rest."

Rest! We women haven't come too far over the years since my mother's days on the prairie, in spite of winning the right to vote and to drive automobiles. We have better sanitation and an anesthetic for pain, but when it comes to birthing a new life, not much has changed.

Feeling despondent and helpless, I gathered up the soiled linen and set it in a washtub outside the back door of the cabin, then gazed toward the distant mountains. *I will lift up mine eyes unto the hills, from whence cometh my help— where's Myrtle's help? Who can now help her infant son? I know, I know, Thy will be done. Thy will be done—*

As I stepped back inside the tiny cabin, an old, familiar promise surfaced in my brain. "*I will never leave thee, nor forsake thee.*" A smile crept onto my face unbidden. *Thanks, Lord, I needed that.*

The hissing and chugging of an automobile engine sent me

flying through the cabin and out the front door. "Dr. Jenkins!" I waved from the top of the porch steps.

The graying, slightly disheveled physician climbed out of his prewar Stanley Steamer and lumbered toward the porch steps. "Nurse Chamberlain, Fred said that he had sent for you. And how is our little mommy doing?"

I shook my head. "The baby—" My voice caught. "—was stillborn. Couldn't have weighed more than a couple of pounds. And Myrtle is hemorrhaging badly."

"Let's see what needs to be done." He plodded past me into the house and through the open bedroom door to the side of the iron bedstead. "Well, well, little lady. What's the big idea? You caught me in my cups, you know."

Hard to catch you in any other condition, Dr. Jenkins! I folded my arms and said nothing.

"Dr. Jenkins," the young girl sobbed, "my baby, my baby."

"I know. Nurse Chamberlain told me about the little tyke." He patted her arm. "But don't you worry none; there'll be more. Trust me, you and Fred will make a passel of kids before you're done."

I could tell by the pain in the woman's eyes that his words hadn't eased the agony of her loss. "What did I do wrong, Doctor? I must have done something wrong."

"Now, now, you didn't do anything wrong. These things happen with pregnancies, and no one knows why. Maybe it's God's way of getting rid of the malformed or the idiots."

I gasped at the man's insensitivity. The doctor glanced at me over his shoulder. "You got a better reason?"

I shrugged. The last thing I wanted was to get into another debate, philosophical or otherwise, with this man on my last day in Oregon. *You are one person, Dr. Jenkins, I will definitely not miss when I think of Oregon.*

He looked at me and snorted. "It's killing you to bite your tongue, isn't it, Nurse Chamberlain? Well, you better learn to do just that if you plan to work anywhere but in this remote outpost of society. You're lucky I've been so patient with you!"

I could tell by his quirky grin that he was goading me. *You're enjoying this, aren't you? You'd love for me to blow up at you one more time. Forget it!*

The sound of the cabin door slamming afforded me the escape I needed. "It sounds like Fred is home. So, if there's nothing else, Doctor, I'll be on my way." I took Myrtle's hand in mine. "I'll be praying for you. God bless."

Tears filled the woman's eyes. "Thank you, Nurse Chamberlain. You're going to be missed."

After Fred burst into the bedroom, I slipped past him and out of the cabin. I didn't want to hear his excuses; the smell on his breath betrayed the true reason for his delay. For the men of the region, drinking moonshine or bathtub gin was as much a part of their daily fare as bread or potatoes. *Another aspect of southern Oregon I won't miss.*

I walked the two miles back into Klamath Falls, where I'd been staying with Uncle Pete and Aunt Faith for a few days before heading south to San Francisco for the wedding. As I walked, I had time to reminisce.

Leaving my friends at the reservation, especially Nina, had torn me apart. The combined farewell party and bridal shower they had held for me was an event to remember. I thought of Nina's gift, a black leather family Bible embossed with gold lettering. *Thad and I will treasure it always.*

When Calvin Blair strode into the decorated recreation hall at the reservation, I had reddened. I hadn't seen him much since we had broken our engagement at Christmastime—my fault, not his. "Can't stay for the party, CeeCee. I have a mare in labor, but I wanted to say goodbye and wish you and Thaddeus God's blessing. He's a great guy."

"Thank you, Cal. I-I don't know what to—"

He lifted a hand to stop me. "Hey, I don't know if you heard, but there's a new schoolmarm over Medford way. They says she hails from Boston. I've been thinking of paying my respects."

"That would be wonderful, Cal." He met and held my gaze for an instant, his eyes revealing both sadness and love. Clearing his throat, he handed me a large mahogany box with a hand-tooled leather insert on the lid.

"Here. This is for your new Bible. Nina and I conspired."

"You two! How can I ever thank you? It's beautiful."

Nina placed her hand on my shoulder. "Cal tooled the leather himself."

"Really?" I fingered the detailed scrollwork.

"Yeah, old Dobbin will never be the same again."

"What? Dobbin?"

"Dobbin, my favorite horse, of course. Gave his all, he did."

I stared, my mouth gaping in horror.

Nina slapped Cal's arm as the two of them doubled over with laughter. "Gotcha a good one that time!" Cal chortled.

Blushing, I sputtered, "That isn't even funny!" The other party guests joined in the laughter. "Well, it isn't!"

I'd learned during the two years I'd spent living among these open and honest westerners that they found nothing more humorous than to put one over on a "foreigner," as they liked to call anyone born and bred in a city.

I smiled to myself on the lonely road back into town and kicked a large pebble with the toe of my boot. Yeah, there's a lot I'll miss—wearing such comfortable boots, for one! I wrinkled my nose at the thought of wearing the white satin pumps with the narrow French heels and pointed toes that my mother had purchased for my wedding day.

"Be advised, CeeCee dear," she'd written, "of the lines 'till death do us part' because this is the only wedding I intend to organize for you. One for you and one for Phoebe—that's it!"

I could only imagine the folderol Mama had gone through doing the things brides usually do while I finished out my contract in Oregon. *Making wedding plans via the U.S. mail will make the job of helping my stepsister plan for her wedding seem like planning for an afternoon tea.*

That night, as I prepared to retire, I wrote my last Oregon entry.

Klamath Falls, Oregon

Dear Emily, It's so strange. What starts out to be so simple—two kids romping on a Cape Cod beach—becomes unbelievably complicated when the subject of marriage enters the picture. I dread exchanging the tranquility of Oregon for the confusion and chaos of the next few weeks. If it weren't for Thad, I'd disappear into the Cascades until the event faded from my memory. In some ways, none of it seems real anyway.

It had been five months since I had kissed Thad goodbye at the railway station in Oakland, and then, two days later left from the same depot for Klamath Falls. Only his constant flow of letters kept him alive to me, the letters and the memories of our two weeks together at my parents' home in San Francisco.

If our two weeks together were dreamlike, the two days in between Thad's departure and mine were an accompanying nightmare of dress fittings, choosing wedding announcements, and making a thousand and one other decisions in preparation for the far-off event. The tension in me eased only with the rumble of the steam engine's wheels taking me north to Oregon. Once back at the reservation, I had little time to think about a Bavarian-lace wedding gown, a fifteen-foot-long silk veil, and a pearl tiara. Thad's letter telling about his assignment as an assistant to a traveling evangelist in the Southwest did little to trigger my excitement, despite his colorful imagery. I'd never seen Texas or Oklahoma, but I remembered Kansas all too well.

However, the night before I said my last goodbye to Oregon, I had more than enough time to face the reality of my situation. *Wedded life? What am I thinking, Lord? Thad and me? During the past four years, we've spent so little time together, and now I'm supposed to follow him across the desert Southwest? I'm supposed to vow to love and honor a man whom I know mostly through letters? Oh, God, what am I doing?*

The next morning, my stomach knotted at the first rumble of the southbound train steaming into the station. My friends from the reservation, Nina, and Cal came to say goodbye. My Aunt Faith kissed me on the cheek, reminding me that she and Uncle Pete would see me at the wedding in two weeks. I nodded, too overcome with emotion to speak, and simply stared tearfully at the loving faces surrounding me, smiling and wishing me well. *Father, where's that peace You promised was mine? I need a major dose right now!*

He must have answered my prayer because once I was settled on board, I slept—past some of the most spectacular scenery in the Western Hemisphere, through the dusty towns of northern California, and past grazing cattle and sheep in the Central

Valley. I awakened in time to straighten my beige felt hat and slip into the jacket of my forest green gabardine traveling suit before the train screeched to a stop at the Oakland station, where I was caught up in a flurry of swirling skirts, excited family members, and last-minute wedding crises.

Parents; brothers and sisters, including Jamie and his bride, Auriel; grandparents; aunts, uncles, cousins—the Oakland depot will never be the same again, and this is only the beginning, I thought. *Cousin Ashley and her brood, along with Uncle Ian and Aunt Drucilla, will be arriving in two days, according to my mother.*

Before my father's shiny new Packard stopped in front of my parents' estate on Russian Hill, I'd chosen the porcelain dove place-card holders over the porcelain cherubs, vetoed beaver top hats for the male attendants, insisted on the already-planned garden reception rather than the one my Grandmother McCall suggested we hold in a downtown hotel ballroom, and settled a disagreement between my mother and Phoebe as to whether the female attendants should wear feather-and-lace headpieces with their pastel-blue-and-lavender gowns or a garland of daisies and forget-me-nots. The garland and my mother won.

I treasured my two escapes during the days and nights that followed—my violin practice time each afternoon and my late-night forays to the gazebo. For years, I'd used my practice time as a mental escape. But with all the guests arriving and wedding arrangements being made, I found that I needed a physical escape as well.

It was there in the garden behind the house where my Granddaddy Spencer, my maternal grandfather, found me the night before Thad's train was to arrive.

The evening had been quiet, with only family members present, one of the last we'd enjoy until after the wedding. Even my stepbrother, Nikolai, had tried to be sociable. After everyone had retired for the night, I ran to my room to get my shawl. The evenings near the bay could be cool even in mid-June.

Pausing to free my hair from the confining pins and combs, I then brushed the snarls and knots from the heavy red strands, vowing for the hundredth time to cut it off—"after the wedding!"

Quickly, I caught it up on the back of my head with a set of turquoise and silver combs Mama had purchased for me at a small shop in town. I twisted my head from side to side in front of the mirror on my dressing table and smiled. *That should hold it in place for a while. Maybe I should change my dress; I'd hate to catch this lavender silk dress on a rosebush or something. Oh, forget it.* I grabbed the white mohair shawl draping the foot of my bed and dashed from the room.

Hidden from view in the shadows of the gazebo, I was enjoying the lights of the city below me, when a familiar voice startled me.

"Nervous, huh?"

"Oh! You startled me, Granddaddy. I didn't hear you coming."

"Mind if I join you?"

"Of course not."

"It's been a rough two weeks for you, hasn't it?"

I shrugged. "There's always so much to do when planning a wedding, you know."

"Quite different from your mother's wedding to Cy."

"Another time, another place," I muttered and leaned my head against one of the gazebo's graceful arches.

"I should say. Getting hitched should be a simple process—say 'I do' and get on with life! The more money one has, the more fuss and bother the event causes."

I chuckled at the ire in his voice.

"Hmmph! Top hats and tails and silk cravats. Puttin' on airs!"

"Mama's done well to control the extravagance, considering her and Daddy's social standing here in the community. You and she are alike in so many ways."

He grunted. "My brown worsted-wool suit should be good enough for any society."

"It's different for a man than it is for a woman, Granddaddy. Mama's filling the role she assumed when she married Daddy." I hugged my arms around my waist. Voicing the thought that had been tumbling inside my mind for weeks gave it substance, a reality.

"And, you, how do you feel about assuming the role Thaddeus

has designed for you?"

How did— I turned toward him but could see only the outline of his sturdy form. Silence hung between us, a veil of fear and doubt. I licked my lips and closed my eyes. "I, uh, I—"

A wave of warmth and love filled me as Granddaddy drew me into his arms. I could feel the soft fleece of his blue plaid flannel shirt against my moist cheek. "Oh, Granddaddy, why did you have to ask me that question? I was doing fine until—"

"Sh-sh-sh, it's all right, child. Everyone's afraid now and then—afraid to confront themselves with the consequences of their decisions."

Needing reassurance, I snuggled deeper into his arms.

"Your mother taught me a lot about being honest with one's self. After she ran away from home, I missed her so much, but I couldn't get past my foolish pride to tell her so."

"This is different."

"Not really. If God is trying to tell you that you're making a mistake committing to this man, you'd better listen."

"Thad and I have prayed, both together and separately, about this decision. And by all indications—"

"You're a long time married, my girl."

"We're not entering this marriage in haste. Maybe it's nothing more than prewedding jitters."

"That's probably closer to the truth—that and your unusual courtship. You must admit that a long-distance love is not the easiest to maintain." His voice grew warm as he rubbed my neck. "Having said all that, I believe you'll have your answer tomorrow when you see him again."

"I hope you're right, Grandpa."

"Aren't I always?" I could hear the mischief in his voice.

"I just wish I could see into the future."

A comforting chuckle arose from deep within his chest. "What? And spoil life's greatest adventure?"

Grandpa turned in the direction of the approaching rumble of an automobile. "Who would be arriving here at this hour?"

I cocked my head toward the noise. "Maybe they're just driving past on the—" I paused at the splay of headlights washing the shrubbery on the north side of the house. "You're right.

They've stopped by the front portico."

Our curiosity drew us to the front of the house, where we spotted a late-model Ford coupe idling in front of the house. I paused behind an oleander bush to watch two men climb out of the car and stretch. Above our heads, interior houselights came on.

"I wonder what they want?" I whispered.

"Guess I'd better go find out, don't you think?" Granddaddy strode toward the strangers. "May I help you, gentlemen?" he called.

"This is the Chamberlain residence, it is not?" The familiar voice sent an electric current through my body, and I steadied myself against the nearest arch.

Once I'd regained my composure, I emerged from the shadows. "Thad! What on earth are you doing here?"

"I think I'm here to get married." His laughter filled the night air.

The porch light blinked on, and my parents stepped out of the house. Feeling suddenly uncertain and scared, my footsteps slowed as I approached the car. *I'm not ready for this, Lord. I was supposed to have until tomorrow, remember?*

My hesitancy triggered a similar response from Thad. While the sound of greetings and laughter echoed off the arches behind us, Thad and I paused six feet apart, staring at one another for what seemed a lifetime. I wondered for an instant if Thad could read the indecision in my eyes. Somewhere in the night, I heard someone call my name, then Thad's, followed by laughter, for neither of us responded. Then the front door closed; the porch light went out, bathing the two of us in darkness.

"CeeCee." Thad's voice trembled. Tentatively, he closed the gap between us, his arms extended. As I lifted my hands to meet his, he caught my hands in his and drew me to him. "I've missed you."

To Love and to Honor

I tried to speak, but the words stuck in my throat. Still holding my hands, Thaddeus took a step closer. "You look so lovely, standing there in the moonlight, that I'm almost afraid to touch you."

I smiled slowly. "Thaddeus, I—"

He kissed my fingertips tenderly, never shifting his gaze from mine. "You are as beautiful as I remembered."

Still grasping my hands, he tipped his head toward me. On tiptoe, I met him halfway. When our lips touched, a familiar warmth flooded through me. As our kiss deepened and Thad gathered me into his arms, my doubts dissolved—just as Granddaddy Spencer had predicted. It felt good to be home. It was as if the months I'd spent in Oregon and he'd spent in Michigan had been only days. Thad kissed me a dozen times between bouts of laughter and excited talk. We had so much to share.

He began with information about our new car. "When my dad showed up at the college with a brand-new car as our wedding present and the invitation to drive across the country together, I could hardly decline," Thad explained as I examined the Ford coupe he'd driven west. "It was good for Dad and me to spend time together. We cleaned out a lot of old wounds, chugging across the plains together, I can tell you. In time, by the grace of God, they'll heal."

"Oh, Thad, I'm glad you each took the time to clear things up between you." I gave his arm a squeeze as we strolled across the red-brick driveway toward the front door. "And I'm delighted that you're finally here!"

"Me too! When did this country get so big?" He opened the front door for me.

I laughed and planted a light kiss on his lips. "I've missed you, Thaddeus Adams."

Sweeping me into his arms, Thad kissed me hard. "And I you, Chloe Celeste Chamberlain, soon-to-be-Adams."

"Hey, you two," a voice behind us boomed. "You'll have the rest of your lives to carry on like that." My father laughed. "Perhaps you could let the rest of us get some sleep."

The rest of our lives— Somehow the idea seemed less intimidating than it had earlier.

As I listened and watched Thad interacting with my family and me during the few days we had left before the wedding, my confidence grew. I loved the twinkle he got in his eyes whenever anyone asked him about his appointment as assistant to evangelist G. L. Millikin. His excitement at the prospect of helping with tent meetings across the Southwest became contagious. Mama and my stepsister Phoebe glowed whenever Thad talked about it. Only my father seemed unimpressed with the prospect.

I wanted to talk with Daddy about his doubts, but parties and fitting appointments kept us apart until the night before the wedding. It had been agreed that Thad would spend the night at Uncle Phillip and Aunt Jenny's place so as not to see me before the wedding. Once I told him good night and he left with my relatives, I slipped up to my room, snagged my shawl from the rocker in my bedroom, and hurried out to my favorite getaway.

As I entered the gazebo, I heard a rustle in the shadows.

"CeeCee." My father stepped out of the shadows. "Don't be alarmed. It's only me."

I whirled about to face him. "Daddy! What are you doing out here?"

"Waiting to see you."

"But how did you—"

He chuckled. "You don't think your evening escapes have gone unnoticed, do you?"

"Daddy! You mean you and Mama knew—" My hand flew to my mouth.

"CeeCee." My father chuckled again. "Of course, we knew. There've been a few late nights these last two weeks."

"What?"

"Your mother wouldn't think of coming to bed until she heard the back door close with you safe inside the house. She takes being a mother hen seriously."

"Oh, I'm so embarrassed."

Slipping his arm around my waist, he strolled with me over to the scenic side of the gazebo. "No, don't be. We understood that you two needed time together, alone."

"I hope you and Mama know that Thaddeus and I did nothing—"

My father whispered in my ear the way he had so often silenced my worries when I was a child. "Shh, do you think I would have stayed in our bedroom if I had thought otherwise?"

I laughed, imagining my father storming the gazebo wearing his nightshirt and brandishing a fireplace poker. "Thad has always been a perfect gentleman, Daddy, like you."

He gave my waist a squeeze. "That's good. If it were otherwise and I found out, the wedding ceremony would not take place. Nature may have made you my stepdaughter, but in my heart, you always have been and always will be wholly and completely my daughter."

I could only imagine how he'd react if he thought any man, Thad or anyone else, had forced himself on me. "So, tell me, why were you waiting to ambush me?"

He didn't answer immediately. When he did, his voice was filled with emotion. "I didn't want to give away my beautiful daughter until I felt confident she understood the life she's chosen and was up to the demands of the task."

"What do you mean, 'up to the demands'? Don't you think I'm ready for marriage?" I studied his profile in the moonlight.

"It won't be an easy life, hopping from town to town, living in dusty little hotel rooms, everything you own contained in two steamer trunks and a couple of suitcases."

"Life on the Klamath Reservation wasn't easy; neither was

the time at Chamonix, living in one room with a bunch of nurses and no hot water," I reminded. "But I survived."

"This will be different. Then, you could always come home. After tomorrow, your home will be with Thaddeus."

Your home will be with Thaddeus— Your home will be with Thaddeus— Your home will be with Thaddeus— My father's words played through my mind the next morning as my cousin Ashley fastened the long row of buttons down the back of the white Bavarian-lace wedding gown. I nervously ran my fingertips over silk embroidered roses on the overskirt while Phoebe buttoned the pearl buttons on the eight-inch lace cuffs.

"Will you stand still and stop fidgeting?" Phoebe demanded. "These nasty little buttons are difficult enough to fasten without your perpetual motion."

I took a deep breath. "I'm sorry. I'm trying, honest. I'm trying."

"Let her be," Ashley defended. "A woman has good reason to be fretful before her wedding. She has no idea what she's getting herself—" My cousin stopped midsentence. I glanced over my shoulder and found her biting her lip and blinking back tears. After swallowing hard, she continued, "Be happy, dear CeeCee. Be happy."

"Thank you, Ashley." I turned and hugged her, and she buried her face in my shoulder.

"Well." Phoebe straightened and adjusted the neckline of her dress. "When Jonathan and I get married—"

My stepsister babbled on about herself and her professor sweetheart, but my cousin and I didn't hear. We stood poised on the threshold of adulthood—Ashley on one side, me on the other. *Your home will be with Thaddeus—*

"—your hair. CeeCee, are you listening?"

"Huh? What?"

"Hello, dear." Ashley laughed and waved one hand before my face. I blinked, surprised to find myself seated at my dressing table, the mirror before me. I could see my mother's reflection. She sat on the end of my bed, the perfect mother of the bride, draped in a lavender print silk gown and dabbing at her eyes with a lace handkerchief.

"Do you still want curls piled on top of your head, even though your veil will cover most of them?" The moment Ashley arrived from the east, she had declared herself my personal hairstylist, much to Phoebe's disgust.

"On top."

"I really think it would be more dramatic—"

"On top."

"OK, OK. On top it is." She grabbed a handful of my hair with one hand and a hairbrush with the other. I endured my cousin's ministrations patiently. When she pinned the mother-of-pearl tiara and the attached multilayered veil on my head, Phoebe sighed and Mama sniffled.

I stood to examine the total effect in the mirror. The scalloped edges of the calf-length gown that tapered into a six-foot train behind me revealed my white silk hose and satin slippers. Phoebe placed a giant bouquet of roses and calla lilies in my hands. *Is this me? Really me?* Big frightened eyes stared back at me as my cousin lowered the blush veil over my face.

Oh, dear God, what have I done this time? I glanced at my cousin's bittersweet smile and gulped. *Please reassure me that I'm not making a mistake.*

"To love and to honor, from this day forward . . ." I recited the words as my father's shiny new Packard eased to a stop in front of the imposing gray stone church my parents had attended since returning to California. The strains of Vivaldi's "Ode to Spring" wafted through the open doors.

At the top of the stairs, Auriel, Ashley, and Phoebe waited, along with my mother and Granddaddy Spencer. The rest of the clan awaited my arrival from inside the sanctuary. As my father took my gloved hand and assisted me from the car, Granddaddy Spencer bounded down the church steps to meet me.

"Before I take my seat—" Granddaddy Spencer grabbed my hand. "—I want to give you something for good luck, as in 'something old, something new, something borrowed, something blue.' Here's a sixpence for your shoe." He pressed a twenty-dollar gold piece into the palm of my hand. My mouth dropped open as I stared in surprise at the rare gold coin. "You might want to carry it in your glove instead of your shoe, or you'll find yourself limping up the center aisle. It's the last of the gold coins your great-grandfather entrusted to me." The old man kissed my cheek, then chuckled.

I glanced at my father, then at Granddaddy. I knew the story of Mama's gold coin—or I should say, her two gold coins, since she had married a second time after my real father died. "Thank you. I will treasure it always."

He shook his finger in my face. "You'll treasure it until you need to trade it for food or for shelter!"

I admired the gold glinting in the sunlight. "Mama still has her gold pieces, you know."

From atop the steps, my mother, as if she'd heard me mention her name, called to my grandfather. "It's time for you to go in, Papa."

He patted my hand. "Your mama has been lucky never to need to use it. God willing, you will experience a similar life." He nodded toward my father, kissed me again, and bounded up the steps with the energy of a man twenty years younger.

Jamie's wife, Auriel, my matron-of-honor, waited from the top of the stairs as Ashley and Phoebe rushed down the steps to gather the yards and yards of rustling silk netting flowing from my tiara while Daddy took my arm and led me solemnly to the top of the church steps.

Some woman I'd never met before whisked me into the church foyer while shushing Phoebe's and Ashley's excited giggles. The woman signaled for my mother and her escort to enter the sanctuary. With tears in her eyes, Mama kissed my cheek, then lowered the blush veil over my face. "Be happy, my darling. Be happy." I could only nod and bite my lip.

When the double doors swung open, I gasped at the beauty of the scene before me. The sunlight streaming through the stained-glass windows sent a kaleidoscope of red, blue, green, and purple lights dancing about the room. The brass candelabras lining the center aisle sparkled, adding a warm glow to the church's gray-stone interior.

My eyes widened at the size of the eager crowd awaiting my appearance. Friends and business associates of my parents whom I did not know, women with whom my mother and Aunt Jenny worked at the clinic, Uncle Pete and Aunt Faith from Oregon, Aunt Bea from Kansas, the Putnams from Denver, Uncle Joe and Aunt Beth, Granddaddy Spencer, Uncle Ian and Aunt Drucilla, Ashley's husband and children, Grandma and Grandpa McCall—so many people had traveled hundreds of miles to celebrate this day with Thad and me. *So many people, so much love.* Grandfather and Grandmother Chamberlain, Uncle Phillip and Aunt Jenny, cousins I hardly knew, all gathered in one place to wish us happiness. Overwhelming gratitude swept through me. *If ever a couple were given a loving send-off—*

I tightened my hold on my father's arm as Pastor Fraelich, my brother Rusty, and my stepbrother Nikolai took their places on the platform, followed by my brother Jamie and a pale Thaddeus. I took a deep breath. *This is it.*

While Ashley, Phoebe, and Auriel strolled down the long center aisle, I spotted Thad's father sitting alone in the front pew and wondered what he felt on the day of his only son's wedding, the son whom time and God had restored to him. A sob caught in my throat.

Daddy looked down at me and patted my arm. "Are you all right?"

I nodded, noting the tears glistening in his eyes.

"You are utterly beautiful, darling. I'm so proud of the woman you've become."

"Don't make me cry!" I sniffled, thankful that my blush veil was of a tighter weave than the rest of the veil's netting.

"Me? You don't need me to make you cry. Between you and your mother, the padding in the shoulders of this suit are waterlogged! I could probably wring out the excess with my bare hands."

I giggled at the idea. Suddenly, my breath caught when, at the front of the church, Dr. Bohn, my first violin teacher, stood and poised his instrument, awaiting the introduction from the organist. As if splashed with ice water, all my levity vanished. I took a deep breath and closed my eyes, allowing the opening chords of "The Bridal March" to wash over me.

I felt a hand urge me forward. I heard the flowers in my bridal bouquet rustle in my quaking hand. And I tasted a bittersweet panic. Like a mechanical doll with a windup key in the middle of her back, I moved stiffly down the aisle. At the end of the aisle, Thad stood waiting, watching.

At the midpoint of my journey, I looked up to find a stream of dazzling sunlight coursing Thad's smiling face. The paleness I'd noted earlier as he entered the sanctuary was gone. Now he stood straight, tall, and confident at the base of the altar steps. As I drew closer, he gave me a lopsided smile and lifted one eyebrow as if to ask a question. *This is the friend who terrified me with visions of razor-tailed snakes, who rescued my shoes from the Atlantic's surging tide, who drew sketches of me while I danced barefoot through the waves.*

That familiar gesture warmed me as little else could at that moment. Tenderness and love filled his eyes. *This is the friend who comforted me after my precious Au Sam died, who kissed me in the shadows under a bridge on the River Seine, who res-cued me from a New York speak-easy, who—* Like the whispering scent of lilacs on a spring morning, peace filled my troubled mind, and my doubts vanished.

The rest of the service, I hardly remember. Nor can I recall much of the garden reception that followed. My memory is blurry about standing in a reception line greeting our guests and thanking them for attending, about cutting the multitiered wedding cake, and about posing with Thad in my parents' impressive foyer for our wedding photo.

My senses returned when my mother and Auriel whisked me away to change into my going-away outfit—the turquoise brocade mandarin wedding dress given to me so many years before by Au Sam.

From the moment I'd announced that I would wear the mandarin-style dress as my going-away outfit, all of my female kith and kin had an opinion on my decision. Aunt Drucilla was horrified, and my Aunt Jenny, fascinated. My Grandma McCall believed the dress to be the garb of a heathen; therefore, my decision was somehow un-Christian. And when Auriel heard, she sniffed into her hankie, "I've never heard of anything more beautiful."

Ashley threw her hands into the air. "I'm surprised you didn't wear it for the wedding ceremony." When I told her that I'd seriously considered it, she shook her head and rolled her eyes.

My mother didn't voice her opinion over the dress, but I knew she was delighted. She quietly watched as I restyled my hair to allow my copper-colored locks to cascade loosely around my face. Then she and Auriel helped me slip the treasured dress over my head.

Immediately, Auriel began fastening the fabric-covered buttons on the tightly fitting sleeves while my mother closed the long row of fabric-covered buttons that trailed down the side of the garment from the high mandarin collar. As she slipped the fabric loops over the buttons, my mother whispered, "Dear Au Sam would be so pleased. She would be so pleased."

I slipped my feet into the turquoise satin slippers my mother had purchased from a shop near her clinic in Chinatown and draped over my arm a shawl that my Grandmother Chamberlain had brought with her from Maryland.

My mother stepped back to inspect the results. "Au Sam would have loved to be here today." Mama brushed an imaginary piece of lint from the skirt. "She would have loved to see you wearing your gift—a perfect fit, I might add." I tried to picture the smiling face of my childhood governess but couldn't.

Has it been that long, Lord?

Auriel kissed me on the cheek. "You will stop by our new home in Springville before you head east for Texas, won't you?"

"Of course, we will. I'm so excited about your and Jamie's new medical practice. And I'm glad you'll be closer to the folks too."

"Well, Springville is still a two- or three-day drive from San Francisco, but that's a lot better than Chamonix, France, I guess."

I glanced down at Auriel's slightly convex abdomen. "And you will have Jamie call me as soon as the baby is born?"

Auriel ran her hand across her stomach and smiled. "Absolutely, Auntie CeeCee."

"It's time," my mother whispered as she handed me the bridal bouquet. "Your luggage is already loaded in the trunk of the

Ford." She kissed my cheek and sniffled. "You look beautiful, darling."

I smiled and blushed.

"Count slowly to ten before you come out of the room," Auriel cautioned as she took my mother's hand and led her into the hallway. "We'll send Thaddeus to meet you at the landing. Throw the bouquet from there."

I breathed deeply two more times and nodded. "*One, two, three*—" As I counted, I could hear the guests assembling at the base of the stairs. "*Four, five, six, oh boy, seven, eight, nine, ten. Here goes.*"

I stepped out into the hallway and saw Thad smiling up at me from the landing. His look of recognition told me he remembered the afternoon in the New York town house when he had caught me modeling the mandarin dress. An audible gasp rippled through the crowd. *Yes, my decision to wear Au Sam's gift had been right.* Smiling, I walked to meet my groom.

After tossing the bouquet directly at Phoebe, I took Thad's hand, and we raced through the gauntlet of streamers, rice, and well-wishers to our waiting automobile. Somewhere along the way, I remember kissing my father and my grandparents goodbye.

Once the car was out of the driveway and on the street, I leaned back against the seat and sighed. "It's finally over!"

Thad drew me across the seat closer to his side. "Ah, but it's only the beginning." He smiled lovingly at me. "Good afternoon, Mrs. Adams."

"Good afternoon, Pastor Adams."

"Have I told you how beautiful you look?"

"Why, no, you haven't."

"When you walked out of your room in that dress, you took my breath away. Your gorgeous red hair, the blue of the dress— a true vision of loveliness. It's a memory I will take to my grave."

"Thank you, Pastor Adams." I shot him a coy smile. "Do you like it better than the wedding gown?"

"That's not a fair question."

"What do you mean?"

"There are no words to describe the almost spiritual awe a

man feels when his beloved comes to him clothed in bridal white. It's a moment unlike any other in a lifetime."

I smiled.

"Yet this dress— I clearly remember the first time I saw you wearing it. In your parents' town house, remember?"

"I remember."

He glanced over at me appreciatively.

I grinned up at him. "Some say the mandarin dress is the most alluring garment in the world."

"They could be right." He winked at me and grinned. "There's something I've been dreaming of doing since the first time I met you."

"Oh?" I eyed him curiously.

"May I?"

I hesitated. "I-I-I guess so."

Removing one hand from the wheel, he reached around behind me and removed one of the turquoise combs holding my hair in place. As a portion of my hair tumbled to my shoulders, thad sucked in his breath. Carefully, he removed the second comb and then the third. I helped him by removing the hairpins myself, until my curls were free and swirling about my face.

"Oh, CeeCee, my imagination didn't do you justice." He ran his fingers through my hair, wrapping one lock around a finger. Slowly, he drew the curl along my chin line. "Have I told you today how much I love you?"

I pursed my lips into a pout. "Actually, I don't think you have, not today, anyway."

"Really? Could I be bold and do so now?"

"W-e-l-l—"

"Chloe Celeste Adams, I love you so very much." He gazed at me, his eyes filled with tenderness.

"And I love you, Thaddeus."

The blare of a horn startled both of us. Thad jerked the wheel to the right, swerving our Ford out of the way of a late-model Cadillac. He shot an embarrassed grin at me. "Guess we'd better save our declarations of love for one another until we safely reach the honeymoon suite."

"That's probably a good idea." I blushed and grinned sheepishly.

The next morning, after breakfast on the private balcony of our suite, we returned to my parents' home to open the rest of our wedding gifts. We had to choose which gifts we could take east to Amarillo with us and which we would have shipped to us later.

Thad and his father drove downtown with my father to take care of some business while my mother and I opened and recorded all our gifts. Silver, pewter, china, linen—I couldn't believe the generosity of our friends and family. Next, I sorted my personal belongings and packed my steamer trunk. With the men gone and the visiting relatives touring the city for the day, I was thankful for some time alone with my mother.

"I can tell by the glow on your faces how happy you two are," she said as she reattached a loose button to my favorite blouse. "I'm glad. I hate having the two of you go so far away, but I am glad you'll be doing the Lord's work." She paused. "Jamie and Auriel will leave on Wednesday. It's hard letting go."

"Do you think I should take this dress with me, Mama?" I held up a wine-colored wool traveling suit with a matching hat. "Isn't it too fancy for Texas?"

"It looks good on you. I think you should take it along. You might be surprised at what the women of Texas are wearing this season."

I laughed and added the dress to the growing pile of clothing. My mother got teary when I packed away the shelf of yearly diaries I'd begun keeping at the age of thirteen. "Don't worry. I'm going to keep them. Or—" I winced. "I was hoping you would keep them for me, along with some of my other treasures."

She grinned. "Like we've been doing all along?"

"Uh-huh—" I nodded.

"Sure, we'll store them in the attic alongside the crates of your old toys that I boxed before we left New York."

That evening the entire family gathered for one last dinner together, since Thad and I would be the first to leave. During one of my Uncle Phillip's tirades against the latest movement for racial equality among the Negro population, he punctuated his remarks with, "Next thing you know, they'll be running for public office!" Having uttered his prophetic remark, he took a sip of water.

"And why not?" my mother asked. "It's been a long time coming, if you ask me. I can see the day when a person of Asian background or American Indian—" Her eyes danced with deviltry, "—maybe even a woman will run for public office and win!"

Uncle Phillip gasped, choking on his drink.

"Hear! Hear!" Uncle Pete pounded his fist on the arm of the chair.

"And who knows, you may one day defend a case before a female judge too." The feather on Aunt Jenny's glittering headband fluttered as she accentuated her predictions with a nod.

Uncle Ian glanced toward Thad and me. "Thaddeus, an old politician like you must have a prediction or two to make."

Thad smiled. "I steer clear of such subjects, sir. But I'll be glad to discuss with you the meaning of the beasts of Daniel two or the horsemen of Revelation."

"Nightmares and horrors!" Uncle Phillip exclaimed in mock dismay. "What have you done to us, CeeCee? We've inducted a preacher into the clan!"

Uncle Joe laughed. "Too bad the young'uns are leaving town tomorrow. From the sound of it, you could use a little churching there, Phillip."

As the two men continued the banter, I whispered into Thad's ear, "Isn't this the craziest family you've ever seen?"

He glanced over at his own father, then back at me. "My father looks totally baffled by it all. But I love it!"

"Good." I settled back against his arm. "For better, for worse, remember?"

Before we ended the evening, my father gathered us together for a prayer.

"Tomorrow, many of you will be heading in different directions—Shinglehouse, Annapolis, Boston, New York, Springville—" He paused and looked across the circle at me. "—and Amarillo, Texas. All of us will pack away the memories of these last few days to resume our daily routines. CeeCee, before you and Thad depart, each of us wants to add one more gift to your wedding memories."

My father reached into his pocket for a piece of note paper, then handed it to me. I opened it and read it out loud, " 'Love one another; as I have loved you.' John 13:34. Wherever you are, wherever you go, I'm but a phone call away. Love, Daddy." My eyes grew misty.

My mother handed me a second note. Inside, it read, " 'Many daughters have done virtuously, but thou excellest them all.' Proverbs 31:29. Always maintain your dignity and your faith in God. Love, Mama."

One after another, the people I love handed me love notes, promises from God's Word. Even Uncle Phillip wrote out the message found in Ecclesiastes 3:1. " 'To everything there is a season, and a time to every purpose under the heaven.' With love, your Uncle Phillip."

When I'd received the last of the love notes, Daddy had prayer. Then Thad and I lingered at the door to wish each of our family good night.

The next morning, after a series of painful goodbyes, Thad and I climbed into our overloaded Ford and headed south and east to Yosemite National Park. For months, Thad had been sending me brochures and articles on the valley's breathtaking scenery. He'd convinced me that the park would be the perfect place to spend our first week together as husband and wife. At the first glimpse of the spectacular valley, I understood why it had become California's most popular tourist spot, with or without President Teddy Roosevelt's famous visit.

Far and Distant Places

Lazy days hiking to the falls, water fights in the icy Yosemite River, taking pictures of Thad preaching (from afar) to a black bear against the evils of stealing our picnic lunch—I will remember always, I wrote in my diary. *Idyllic evenings popping corn over a campfire, playing hide-and-seek among the giant trees, dressing in the confines of a four-man tent, and cuddling beneath three quilts to ward off the cool mountain temperatures.*

When the week came to an end, neither of us wanted to leave our mountain hideaway. It had truly been the perfect place to begin our life together. Not until the morning I was packing my smallest suitcase in the car and spotted the box that held the hand-crocheted bedspread made by Aunt Faith did I remember her advice about talking out my feelings of anger with Thad. *No, now is not the time. Everything's been too perfect. I don't want to tamper with perfection.*

"Hey, honey." I felt Thad's warm breath on my neck and his hands around my waist. "What's the matter? I called to you, but you didn't answer. Is something wrong?"

"Huh?"

"Is anything wrong?"

I turned into his arms. "I guess I dread leaving here. Everything is so perfect."

He slid his arms around me and drew me closer. "The closest to heaven that I've ever been."

"If only we could stay another week."

"Afraid not. Elder Millikin is expecting us to be in Amarillo before the end of this week. Stopping in Springville at your brother's is already going to put us behind a day or two."

I sighed and rested my head against his shoulder. "I know. I know."

"But what do you say to a last hike up Bridalveil Fall?"

More than once we had hiked up behind the shroud of mist sweeping down the mountainside. It didn't matter. I was always eager to do it once again.

We climbed to our favorite spot on the trail, where we could look out over the valley through the mist. By this point, my hair hung in soggy ringlets. And my blouse and knickers hung limp on my slender body.

"This is my favorite spot in the entire valley," Thad said, coming up behind me and slipping his arms about my waist.

"I know. But why? You can't see either Half Dome or El Capitan from here."

"That's why I like it. I can easily imagine the Garden of Eden must have looked much like this to Adam and Eve. All fresh and clean, without a trace of sin."

I relaxed against his shoulder and pressed my ear to his chest, listening to the deep rumble as he spoke. "You are now 'bone of my bones, and flesh of my flesh.' For this reason, I chose to leave my father and be united to you as one flesh. Chloe Celeste, I vow in the presence of God and in the sacredness of this place to give myself totally and irrevocably to you."

Turning to face him, a devilish twinkle in my eyes, I started to say, "I thought you did that a week ago," but he placed his finger over my lips and shook his head gently.

"Sh-sh-sh, don't. Just make me the same vow."

I placed my hands behind his neck. "All right, I'll be serious. Let's see. You are now 'bone of my bones, and flesh of my flesh.' For this reason, I chose to leave my father and mother and be united to you as one flesh." I licked my lips, then continued. "Thaddeus, I vow in the presence of God and in the sacredness of this place that 'whither thou goest, I will go; and where thou lodgest, I will lodge: thy people shall be my people, and thy God my God: and where thou diest, will I die, and there will I be buried.' "

The kiss lingered on my lips throughout the descent down the trail. I hated leaving behind our very own paradise. During the long ride out of the valley, I wrote in my diary, *It's as if the vows we made in the church before our family and friends were but a rehearsal for the true marriage of our spirits and our minds beside the waterfall.*

Traversing the great Central Valley took the rest of the day. One hundred plus miles and six flat tires later we pulled into the bustling town of Porterville. I was hot, tired, and hungry. With the sleeve of my dress, I wiped the rivulets of perspiration off the sides of my face. "I'm glad we're almost at Jamie's. It must be ninety degrees or more. I can hardly wait to get there."

Thad eyed me with concern. "Your face is beet red. And we still have twenty miles or so to drive."

"Twenty miles? I thought Auriel said Springville was only a few miles from Porterville."

He shrugged, then reached over and touched the back of his hand to my cheek. "You're much too overheated, honey. I don't like it. Maybe we'd better stop here in town for a bite to eat."

"Me?" I noted the muddy canals of sweat streaking his face. "You should see yourself. Your face is a topographical map."

He laughed. "Let's rest until the worst heat of the day passes. I spotted the Porterville Inn when we drove through the center of town. It looked like there was a restaurant too."

"Good idea. I'm starved!"

Once settled in the eight-table restaurant, we lingered over our meal, enjoying the cool air generated by the three ceiling fans. Finally, as the giant golden sun dipped beyond the horizon, we climbed back into the car and completed our journey to Springville.

I fell instantly in love with Auriel and Jamie's little cottage. After a bath and a couple hours of good conversation, we said good night to Auriel and Jamie.

A cool breeze blew through the closet-sized guest room. A double bed, a small dresser, a small wooden chair, a lamp stand, and a lamp filled the room. I recognized the tulip-patterned quilt that had been in my parents' home since I was a child and thought of the wedding-ring quilt packed in the trunk of our car and smiled.

As I undid my hair and brushed out the snarls, I couldn't contain my enthusiasm. "Oh, Thad, isn't this place adorable? Auriel has done so much in the short time they've been here. I'm getting excited about fixing up our first home." In my babbling I failed to notice how quiet he'd been.

"Thad?" I turned and discovered him sitting on the edge of the bed, staring at his hands. "Thad? What's wrong?"

Slowly, he lifted his head. "You do understand that, as part of an evangelistic team, we'll stay for only a few weeks in one location, then move on to the next, don't you? I explained it in my letters."

I drew the brush partway through my heavy locks, then paused. "Y-e-s, I know."

"It may be years before we move into a regular house, and then, it probably won't belong to us." His stare unnerved me.

"I understand all of that, but you need to understand something also." I whirled about to face him. "In two years, on my twenty-fifth birthday, I will come into my inheritance from my real father, James McCall. And from what I understand, the purchase of a house will not be a problem."

Thad dropped his gaze to his hands once more. "I'm not sure I want to live off my wife's largess."

"Largess? Is that what you call it?" I planted my hands firmly on my hips. "Didn't you and I become one flesh less than two weeks ago? What's mine is yours, and so forth?"

"That's not the point."

"Not the point? Then what is the point, may I ask?"

He pounded a fist into the palm of his other hand. "I won't be a kept man!"

"A kept man?"

"That's right, a kept man! I will support and provide for my family." He stood up and walked to the door.

"You knew before you married me that I come from a wealthy family."

Pointing his finger at me, he growled, "I thought long and hard about that before asking you to marry me."

I inhaled sharply. "If it bothers you, then why did you decide to go ahead with it?"

"From the way you described your experience in Chamonix and in Oregon, it was obvious that you could adapt to primitive living conditions." He shoved his hands in his pants pockets.

"Look, I'm sorry I'm such a disappointment as a wife. All I did was say how much fun it would be to fix up our first home."

"I could tell where the conversation was heading."

"Oh, you could, could you? I'm that predictable, after only a week of marriage? Trust me, Thaddeus, you've got a lot to learn about me, and one thing is, never presume anything!"

"Fine!"

"Fine!" We froze, trapped in a daring stare down, neither of us willing to give.

"Fine!" He yanked open the bedroom door.

"Just where do you think you're going?" I hissed. "Someone's going to hear you."

"I need to get some fresh air."

Tears of anger filled my eyes, and I turned my back to him. The door closed none too silently.

Married less than two weeks, and we have our first argument. And I'm not sure I know what it was about! I sank to the floor, my stomach heaving as if I'd lose my supper. Tears poured from my eyes as I sobbed in silence, afraid my brother or his wife would hear. During a pause in my tears, I looked at my wristwatch. A half-hour had passed, and Thad hadn't returned.

I was too tired to cry any longer. The coolness of the linoleum soothed and relaxed me, and finally my exhaustion overcame my sorrow. I awoke with a start at being lifted from the floor and struggled to break free.

"Thad!" My voice rang out in the darkness.

"Shh, I'm just tucking you in bed, darling." He laid me on the cool cotton sheet. "You'll catch your death down there."

"Where, what time is it?"

"Late, honey. Late." He slid into bed beside me and pulled the covers over us.

"How late? Where've you been?"

"Shh, voices carry in this house. I took a walk."

I glanced toward the window. A tangerine glow filled the sky over the mountains. "It must have been some walk. It's day-break."

"I had a lot of thinking to do." We snuggled close, like spoons in the utility drawer. "I want you to know that I forgive you."

"Forgive me?" The fingers of my one hand started tapping against the edge of the bed.

"After I cooled off, I realized that you were exhausted after our long ride. It's only natural for one to get a little grumpy under the circumstances." As he kissed my neck several times, I stiffened.

"How very understanding you are of my little foibles," I hissed through my teeth.

He brushed my hair aside and continued by kissing my shoulder. "That's what it takes to make a good marriage— understanding and patience."

"Of which you have an abundance, I suppose?"

He paused. "Do I detect a little edge in your voice?"

"Oh—" I chuckled, sarcastically, "you could say that." I lifted his arm from around my waist. "Now, if you'll excuse me, your exhausted and grumpy little wife must get her sleep." Even as I thumped his arm down on his thigh and burrowed under the blankets, I could hear my mother's voice, *Never let the sun set on a quarrel.*

The next morning we bade Jamie and Auriel an awkward goodbye and left for Porterville. There, we stopped to have our spare tires repaired before heading south to Bakersfield and out across the Mojave Desert. While one-hundred-degree temperatures soared outside our automobile, inside, it never got above freezing.

We maintained an uneasy truce, speaking only when necessary. Except when we stopped for food or for fuel, or when a tire blew, I slept. And when I couldn't sleep, I pretended.

That evening as the molten sun disappeared from view, we parked the car beside the road, and Thad began to set up camp. He lighted the kerosene lamp and set it on the hood of the car, then dug the tent out of the trunk and spread it out on the desert floor. I offered to help, but he refused my offer. While he struggled with the tent, I recorded in my diary, *Poor road conditions and an unusually high number of blown tires reduced the number of miles we covered on our first day out. The chill from the evening desert breeze is nothing compared to the chill I get from Thad whenever our eyes meet.*

While I waited for him to finish pitching the tent, I took out my hairbrush and began brushing out the snarls. I chuckled to myself as I watched his frustrated efforts. *If he'd swallow his pride a little, I'd be glad to help.* When the tent caved in on him for the third time, I set my brush on the seat of the car. "OK, what do you want me to do?"

Grudgingly, he directed me to hold the pole at one end of the canvas while he climbed inside the tent and secured the pole at the opposite end. I gazed out over the broad desert floor, covered with the same sagebrush and cactuses that we'd driven past all day. In my mind, I compared the landscape to the high desert of southeastern Oregon. *I miss the distant purple mountains. I miss the red splashes of Indian paintbrush sweeping up the hillsides and the quail darting across the roads. I miss Nina, the children, Cal— No! Stop it, CeeCee! You're a married woman!* I shook my head in disgust.

A muffled sound came from inside the tent. "What?" I called. "Did you call me?"

The garble grew louder, more insistent. Holding onto the tent pole, I knelt down and stuck my head into the tent. "I'm sorry, but I couldn't understand you. What did you want?"

"I said, 'I need you to hold this other pole in place while I stake the ropes.'" His exaggerated tone of tolerance irked me.

"How can I possibly hold both poles at the same time?" I had the unreasonable urge to slap the condescending smile from his face. *Oh, dear God. Forgive me. I'm hardly a violent person. How can I think such thoughts?* At that moment, I didn't like myself very much. I prayed a quick prayer for patience and measured my words carefully. "OK, how shall we do this? We didn't have this much trouble pitching the tent in Yosemite."

"That's because the ground was softer there. This stuff is solid like rock!" Thad wiped beads of sweat from his forehead.

I peered into the tent's dark interior. "Basically, we need to switch poles."

"Hmm, maybe if I scoot to the right, there'll be enough room for you to crawl in on the left. Then on the count of three, we can switch poles. What do you think?"

"Sounds good."

I scooted into the tent on my knees, all the while struggling to keep my tent pole vertical. "Ow," I grumbled. Pebbles protruding through the tent's canvas floor bruised my knees. With my free hand, I poked at the canvas, trying to lift it off my head. "There, that should do it. Let's get this over with. My knees are killing me!"

"Stop complaining," Thad whispered, his breath brushing against my face.

"Oh!" I started, surprised to find us kneeling face to face.

He caressed my cheek with his free hand, then pressed his lips to mine. When the kiss ended, I felt bereft. "I missed you today, darling."

Tears filled my eyes. Timidly, I touched his face with my free hand. "I missed you too."

"I'm so sorr—" We both spoke at once. We laughed and tried again.

"Please, let's promise never to allow a problem or misunderstanding to come between us again," he begged.

"I'd like that." My voice caught.

"You're crying?" He wiped away the tears from my cheeks. "Oh, my darling, I am so, so sorry for everything that happened."

"Oh, Thad, I love you so much!" My arms flew around his neck as I threw myself into his arms.

"Hey, what—" He fell backward, and I tumbled on top of him.

As the tent and the poles trapped us in a cocoon of canvas, I realized my mistake. "Oh no!" I wailed, pawing the veil of my freed hair from my mouth and face.

Suddenly, Thad chuckled.

"We've got to get out of here. We'll suffocate!" I struggled, but he continued holding me in his arms. His chuckle grew to laughter, then to hilarity.

"Stop laughing, you—you ninny!" I pounded his chest. I think he would have let me go at that point if I hadn't giggled. And, as usual, once I started laughing, I couldn't stop. Neither could he. I don't know what the night creatures must have thought as our laughter rang across the desert floor.

Later, as we sat on the car's running board, eating crackers and cheese, I tried to broach the cause of our earlier disagreement.

"Honey—" Thad took a gulp of water from the Thermos bottle we'd received from one of my parents' friends. "—not now. I feel so at peace and so in love with you. Not now."

"But, Thad, we have to talk these things out, or they'll just come back again. You know that."

"I know. I know." He kissed my lips gently. "Just not now."

"I really think—"

"Can't you let it go?"

Shrinking from the agitation in his voice, I needed to go off by myself to nurse my wounded feelings. "I, uh, need to, uh, take a walk before we turn in for the night."

Later, I wrote in my diary, *I didn't realize how much of the pattern for our marriage was set that night. Coming from a family where honesty and open discussion were encouraged, I couldn't understand Thad's reluctance to talk out our problems together. He'd rather pretend they don't exist.*

Six days after leaving Jamie and Auriel's place, we arrived on the outskirts of Amarillo, Texas, eager for a cool bath and a hot meal. I was the first to spot the big canvas tent.

"Is that it? Are we finally here?" I shivered with excitement. Then a wave of fear washed over me. "What if the Millikins don't like me?"

"They'll love you, darling, and you'll love them. Elder Millikin is a great man of God and a fiery preacher." Thad sent me a reassuring smile. "And Mrs. Millikin, well, Mrs. Millikin is a kind, gentle lady. The two of you will become fast friends right away."

Thad was right. I fell instantly in love with the gray-haired and dimpled Mrs. Millikin, or Genevieve, as she insisted I call her. And I had to admit Elder Millikin could stir up the fires of his congregation when he preached. As to liking the man, well, what can I say? He had one goal in life, and one goal only—to preach and to baptize. Nothing else mattered, not his wife, not

Thad, not me—no one. He worked from dawn till midnight, seven days a week, and expected everyone else to do the same. Though he held meetings only five nights a week, the evangelist insisted he and Thad use whatever free time to visit their converts. I used the days alone to practice my violin.

Elder Millikin decided it would be best if Thad and I lived in a two-room tent behind the main tent, for security reasons. Thad agreed, then told me. "Just until September, of course, when the weather turns cold." Since we'd been renting a room in a flea-infested boardinghouse whose walls quaked every time a train passed through town, I went along with the plan.

While I provided the special music on my violin at each evening meeting, Thad acted as a general handyman and lackey to the great evangelist. After three weeks, I asked Thad, "When will you get to preach?"

"In time, in time. Elder Millikin has assured me that he'll use me when I'm ready."

The routine continued throughout July and into August— two weeks in a town, then on to the next. Lubbock, Abilene, San Angelo, Fort Stockton, Pecos—they all were the same, hot, dusty, exhausting. Whenever I complained about Thad's absence or about our wedding gifts still unpacked in the back of the Ford or his not getting to preach or about the incredibly high temperatures or the hole in the canvas directly over our bed, Thad would remind me that such sacrifices were necessary when doing the work of the Lord. Then he would leave on another important mission.

At that point I would take out my violin and play what quickly became my protest song, Bach's "Jesu, Joy of Man's Desiring." The song, meant to be gentle and ethereal, took on a strident, militaristic tone. And that was the closest I came to protesting my lot. After that first disagreement we had, I'd determined to be as good a wife as possible.

In my letters to my parents, I wrote of the great number of people saved at each crusade, but nothing about our living conditions. They'd be horrified if they knew.

When I received letters from Ashley, telling me about her terribly unhappy marriage to Charles and about his philandering, I thanked God that Thad and I were not like them, that our marriage was solid and happy. I refused to admit to myself that I was more than unhappy living as we did and that I was also furiously angry at Thad, at Elder Millikin, and, on particularly bad days, at God, since He was the One I held responsible for my discomfort.

The beginning of the end of tent life came one night when I found a rattler coiled beneath our bed. To say that I went slightly crazy at the sight of the six-foot beast shaking his rattle at me would be an understatement. I spent the night sleeping in the front seat of the Ford. A week later, I came within two inches of stepping, barefooted, on a scorpion. But it was the rabbit and the coyote that finally did it for me.

It was after eleven, and Thad wasn't back from his visitation appointments. I'd walked to town earlier and bought myself a meal of chili beans and corn bread. As I sat alone in the tent waiting for Thad, my stomach began to churn from anger or from those beans, I'm not sure which. In my haste to make a run for the makeshift outhouse behind our living quarters, I grabbed the kerosene lantern and rushed from the tent, accidentally leaving open the tent flap.

I returned to the sound of scratching and scampering inside the tent. "Thad? Is that you?"

Holding the lantern in front of me, I peered inside the tent as a streak of gray darted past me. My scream must have terrified the coyote, for instead of running, he backed into the corner of the tent at the foot of our bed. All I could see in the lamplight were his glistening yellow eyes and his bared fangs.

"Good boy," I gasped. "No one's going to hurt you, I promise." I backed out slowly, knocking over the washbasin sitting on top of Thad's trunk. Water, crockery, and shaving gear crashed to the floor of the tent. When I stooped to pick up Thad's razor, the cornered coyote snarled and lunged at me.

Clutching the kerosene lamp, I screamed and ran out into the night. Too frightened to return, I sneaked inside the large meeting tent; made my way to the rickety, out-of-tune piano; and began pounding out the familiar strains of "Jesu, Joy of Man's Desiring." Tears streamed down my cheeks as I pounded out the notes with a deliberation Bach never intended. If it had been meeting time, the volume alone would have drawn people from three or more counties.

"Thaddeus Adams! I have had it! Tonight is the last straw. Tomorrow morning we are moving into a decent, and I do mean decent, boardinghouse, where we can eat decent meals and sleep in a decent bed and take decent baths!" I shouted my demands between hiccups.

I switched to a vengeful rendition of "Joyful, Joyful, We Adore Thee." But the hymn I found the most pleasure playing was "Sound the Battle Cry."

"And if you can't see your way clear to—"

"Hello? Are you all right?" Thad walked cautiously up the center aisle toward me. I'd been so intent on reciting my diatribe and playing my thunderous music I neither heard the Ford pull up or Thad enter the tent.

All I saw was the shadow of a man coming toward me from the rear of the tent. Grabbing the nearest object, I screamed and threw a hymnal straight at his head. He ducked and shouted, but my continued screams drowned out his calls. I sent five more hymnals sailing, in Gatling-gun succession, through the air, forcing Thad to scramble for cover.

I raised my hand to fire a large vase of cut roses sitting beside the piano, when he lunged at me, catching my arm and me in a paralyzing death grip. My screams caught in my throat from the sudden dousing of water from the vase.

"Huh? What in the—" I gaped at his distressed face and at the rose petals dotting his shoulders and chest.

"What is the matter with you, woman? Have you gone loco? I could hear you a half mile down the road, over the noise of the flivver, I might add."

Before I could answer, the wail of a siren rose and fell outside the tent. Seconds later, the local sheriff and three of his deputies burst through the tent flaps, with guns drawn.

Thad and I moved into Rosa's Boardinghouse the next morning. Neither Elder Millikin nor Genevieve said a word. And, fortunately, no one tried to vandalize the unguarded evangelistic equipment.

Two days later, we finished our meetings in Sheffield and moved on to Sonora. The first thing Thad did this time, even before pitching the meeting tent or handing out fliers, was to find a suitable room for me. Unfortunately, the only rooming house in town was less than desirable as rooming houses go, but I didn't complain, for it was far better than the two-room tent, now permanently stashed in the back of the Millikins' truck.

In Del Rio, I first suspected that my queasy stomach might be due to more than a bad batch of chili beans. Mrs. Millikin was the first to suggest that I might be pregnant. I stared at her in horror.

"No, I can't bring up a baby traipsing from town to town across the Southwest," I wailed.

She smiled sweetly and patted my hand with grandmotherly concern. "Honey, of course, you can. I raised four girls and three boys, living out of the back of Gideon's truck. It's just been since his arthritis has been kicking up that we've taken to staying in boardinghouses."

"His arthritis? What about yours?" I glanced down at her gnarled fingers.

"Oh, pay no mind to this." She held up one hand. "God's work is important to me. I don't want to hinder it in any way." She smiled self-consciously. "This is my ministry as much as it is Gideon's. And, besides, I don't like to fuss."

I shook my head. "You're a better woman than I, Genevieve."

"You don't really like this life on the road, do you?" Her soft southern drawl was neither hurried nor judgmental.

I reddened and avoided her gaze. "I love Thad very much."

"I didn't ask you that."

I swallowed hard. *How much can I trust you, Genevieve? Will you tell your husband about our conversation and get Thad fired?*

"When I married Thad, I vowed for better, for worse; in sickness and in health; and as long as we both shall live."

"I am familiar with the wedding vows, CeeCee dear. But, then, I have your answer, don't I?" A mixture of sadness and compassion filled her eyes. "I'm lucky because I genuinely like moving from town to town with Gideon, seeing new places, meeting new people. After all these years, the beginning of every crusade excites me, and I eagerly look forward to the next one farther down the road."

"You are lucky. More than that, you are the closest thing to a saint whom I've ever known."

The little woman threw back her head and laughed. "Oh, my dear, I'm as much a saint as you, since *saint* simply means 'set apart.' Otherwise, I can be as difficult to live with as the next woman, or man, I might add. No, don't make me to be more than I am."

Alone in my room that night, I thought about Genevieve raising seven children from the tailgate of a truck. I opened my Bible to Hannah's prayer in 1 Samuel, then read Mary's song in Luke. But neither made me feel better about my possible condition. *Oh, dear Lord, I should be singing songs of praise to You for this new life growing inside me. I should be, but I can't. Please, please help me to feel grateful for this miracle of love.*

I glanced toward my diary sitting on the edge of the night stand. *No, I can't even tell you yet.* A letter I'd received that day from Auriel announced the birth of Jamie's and her first child, James Cyrus McCall, my first nephew. *Oh, dear God, I'm not ready for this. This isn't how I imagined things would be.*

Before turning out the light, I went through my nightly ritual of throwing back the covers and checking for any vermin that might have slithered in from the desert. It would be at least two more hours before Thad returned home.

As darkness settled into the room, I burrowed under the quilts and squeezed my eyes shut. *I could be wrong; there are dozens of possible causes. Maybe I drank some bad water.* I thought over all the horrid diseases I'd ever studied, from the trivial to the deadly. I didn't like the sound of any of them. *Maybe—maybe—maybe my nausea really is from the beans, or perhaps the grits I ate for breakfast. Oh, Lord, please make it be so. Please make it be the grits.*

Storm Warnings

I waited two weeks before informing Thad of my suspicions. I had to be certain. Being a nurse, I didn't want to look foolish by leaping to false conclusions. By the end of the two weeks, I knew, without a doubt, that I was indeed pregnant. And according to my calculation, our baby would arrive toward the end of May, sometime around my twenty-fourth birthday.

Thad noticed nothing, suspected nothing. The evangelistic meetings were his life. Long days, short nights—whether pitching the tent or passing out fliers, Thad gave his all. Sometimes I wondered during those days, if I had hopped a freight train west, how long would it have taken him to notice my absence. *I'm sure that's the exaggeration of a slightly spoiled woman*, I told myself whenever the thought lingered long enough to become a threat.

The night I planned to tell Thad the news, we were beginning a new series of meetings in Laredo. I finished the musical portion of the program for the evening meeting, then hurried back to the boardinghouse to prepare for Thad's arrival. He'd promised to come straight home after the meeting—no matter what.

I wanted everything to be perfect. After clearing the clutter from the secretary, I spread a square damask tablecloth over it. On my makeshift table, I arranged fruit in a silver compote, a single red rose in a silver bud vase, two candles in crystal holders, and a crystal candy dish heaped with bonbons. It had taken most of the afternoon to gather the items. The tablecloth, the crystal, and the silver I dug out of the trunk of our car. And the goodies I collected from shops around town, with the exception of the rose. That, I found in an old lady's kitchen garden. When I told the woman what I was doing, she gladly gave me one of her roses.

I inspected the desk from every angle. *Perfect!* Next I trotted down the hall to the community bathroom and indulged in a luxurious bubble bath. After powdering myself from head to toe, I brushed my hair until it gleamed, then left it hanging loose, down my back, the way Thad most liked it.

Slipping into the Mandarin wedding dress, Thad's favorite, I climbed, barefoot, onto the bed to get a full-length view of myself in the mirror over the washstand. I patted my still-flat stomach and smiled.

Somewhere in the rooming house, a clock gonged nine times. *Elder Millikin always stops speaking at nine o'clock.* Aloud I mimicked the man's deep base voice. "The devil comes in after nine—ha, ha, ha." In spite of the minister's relentless drive, I had to admit I genuinely liked the man. *And I'd like you a lot more, Elder Millikin, if you didn't keep Thad away from me so much!*

In truth I was lonely, cooped up in rooming houses most of the day. *At least when we were living in the tent, I was involved in the excitement of the meetings. Stop complaining, Chloe Celeste. You'll develop wrinkles before your time.*

Beyond the rooming-house window, a siren wailed. I climbed off the bed, ambled over to the window, and looked down on the otherwise quiet town. Sighing, I strolled over to the mirror again. *Peaches and cream, that's how Thad likes to describe my complexion.* With my fingers, I traced along the corners of my mouth and the outer edges of my eyes. *Wrinkles? Maybe in twenty years or so.* My forty-two-year-old mother's face was still virtually free from crow's-feet.

"Chloe Celeste, if you want to postpone developing wrinkles, there are three things that help." I could hear her voice clearly. "First, scrub your face twice every day with a linen face cloth and warm water. Second, rub the peel of a lemon on your face each evening. Third, smile and think happy thoughts; then the lines you develop will be pleasing to your visage." *Lines? I'm worrying about lines at twenty-three? Next thing you know I'll be imagining gray hairs!* My attention shifted to my hair. I found one strand that didn't match my normally copper tones. *Blond, probably.* I yanked it out anyway.

Glancing at my watch, I wondered, *What's keeping Thad?* The tent was pitched in a vacant lot less than a ten-minute walk from the boardinghouse. Irritated, I lighted the candles and turned out the lamp, then sat on the edge of the bed in the semi-darkness to await his arrival. I took several deep breaths. *Think of the baby. Think tranquil thoughts, Chloe Celeste.*

I heard the wail of another siren. *Hmm, I wonder what's happening? Nothing much ever happens in these small Texas towns. That's why the evangelistic meetings are so popular.* I yawned. *I'm so sleepy. One of the sure signs of pregnancy*, I mused as I stretched out on top of the bedcovers. *I'll just close my eyes. Thad should be here any minute.*

Sometime later, I awoke slowly to Thad's gentle touch. "CeeCee, wake up, honey. Wake up."

"Hmm?" I smiled up into his concerned face. "What's the matter? What time is it?"

"It's after one o'clock in the morning."

I purred again. "That's nice. Then I can go back to sleep for a few more hours."

"No, honey, you can't. Genevieve is asking for you. Something's happened."

My eyes blinked open at the mention of Mrs. Millikin. I struggled to sit up, but my garment constricted my movements. I glanced down in frustration, then remembered the planned tête-à-tête. "Where have you been?" I swung my legs around and then sat up. "I expected you home hours ago. You promised."

"What are you dressed in—?" He noticed my costume for the first time. Then he turned and looked at the carefully set desk and the burned-out candles. His face paled. "Oh no, I'm so sorry."

I could tell that he expected me to be angry, but I was still too drowsy.

"CeeCee, darling, you must change clothing and go with me to the hospital. Gideon was lucky we were here in Laredo and not one of the little backwater towns like Rocksprings."

"Gideon?" I stared at him uncomprehendingly.

"Gideon, Gideon Millikin. Are you sure you're awake?"

"Hospital?"

"Yes, hospital." He took hold of my shoulders and stared into my eyes. "CeeCee, please wake up."

When the word *hospital* sank into my brain, I leapt from the bed and began unbuttoning the dress. "What? What happened?"

"Elder Millikin collapsed tonight at the end of his sermon. They've rushed him to the community hospital. His wife asked for you."

"Oh, dear. That's what the sirens were about."

"I'll start the car while you get ready."

My medical training overcame my sleepiness. I rushed to dress and brush my hair into place. Within a couple of minutes, I was hurrying down the steps into the waiting Ford. It took another five minutes to reach the hospital.

"Where's Mrs. Millikin?" I called to the nurse on duty as I barged through the hospital entrance with Thad close behind me. "Who's the attending physician?"

The startled nurse rounded the nurses' station. "Madam, you can't see the patients until visiting hours. Please—"

Thad started to speak, but I raised my hand to silence him. "I'm a registered nurse—Gideon Millikin's private nurse, Miss, Miss—" I glanced at her name tag. "—Miss Tatum. Now please direct me to Elder Millikin's room or to his doctor." I brushed her aside and continued down the hallway. I was glad I had thought to wear my nurse's uniform.

"Oh, oh, I didn't know. Of course, Miss—what did you say your name was?"

Thad trailed behind us, looking surprisingly uncomfortable and dismayed. He'd never seen me in my element.

The pretty blond nurse matched me stride for stride. "Are you new in town?"

I brushed her question aside. "Who did you say is the attending physician?"

"Doctor Raleigh, ma'am."

"Is he still in the hospital?"

"He's with the patient now, I believe. This way."

"Did you see Elder Millikin when they brought him in?"

The woman nodded. "Heart attack, if you ask me."

"Has his condition stabilized?"

"You'll have to ask the doctor, I'm afraid."

At the end of the hall, she paused. "I can't leave my ward, but if you'll go down to the end of this hall and turn right, you'll find them in room 133."

"Thank you, Miss Tatum." My thick Cuban heels clicked on the tile floor as I followed the young nurse's directions. I could hear Thad's footsteps somewhere behind me.

It felt good to be back in a hospital again. The odor of disinfectant, the sparkling clean floors, the atmosphere of efficiency, it was like entering another world, one I'd missed more than I'd imagined.

Before I reached the room, Genevieve saw me coming down the hallway. "Oh, Chloe Celeste, thank you for coming. I hope you didn't mind."

"Of course not." I hugged her. "What has the doctor told you?"

"The doctor won't tell me anything. But I knew it was a heart attack the moment I saw Gideon double over and crumble to the floor during the altar call. My husband had a small heart attack a few months before you two joined us, but he refused to see a doctor."

I raised my eyebrows. "This time, I guess he didn't have a choice." I led her to a nearby chair. "Thad, why don't you stay with Mrs. Millikin while I go see what's happening."

"The doctor won't let you in there," Genevieve warned.

"I'm a registered nurse."

"Oh." She noticed my uniform for the first time.

Doctor Raleigh proved to be a competent and likable physician. He seemed relieved that I could supply Elder Millikin with the special attention the man would need over the next few hours.

During the weeks that followed, I spent as much time as possible with my patient while Thad conducted the evening meetings alone. Hector, the Millikins' eldest son, drove down from Tulsa to be with his parents. When it became obvious that Elder Millikin would have a long recovery period once he was released from the hospital, Hector insisted on taking his parents to his home in Oklahoma. As expected, Elder Millikin argued that the schedule of meetings must be met. "I've made commitments straight through November. I can't break my word."

The patient became so agitated that the doctor was concerned he'd have another attack.

"Thad and I can complete the appointments for you," I volunteered. Once I made the suggestion, nothing could have stopped the chain of events that followed. Within three days, the Millikins were on their way to their son's house, and Thad and I were left behind to carry on as best we could. Instead of exhausting Thad, the heavy schedule of preaching and visiting interested people charged him even more. "The entire Harrington family gave their hearts to Christ tonight—sixteen of them, counting the five-year-old. Isn't that exciting?"

I did the best I could to keep up with him. But in the rush, I never could find a quiet, private moment to tell him about the baby. The day came in mid-November when I no longer had a choice. I'd been helping him set up the main tent in Santa Elena for the next series of meetings. We were stringing the electric lights when one of the legs on the rickety ladder on which I was standing split, sending me crashing to the floor.

Thad rushed to my side. "Darling, are you all right?"

"I think I might have twisted my ankle."

After examining my ankle, he scooped me into his arms and carried me to the car. "I'm taking you to a doctor."

I didn't object. He had to drive me to San Isidro to the nearest doctor. While the physician examined my foot, I became increasingly certain that my ankle was the least of my problems.

The man straightened and assured me my ankle wasn't broken. "Stay off it for a few days, and you'll be all right."

"Uh, Doctor, I think I have another, more urgent problem from the fall."

"Oh?" He raised his bushy eyebrows over the tops of his dark-rimmed spectacles.

"I'm at least two, perhaps two and a half months, pregnant. And, well, I'm having contractions."

After a thorough exam, I went to dress while the doctor spoke with Thad.

When I came out of the dressing room, Thad met me at the door. "Why haven't you told me you were pregnant? I never would have allowed you to climb that ladder or carry the hymnbooks. How long have you known?"

Embarrassed at having the doctor overhear Thad's questions, I tried to hurry Thad from the office. The two men carried me to the car and set me in the front seat.

Then Thad hopped in beside me. "I am furious with you for not telling me about the baby, CeeCee."

"When? When would I have had time to tell you? Between meetings? While pitching the tent or tearing it down? When?"

"When did you plan to tell me—on the child's first birthday?"

"Thad, I'm sorry. I planned to tell you the night of Elder Millikin's heart attack. Since then, we've not had much time together, you must admit."

"You're right, of course. But you could have taken things easy, at the very least."

"Are you saying it's my fault that we might lose our baby?" I shrank down in the seat, wishing I could disappear.

He took my hand in his and brought it to his lips. "No, of course not."

My tears fell unbidden. "Oh, Thad, I'm so sorry. I never dreamed I'd have any trouble carrying the baby. My mother never did. My grandmother bore fourteen before she died. I just never thought—"

"Honey, it's OK. I love you so much. Thank God, this is the last series of meetings!"

We'd promised to return the equipment to Elder Millikin once we'd completed his appointments. After that, we had no idea where God would send us. I'd been hoping for time off so we could visit my parents in San Francisco.

That night I lost our baby. The pains from the miscarriage were nothing compared to the pain inside my soul. When Thad returned from the evening meeting and found me sitting in the middle of the bed, hugging a pillow, rocking back and forth and sobbing, he knew instantly what had happened. Patiently, he held me in his arms and stroked my head and back until morning broke over the Texas plains. The next day he canceled the rest of the meetings and hired a team of workers to pack up the equipment.

Two days later, when I was strong enough to drive the Ford while he drove the equipment truck, we headed north to Tulsa. I cried all the way across Texas for the baby I was leaving behind. As the tears flowed, I told myself over and over again, *CeeCee, someday, in God's kingdom, you will have that baby to hold and to love—someday—someday—*

A surprise awaited us in Tulsa, a surprise that eased Thad's mind and disturbed mine. Without our knowledge, Hector Millikin had arranged for Thad to pastor a small church in Grants, New Mexico. "I have a friend who told me about a church needing a pastor, and I knew you folks would be needing somewhere to go after finishing my father's circuit, so I told him to hold the position open for you. I hope you don't mind."

"Mind?" Thad assured him. "We're delighted, aren't we, darling?"

I smiled weakly, keeping my groans to myself.

The next morning, as we set out on our tedious journey across the red hills of Oklahoma and the barren plains of the Texas panhandle, a wave of relief, of freedom engulfed me, freedom at leaving the tent and the meetings behind. I was heading west, and, for the moment, that was enough.

The dusty little adobe church in Grants blended into its surroundings. In no time, the friendly people who worshiped there won my heart. But the best part of living in Grants was being able to volunteer my nursing skills at the nearby Acoma Indian Reservation. My red hair never ceased being an object of amazement for the precious little children on the reservation.

Over the next six months, I filled my letters home with humorous and exciting anecdotes about life on the southwestern desert. If anything, after losing the baby, Thad and I grew closer, and I couldn't have been more content.

I decorated what I called our adobe hacienda parsonage with bright blankets and baskets made on the reservation. My favorite discovery was a heavy pine trestle table that dominated our main living space. I found it, covered with ugly green paint, in a secondhand store in Albuquerque.

I scoured and sanded, then scoured some more to remove the many layers of paint that had been applied to the top. Finally, I uncovered the rich natural tone of the wood, which I oiled to a deep, lustrous shine.

Thad took up sketching again in his spare time. We tried to take some time each week to drive out into the desert so he could sketch and I could collect my treasures. His best sketches I framed and hung over the round adobe fireplace in the corner of our kitchen. I didn't mind so much that he was often gone in the evenings, visiting his parishioners, and I often chose to go along with him.

Nothing could have pleased me more than to discover, in July, that I was pregnant once again. This time, I alerted Thad as soon as I was sure. We both couldn't have been happier. Immediately, I ordered pink and blue yarn from the Montgomery Ward catalog. *This time*, I vowed, *I will stay off all ladders and tend to my knitting!*

I continued to help at the reservation one day a week until winter came and made the trip over the unpaved roads more difficult. Thad didn't want me changing automobile tires "out in the middle of nowhere," as he put it. *Being pregnant has its benefits*, I decided. I liked having him fuss over me.

At Christmas, Thad and I dragged a scraggly mesquite tree indoors and decorated it with ornaments I made from natural objects I had found on the desert. My parents sent a large package of goodies to add to our holiday cheer, since we couldn't afford to make the long trip to San Francisco. Along with the apples and the cookies, my mother included a letter inquiring of my health, making certain I'd gone to see a physician. She also assured me that she would reach New Mexico in plenty of time before the baby was due. "I was thrilled to be one of the first to hold my first grandson, James Cyrus. You do know that his nickname is JC? I look forward to enjoying that same pleasure with my second grandchild."

She went on to tell me about Phoebe's wedding to her young professor and about Nikolai's abrupt departure after the wedding. "We have no idea where he went or why he left, and Phoebe isn't talking. I'm sure she knows exactly where he went. Your father hired a Pinkerton agent to find him. All we know is that Nikolai boarded a ship for England."

Two days before Christmas, a second box arrived from them—a Victrola, with twenty-four records, including my favorite operettas by Gilbert and Sullivan. I cried when I read the note inside the box. "May your home always be filled with music and with laughter." That evening, Thad and I roasted piñon nuts in the fireplace and listened to *H.M.S. Pinafore.*

My contentment lasted until one bitterly cold day toward the end of January. A storm out of the northwest swept in during the night, dumping thirteen inches of snow on the ground by morning. After Thad cleared a path from the house to the church steps, he spent the morning working on his sermon for the weekend service while I cut out the patterns for baby jackets from five yards of blue polka-dot cotton flannel that Auriel and Jamie had included in their Christmas package to us.

When Thad hadn't come home to eat lunch by one o'clock, I decided to pack a couple of sandwiches and an orange and take them to him at the church office. Halfway across the yard, I slipped. Instead of landing on the soft mound of shoveled snow, I hit the frozen path he'd cleared.

The moment I hit, I felt something tear inside me. "No," I wailed. "No, God, don't take this baby too."

I tried to struggle to my feet, but the pain in my abdomen kept me doubled over. I screamed for help, all the while realizing that the church's twelve-inch-thick adobe walls would deaden any sound I might make. *I can't just lie here and freeze to death.*

Unable to stand, I crawled a few yards on my hands and knees, leaving a trail of blood behind. Please, God, help Thad to hear me.

When I paused to rest, I heard the jangle of sleigh bells. *Someone's coming!* I screamed until my throat hurt. *Oh, dear God, let them hear me.* Another pain gripped my stomach, and I doubled over, my forehead touching the snow. I crouched there for some time, waiting for the pain to subside. *Please, heavenly Father, pl-e-e-ease!*

I'd almost given up when I felt strong hands lifting me from the pathway. When I opened my eyes, I looked into the face of Black Hawk, the medicine man at the reservation. Unable to speak, I closed my eyes, trying to stop my world from spinning out of control.

When the spinning stopped, I found myself lying in my own bed and Black Hawk staring down at me. "Preacher go get white doctor. Here—" He lifted me to a sitting position. "—drink this."

I sipped the murky liquid in the cup and grimaced. *And I thought some of my mama's teas tasted foul!*

"Drink more."

"What is it?"

He answered me in his language.

Remembering my mother's concoctions for stopping the flow of blood, I obeyed. Only when the cup was empty did Black Hawk allow me to rest again. I slept until I heard the town doctor and Thad enter the front door. A glance about the room revealed that Black Hawk had already gone. The doctor examined me, shook his head, and conferred quietly with Thad in the next room.

Two days later our son was born. For twelve hours, he struggled to breathe, but his tiny lungs were not developed enough to sustain life. Thad took the still, white infant from my arms. After staring down at the bundle for a long moment, he sighed and drew the corner of the blanket over the baby's face. "Thy will be done, O Lord."

Anger like molten lead rose in my throat. "Oh, and do you think that fills a mother's heart and arms?" I spat back in his stunned face. "You did not bear this baby. You cannot imagine what it is like to give life and then see it die. I hate it here! I hate it here!" I turned my face to the wall. *Where are You, God? Once, I knew. Once, I shouted Your goodness and power from the mountaintop. Now, tell me, Father, how can I shout Your praises? Tell me how!* I buried my face in the pillow. *If I could only hold my breath long enough—* I heard the door to our bedroom close. "Don't talk to me about God!" I shouted. "Never again!"

Like the mothers of Israel weeping over their slain children, I wailed, not caring who might hear me or who might not understand. After the anger passed, a coldness settled within me like nothing I'd ever experienced. It was as if there were a hole inside my soul that could never be filled. Heavy apathy controlled me. I didn't leave my bed to attend our son's funeral. I refused all visitors. Women with whom I'd made friends at the Indian reservation brought loaves of Navajo bread and jars of honey, but I refused to go out to meet them. Thad was left to extend my thanks and my apologies. The cards and letters of sympathy we received from our friends and family members I crumpled and threw across the room without reading.

In the night, while Thad slept on the horsehair sofa I'd re-covered during happier days and I lay awake in our bed, I blamed him for the death of our son. When my anger against my husband exhausted itself, I blamed Black Hawk. I blamed the town doctor. I blamed God. But most often, I blamed myself.

When I slept, which was around the clock, I dreamed of far-away places. The distorted faces of Sarge, of Paul, of Au Sam, of Nina, and so many more rolled through my mind like a movie film. Occasionally, I was afraid I might be losing my mind, yet I had no strength to resist the terrifying lethargy.

Early February I developed a cough that persisted. March followed without much change. Warm April breezes blew outside our hacienda before Thad returned to sleep on his side of our bed. On the morning that followed, after he left to visit one of our aging parishioners, I wrote in my diary for the first time since my child's death.

"Because I could not stop for Death." I quoted the first line of a poem written by my favorite poet, then continued to express on paper what I'd been thinking for months. *Oh, how I wish death could stop for me. Better to lie cold and forgotten in the earth than to live with a cold, dead spirit. Thaddeus expects a warm, loving wife. Unfortunately, I feel no warmth, and I have no love to give.*

Placing my diary in my desk drawer, I caught a glimpse of my gaunt face in the mirror. The eyes looking at me appeared as lifeless as I felt. I pulled back my dull hair and fastened it into a bun at the back of my neck.

Knowing Thad would be home for lunch, I prepared a sandwich for him, wrote him a note, then fled the cabin. Any excuse to avoid him was worth a try. As I hurried from the house, I considered taking my Bible with me. *No, no!* The sun warmed my back as I hiked to the top of the mesa behind the chapel. As a breeze cooled my flushed face, I spread my shawl on the ground, then sat down to view the valley and the series of gray ridges leading off to the horizon. It felt good to be outside again. And it felt good to feel something other than hollow once more too.

I counted the ridges—seven mountain ranges. The words from Psalm 121 teased the recesses of my mind. "I will lift up mine eyes unto the hills, from whence cometh my help—" I'd not opened God's Word since the death of my son. Somehow I felt very old as I studied the varying shades of gray as the ranges disappeared into a cloud bank.

How different these hills are from the mountains near Chamonix. Smiling, I recalled my perch over the gorge. I could recite from memory the psalm I had shouted to my echo over the canyon, but this time I remained mute. *Those were happy days, days filled with purpose and excitement. If only I could go back—* I buried my face in my skirt, wanting to weep, but remained tearless. Even after clouds moved in from the north, covering the sun, I stayed on the mesa, trying to postpone returning to the house.

I stayed on the mesa until large drops of rain hit my bare arms. The storm came up so quickly that I was drenched by the time I entered the empty house. During my absence, Thad had eaten his sandwich and left. I smiled to myself and fixed myself a cup of hot rosemary tea.

That evening, like so many others we'd endured over the previous three months, Thad spoke only when necessary. Otherwise, he didn't challenge the cold barrier I had constructed after losing the baby. As I washed the evening dishes, I watched him out of the corner of my eye. He sat in his favorite chair, reading his Bible. For the first time, it occurred to me that he might be hurting too. Yet I resisted the urge to reach out to him. *After all*, I argued, *he didn't carry our son for six-and-a-half months. He didn't suffer the pain of childbirth for naught.*

As I placed a large serving platter on the high pantry shelf, I sneezed. I could feel a cold coming on.

"God bless you," I heard from the other room.

Over the next three days, I developed a major cold, which settled in my chest and refused to leave. After a month of deep, racking coughs; splitting headaches; and frightening weight loss, I began to suspect that I'd contracted consumption. By the way Thad watched me whenever I started coughing, I could tell that he had similar fears.

One morning, when I couldn't bring myself to get up and fix Thad's breakfast, he came into our bedroom and announced that he was driving into Albuquerque for supplies. "I wondered if you'd like to go with me. It would do you good; you've been cooped up in the house too long."

I thought for a moment. The idea appealed to a part of me, but the thought of riding such a long distance in the car didn't. "I'm sorry, but I'm just not up to making the trip right now."

I spent the day sleeping on the sofa. Late in the afternoon I heard the Ford stop in front of the house, and Thad bounded inside. "Wake up, honey. You're going home." He'd automatically assumed I would be sleeping.

I opened my eyes wide in surprise. "I am home."

"No, I mean to San Francisco. Because you need some proper medical attention, I've asked for and received time off from the parish." He took a deep breath. "I'm taking you home tomorrow on the morning train. I already bought the tickets."

Home to California? Tomorrow? I stared at him, bewildered.

"Come on. Get up and start packing. We have to be down at the station before seven o'clock."

Fear struck at my heart. "Are you sending me away?"

"Of course not, silly. Your mother and I simply think that a little California sunshine will do you good."

"My mother?"

"Yes, your mother. I talked with her on the telephone this morning. She's been visiting Jamie and Auriel during the last few weeks." He took my hands and helped me to my feet. "Jamie will meet our train in Bakersfield, then take you to Springville until you're rested. Then you and your mother will complete the trip to San Francisco."

"What about you?"

"I'll head back here, of course. It will be only until you're feeling better, darling. I believe that it's for the best." He searched my eyes for several seconds before continuing. "When you're feeling better, you can give me a call, and you can take the train back to Grants—" His voice broke. "—back to me."

"I-I-I don't know what to say."

"There's nothing to say. I only hope your mother will be able to accomplish what I've failed to do—put some roses back in your cheeks." His fingers lingered on the side of my face. "Now, what will you need to take with you?"

I slept little that night. I insisted on bathing and shampooing my hair, which meant dragging the big oak washtub in from the car barn and heating the water on the stove. But it was worth it. I even found a sprinkling of lemon verbena in my dresser drawer to add to the bath water. After the bath, I wrapped up in my favorite flannel robe, sat on a stool by the fire, and towel dried my hair as best I could. After a few minutes, I started brushing out the tangles. I couldn't believe how quickly my strength gave out. Thad noticed too. He gently removed the brush from my hand, sat down in the armchair behind me, and brushed the back of my hair.

Once my hair was dried and snarl free, he braided it in one long braid down my back. "Here, I'll let you tie this off." He handed me the end of the braid.

"You'd better climb into bed before you catch another chill. I'll sleep on the sofa tonight so you can get a good night's sleep before we begin the trip."

I didn't argue. I allowed him to tuck me in, pray for us both, then kiss me good night. "I love you, CeeCee. I hope you won't forget that."

My eyes filled with tears. "I know," I whispered before breaking into a fierce attack of coughing. He held me in his arms, gently massaging my shoulders and back until the coughing stopped. As tears rolled down my cheeks from the pain in my chest, I caught a glimpse of my husband's face, stricken and white.

"There, there," he soothed. "It's OK. You're going to be OK. We're going to be OK."

Healing Old Wounds

I stood in the doorway, my portmanteau in hand, and glanced about the little parish home, remembering both the joy and sadness I'd experienced within its adobe walls. The rag rug I had made to cover the Mexican tile in front of the fireplace, Thad's framed sketches hanging on whitewashed walls, dried weed-and-flower arrangements sprouting from hand-woven baskets, and the vivid red-and-yellow wool runner covering my beloved trestle table—all reached out to me as I prepared to leave. *Will I ever see this place again?* I wondered as another coughing attack wracked my body. When I regained my composure, I closed my eyes and scolded myself for having such thoughts. *Of course, you will. You'll get well and come home, just as Thad said.* Yet a part of me continued to wonder whether, if I had a chance to not return, would I take it?

"Come on, honey," Thad called from the waiting car. "We don't want to miss the train." He bounded across the sandy front yard toward me. "Here, let me get that for you." He took the case from my hand and led me to the car.

We boarded the train immediately upon arriving at the station, for the passenger train heading west stopped only briefly in Grants. I marveled at how modern the Atcheson, Topeka, and Santa Fe passenger cars were compared to the one I'd taken from Klamath Falls to San Francisco less than two years previously. As the sleek black monster sped over the mountains and across the high desert, I settled back and enjoyed the comfort of our private compartment, surprised that Thad hadn't purchased coach-class tickets for our journey.

In spite of the numerous times we pulled onto a siding to allow the express trains to pass or stopped at watering tanks across the desert, it was a pleasant journey. When we pulled into the Bakersfield station, I spotted Jamie and Mama waiting for us. I was surprised to discover that I didn't feel much more tired than I had when we left Grants.

After dining in a local eatery, we drove Thad back to the depot, since he felt obligated to return to Grants as soon as possible. I tried to hide my eagerness for him to leave, but I doubt I fooled anyone, least of all him. From the displeased look on my mother's face, I knew she didn't buy my mock remorse.

"You take care, now, you hear?" I adjusted his tie. "Be sure to eat right while I'm gone."

I reddened when he shot me a quizzical smile. I hadn't been cooking for him or me in quite some time. "I'll do fine," he assured me. "Mrs. Bowman has invited me to eat with William and her each evening. The rest of the time, I can fend for myself."

"It eases my mind to hear that," I admitted. On the trip west, we'd been silent beyond the necessary pleasantries. And now, it seemed, as we were about to part, there still was nothing to say.

When the conductor called "All aboard" and Thad kissed me goodbye, I sensed a desperation in his touch.

"It's going to be all right! Weren't you the one telling me that?" I reminded.

He nodded. "I'm sorry," he whispered, his lips brushing against the side of my face. "I am sorry, you know."

"Sorry?" I looked at Thad in surprise.

"For everything." Tears filled his eyes before he cleared his throat and averted his gaze. "And I do love you, Chloe Celeste. Remember that. I do love you."

Now my remorse was genuine as I watched him board the train. *What happened to us since Paris, since Cape Cod?* I felt a hundred-pound weight resting on my soul. Preoccupied with waving until the train disappeared from view, I didn't notice the tears coursing my face until they brought on a coughing attack. Mama appeared at my side and handed me a linen handkerchief from her purse. She and my brother had waited in the depot while Thad and I said our farewells. Slipping her arm around my waist, she led me to the little train that would take the three of us to Springville.

During the ride to the rural mountain community, I sat hunched over and silent. I missed Thad more than I'd imagined I would, and I dreaded seeing my nephew, JC, for the first time. *I won't try to hold him,* I told myself. *I don't think I could stand to do that. Besides, I don't want to expose him to whatever it is I have.*

The baby was sleeping when we arrived at Jamie and Auriel's house. We'd been there but a few minutes when I had another bout of coughing. Mama insisted I rest while she and Jamie walked to the clinic where he worked.

Auriel led me to the guest room where Thad and I had slept during our previous visit, the memory of which brought a heavy pain to my heart. "Are you still working at the clinic?" I asked as Auriel turned down the bedding and I slipped out of my travel suit and put it on a hanger.

"Two afternoons a week," she replied, glancing my way. A look of shock spread over her face.

I looked down at my emaciated form and admitted, "I guess I've lost a little weight since losing the baby."

She nodded, then tried to cover up her shock. "Mama will fatten you up, never fear. A few weeks of her creamy buttermilk and the cook's Bavarian pastries, and you'll be bursting the seams of your clothing."

Suddenly I froze at the cries of the baby. "My baby," she whispered, her eyes flooding with tears. "Excuse me, please. He needs me."

I managed to choke out, "I'd come with you, but—" I coughed delicately. "—this cough. I'd hate to—"

She nodded and slipped from the room.

I fought the envy that bubbled up from deep within me. *I'm happy for my brother and Auriel. Truly, I am. Oh, God, it's not fair. It's not fair! You have enough life to sustain both of the boys. There didn't need to be a choice made.*

Just knowing that my healthy little nephew was in the next

room disturbed my sleep that night. In the morning, my red, puffy eyes must have given me away. One look at me over the breakfast table, and Mama insisted we continue our trip to San Francisco. "I need to get home to your father. I've been gone far too long."

Jamie and Auriel readily agreed. The concern and worry in their faces for their son was all too evident. And I didn't blame them one bit. As I watched the happy little boy sitting in the highchair on the far end of the breakfast table, I knew I'd be the same way were it my son. If he were mine, I'd protect him with the ferocity of a mother grizzly.

On the ride north to San Francisco, my mother said nothing about either my health or Thad's strange goodbye. She did tell me all the latest about kith and kin scattered across the continent. "Your Aunt Drucilla says Ashley's husband Charles is making money hand over fist in the stock market, but they're not happy together."

Late that night, ensconced in my bedroom, with Meeker sleeping by my feet and Sundance curled up on the rug beside my bed, I felt at peace for the first time in months. The heavy sorrow that had weakened my body and wounded my spirit receded as I closed my eyes and inhaled the familiar aromas of home.

From the moment I awakened the next morning, my parents began spoiling me. Daddy brought home books for me to read and musical recordings for the Victrola. Mama came home from the clinic carrying shopping bags of luscious fruit and exotic vegetables. She plied me each evening with her famous elixirs and herbal teas until I thought I might float away. Hilda, the cook, stuffed me with heavy desserts and main dishes swimming in rich cream sauce. I loved it. I'd had enough of adult troubles; I enjoyed being a child again, if only for a short time.

I had been home for an entire week before I realized that I'd left my beloved violin behind in New Mexico. Since the age of thirteen, I'd seldom allowed the instrument from my side. The shock that I didn't remember to bring it with me triggered my desire to get well. And I did begin to get better. My coughing attacks grew farther and farther apart.

Each day, after receiving Thad's letter in the mail, I took a walk in the garden. Each evening, I watched the city from my favorite arch in the gazebo and thought about him.

His letters came faithfully. He told about the visits he made, about the sermons he was writing, about the generosity of the Bowman family, and about their boarder, the new schoolteacher. I had to admit that it disturbed me when he wrote how he and Miss Masters would discuss points of church doctrine long after Mr. and Mrs. Bowman had retired for the night. *Foolish woman*, I thought, *as if Thad can't figure out what you're after*.

On weekends my mother bundled me up, and we went to visit Granddaddy Spencer and my younger brother, Rusty, at Uncle Joe's ranch. Rusty had decided to work at the ranch for the summer, hoping to earn enough money to buy a car.

At the ranch I'd sleep in the warm patio, take long walks with my grandfather, and enjoy relaxing evenings with the family. Nothing could have been better for my recovery. I'd been recuperating in California for a month, when Phoebe, my stepsister, noted my improved health and invited me to a dinner party for her husband's colleagues. "Come on, CeeCee. I need an extra woman at the table," she coaxed.

The day before the party, I tried on one of the evening dresses I'd worn in England. Finding that it hung like a tent from my shoulders, I ran downstairs to show my mother. "What am I going to do?" I cried. "I can't show up at Phoebe's party looking like this."

Mama took one look at the dress and declared, "CeeCee, you and I are going shopping."

Our shopping foray proved successful. I found a modest little midnight blue evening dress that would hide my thinness. With a little urging from my mother, I cut my hair to shoulder length. As the first lock fell to the floor, I wondered, for a moment, what Thad would think when he saw me again. Later, when the hairstylist finished and I examined myself in the mirror, I decided that I liked the new me. The new hairdo complimented my protruding cheek bones. I turned toward my mother. "What do you think?" I asked, gently shaking the loose locks.

"I like it. I think I'll have the woman cut mine too." Delighted with our new looks, she and I bought several additional outfits. We laughed and giggled like schoolgirls playing hooky. That evening, when I thought about our day together, I realized I'd seen a side of my mother that I'd never known before—and I liked it.

The first few minutes after I arrived at the dinner party, I felt uncomfortable not having Thad by my side, but soon I relaxed. The gentlemen between whom I sat at the dinner table were engaging, especially the man on my right, Dr. Morton Rayburn, a professor of music history at the university where Phoebe's husband taught. We had a great time discussing our preferences in baroque and classical music. It had been so long since I'd been around an individual versed in the arts that I felt as though I'd been resurrected from the dead.

In the course of the evening, I was careful to mention my husband Thad and his growing church in New Mexico a number of times. Dr. Rayburn, in turn, talked about his wife Fern, who was spending the season on the French Riviera. This led to my telling him about the months I spent at the clinic in Chamonix and about Sarge, the classically trained pianist, from whom a budding concert career had been snatched by the war. "He's a remarkable man. The last I knew, he was returning to school for his doctorate in music education."

"Incredible!" The way Dr. Rayburn hung on my every word was exhilarating. Toward the end of the evening, after I expressed an interest in seeing the campus, he volunteered to escort me about the following day. "Why don't I meet you here at your stepsister's house around eleven tomorrow morning? We'll tour the campus, and I can take you to lunch afterward. There's a fabulous little seafood place by the bay. You'll love it."

Fish? Hardly! Besides— I hesitated a moment. *This is just a professional contact, silly. It's all right for him to show you the campus and have lunch together later. After all, it's broad daylight.* "I would like that, if you can assure me that your restaurant serves something other than fish."

"What? You don't like fish? A longtime resident of the City by the Bay?"

I laughed and shook my head. "One lifetime wouldn't be long

enough for me to develop a tolerance for the taste of seafood, Dr. Rayburn."

"Call me Mort."

"Perhaps we'd better stick with Dr. Rayburn and Mrs. Adams," I demurred.

His eyes twinkled as he bowed slightly. "As you wish, Mrs. Adams. And bring your violin along. I would love to hear you play."

I shrugged and smiled sadly. "I would, but I left it at my home in New Mexico, I'm afraid."

"No problem, I'm sure we have a practice fiddle in the music department somewhere."

Dr. Rayburn volunteered to drive me home, but I declined his offer. "My parents lent me the family car this evening. Thank you anyway."

As I prepared to leave, Phoebe whispered in my ear, "Wait, I need to talk to you about something important."

I lingered in her parlor until after their other guests had left. When she and her husband returned, Phoebe paused in the doorway, her face suffused with anger. "CeeCee, please tell the folks not to worry about Nikolai any longer. He sent me a telegram from England."

"Oh!" I clasped my hands together with delight. "They will be so relieved."

"Hardly! The scoundrel is living off the money our mother placed in a Swiss bank account for us before she died. I knew nothing about the money or the secret account."

Sensing Phoebe's frustration, her husband put his arm around her shoulders. "It's all right, honey. We don't need the money anyway."

"What my husband is saying is that dear, sweet Nikolai has no intention of sharing the wealth with me. He says it was his father's money, not mine. By the sound of it, he's squandering the inheritance all over London."

"Can't you do anything?"

Phoebe glanced over her shoulder at her husband. "I would, but Jonathan disapproves."

"I'm sure there's little one can do while he's out of the country. That's the beauty of Swiss bank accounts, my dear."

After I arrived home, I told my parents the news about Nikolai's deception. My father stared into the fireplace embers while Mama exploded. "Now I understand why Nikolai didn't fight you about turning the smuggled items over to the French government!" she sputtered. "After all we did for the boy! He lied to everyone. And to think how he risked your life, CeeCee."

Daddy stood up and scattered the embers with the poker. "Well, I guess I don't have to feel guilty any longer that I found the lad totally intolerable!"

I laughed at my father's ironic sense of humor, then changed the subject. "Oh, Daddy, I have a lunch invitation for tomorrow, and I wonder if I could borrow the car again. I'll drive you to work first, if you like."

Mama gave a pleased smile. "I'm glad to see that you and Phoebe are becoming friends."

I reddened a bit. "We are, but I'm not having lunch with her. One of the professors who sat next to me at the dinner party volunteered to show me the campus, especially the music department."

My mother pursed her lips thoughtfully. "Oh? I didn't know the university employed female professors. How progressive."

My color deepened. "Dr. Rayburn is a man, Mother."

Now my father's smile disappeared into a frown. "Do you think it's wise to be seen in public with another man? Your being a married woman?"

"Daddy, I'm not romantically involved with the man. He's only going to show me the campus. That's all. I don't believe this." I shook my head in wonder. "I'm not a child anymore. And I certainly have no intentions of being unfaithful to my husband." I waited for a reply, but none came. "If you'd prefer I not use the car, I will call a taxi."

"You're right, my dear. It's sometimes hard to remember that you are indeed a mature woman and don't need us to think for you." My father put his arm about my shoulders and led me toward the stairs. "Of course, you may use the car." As we reached the first step, he paused. "But please remember, darling, men think differently than women about such things."

"Daddy! We had this talk when I was sixteen, remember?"

"You're right. Come on, Chloe, it's time to get some sleep."

Without a word, my mother climbed the stairs behind my father.

"I'll be up in a few minutes. I want to take my evening walk out to the gazebo. Good night."

"Good night," they called, their bedroom door closing behind them.

I thought of Thad as I gazed out over the sparkling lights of the city. *How ironic,* I thought. *Thad is probably looking up at a canopy of desert stars right now while I look down at a blanket of city lights. And most likely, that spinster teacher is right by his side, correcting him when he mistakes the evening star for the north star.* A cool breeze ruffled the loose hairs on my neck, sending a chill through my body. *Thad, I do love you, you know. I really do—* Reluctantly, I ambled back inside the house. Though my cough was lessening and my strength returning, I couldn't risk a relapse.

The next morning, while I was dressing for my appointment with Dr. Rayburn, my mother knocked on my door. "Today's mail arrived. You have a letter from Thad."

"Come on in." I held up two new outfits, a gray flowered chiffon dress and a pale green silk shantung suit. "Which should I wear today?"

"It's up to you. I won't be a party to your liaison with a man other than your husband." She laid Thad's letter on the edge of the bed and turned to walk from the room. "I'm so happy you're feeling so much better. Perhaps you're strong enough to make the trip home now."

I whirled about in surprise. "Are you saying that I've overstayed my welcome? That you want me to leave?"

Mama lifted her hand in denial. "No, darling, I would never say that to any of my children. It's just that a wife belongs by her husband's side. Thaddeus needs you."

"Not really, Mother." I held up the gray flowered dress and examined my reflection in the mirror. Even I couldn't miss seeing the hardness in my eyes. "My husband would be content with or without me, I assure you."

I heard her walk toward me, then saw her reflection behind me in the mirror. "CeeCee, I've waited for you to talk about the baby. I could tell things were tense between you and Thad at the depot. You have to let it go, darling." She placed her hands on my shoulders and gazed at our reflections, so similar, yet different. "Whatever anger and bitterness you're holding inside you, you must, sooner or later, let it go."

I stared into the mirror, watching hard lines form at the corners of my lips. *Here goes. This is the talk I was dreading.* I straightened my shoulders and barricaded my mind.

She searched my face as she spoke. "You've changed so. What happened to the young girl who returned from France praising God and eager to live life?"

"You're right! I am no longer the adoring little girl who could be coaxed from a frown into a smile. Mother, I'm a woman who has lost two children. I'm a woman who lived for a time in a canvas tent, a woman who followed her husband from one backwater Texas town to the next. I'm the woman who spent night after lonely night in cheap boardinghouses, waiting for her husband to return after 'doing the Lord's work'!" I spat the words at her mirrored reflection. My eyes brimmed with tears. "That's who I am now, Mother. That's who I am!"

Tears spilled down my mother's cheeks. But instead of backing away from me as I expected her to do, Mama hugged my shoulders more tightly. "Oh, CeeCee darling, I'm so sorry you are hurting. If I could, I would lift your load of pain from your shoulders and carry it for you." She choked out the words through her tears. "Life plays rough sometimes, doesn't it?"

Suddenly, the dam of tears that had been building since the day I stopped crying over my lost son broke loose. Tossing the dress on the bed, I turned and found myself engulfed in my mother's waiting arms. "He was a beautiful baby boy, Mama. Perfect in every detail. It's not fair!" I sobbed. "It's just not fair!"

"I know, honey. I know." She massaged my back and let me cry.

"Why does God snatch an innocent child from his mother's arms? I mean, I could understand when Au Sam died. As much as I loved her, I could understand. And the casualties of war I could understand."

"I don't know, darling." My mother led me to the bed. "I wish I did, but I don't. However, I do know that God loves you, and He never leaves you to bear your problems alone. And I believe you'll hold that sweet little babe in your arms once again in the perfect environment of heaven."

I shook my head in despair. It all sounded so fairy-tale lovely— and so unbelievable. "I want to believe. Honest, I do." I remembered the joy I had once experienced and the peace. *Oh, to enjoy that peace again!*

"Darling, I know this is little comfort now, but God will give you another baby to hold and to love. And while that child can never take the place of—"

"Mama," I interrupted, "there will be no more babies!"

"Of course there will, sweetheart."

"No, there won't! I won't let it happen again. I won't!"

She held me at arm's length and gazed into my eyes. "Honey, you can't be sure of that."

"Oh yes, I can. And I will prevent it!"

"Are you saying what I think you're saying?"

I nodded my head defiantly. "Absolutely!"

"Have you discussed your decision with Thad?"

"Of course not." I folded my arms, waiting for her stream of protest.

"Are you ready to betray your marriage vows? The physical side of marriage is, as one preacher put it, the lubricant that keeps the engine running smoothly."

I turned my shoulder from her. "I don't care. I can't risk another pregnancy." When she didn't reply, I turned to face her again. "I haven't told Thad, but the physician who cared for me after, after our son died—" I swallowed hard several times. "—said that I would probably have trouble delivering another baby to full term. In other words, the next one will die too!"

My mother frowned, absorbing the meaning of my words. "Are you sure? Have you seen any other doctors?"

"No, I don't have to." I avoided her gaze while we listened to the gong from the grandfather clock at the top of the stairs sounding ten times.

"I'm sorry, sweetheart, but I'm due at the clinic in a few minutes. But I can call and tell them I'll be late, if you—"

I shook my head. Slowly, my mother stood, resting her hand on my shoulder. "Then I'll leave you alone to read your letter from Thad. You'd better start getting dressed if you want to be on time for your, uh, appointment."

As the door closed behind her, I opened the letter. "Dearest CeeCee," it began. "You asked in your last letter about the rosebush you planted last fall. I haven't checked it lately since I don't go home until after dark most nights. Most of the time I'm either at the church office, making visitation calls, or at the Bowmans'."

"Hmmph! Might know," I grunted.

"I promise that I'll water the bush as soon as I post this letter. After that, Elizabeth asked me to stop by the school and help her choose a new biology book. She wants to be certain there's not a taint of evolution in the text before she orders them."

"Hmmph!" I grunted again. "Can't you see that the only evolution she's concerned about is her evolving relationship with you?" I hurriedly read the rest of his letter and tossed it on the bed.

After a quick scrub, I splashed astringent on my face to relieve the puffiness around my eyes, patted on a little face powder, and brushed my hair to a rich shine. Then I slipped into the gray flowered chiffon and added a wide-brimmed straw hat. A pair of black patent leather pumps and matching purse completed the ensemble.

Hmmm. I sashayed one direction, then the other in front of the mirror. I felt five years younger. *You look pretty good, Mrs. Adams, for an old married woman of twenty-five.*

As I glided down the stairs to the foyer, I could hear my mother talking with someone as I passed the open library doors. "Mama?" I peeked into the room. "How do I look? Oh, sorry. I didn't know you were on the telephone." I turned to tiptoe away.

"No, CeeCee, wait. It's for you." She extended the receiver toward me. "It's Thaddeus."

"Thad?" I froze midstep, then whirled about in panic. "Please, I don't want to talk with him right now," I hissed, staring at the receiver as if it were a cobra. "You didn't tell him about my luncheon, er, appointment, did you?"

She shook her head and placed the receiver in my hand. I took a deep breath and lifted it to my ear.

"Thad? What a pleasant surprise. What prompted you to call at this time of day?"

"Hello, darling. I miss you too," he replied over the scratchy-sounding connection.

"Oh, I'm sorry. I can hardly hear you. Are you calling from the mercantile?" I plugged my one ear so as to focus on his voice.

"No, the church board voted to allow me to attend a Bible conference in Los Angeles. I'm in Los Angeles. I spent Tuesday night in Springville with Jamie and Auriel."

"What?"

"I'm in Los Angeles at some meetings. It all happened so suddenly I didn't have time to tell you about it in a letter."

"Los Angeles? Did you say Los Angeles? I can barely make out what you're saying." I hurried on, knowing that I'd be late for my appointment if we talked very long. Having Thad intrude on my safe little world irritated me. "How long will your meetings last? When do you head back home?"

"The last meeting is Saturday night—"

"Honey, I'm sorry to interrupt, but could you call me back this evening? I have a luncheon engagement for which I'm already late. And, besides, this connection is terrible."

The reluctance in his voice was obvious as he accommodated my wishes. But I didn't even wait to hear the click before I placed the receiver in its cradle and hurried from the house. Despite the delay Thad's call had caused, I still arrived at Phoebe's home three minutes before Dr. Rayburn. I'd barely finished telling her about my parents' reaction to Nikolai's secret stash of wealth when the tall, engaging professor arrived at her front door.

She arched her eyebrows when I explained Dr. Rayburn's reason for being there. "Your husband doesn't mind?" she hissed.

I laughed. "Of course not. You and Mother are making more of this than necessary." After extending the proper greetings, Dr. Rayburn took my arm and escorted me down the steps in front of the house.

"I thought we'd leave your car here until later, since your sister's house is right on the edge of campus." He glanced admiringly at the shiny new forest-green-and-black Packard. "My father-in-law owns a maroon Packard similar to that." I couldn't miss the sharp edge in his voice. "Fern's papa paid for her trip to the Riviera too. University professors, like pastors, don't travel in those circles."

I laughed and fell into step beside him. "I didn't realize until after we were married that my father's money bothered Thaddeus."

Dr. Rayburn tossed a wry smile my direction. "A woman can't understand how emasculating it is for a man to live off her inheritance, I assure you." He shrugged and grinned a hapless grin. "Hey, but what can I do? I like expensive things, and I love teaching music."

"If it really bothers you, why don't you find other employment?"

He laughed sardonically. "There aren't too many employers eager to hire a man who's skilled at playing medieval woodwind instruments."

"I guess you have a point there." I thought to myself, *At least Thad has a calling from God*. About that I had no doubt.

I enjoyed my tour of the university campus. Dr. Rayburn was an engaging guide, full of interesting trivia and anecdotes. He saved the music department for last. The studios were much like the ones where I studied in New York and the ones I had toured in Boston. When we arrived at the last studio, he placed a violin in my hands. "Here. I could tell by the longing in your voice last night that you missed playing. Why don't you play something for me?"

I took the treasured instrument and tuned the strings. Then, reverently, I began to play the familiar melody of "Jesu, Joy of Man's Desiring." Squawky at first, revealing how out of practice I was, the notes sweetened after the first movement. I glided into Beethoven's "Pathétique" and the "Coriolan Overture." I became so absorbed in my music that I forgot Dr. Rayburn was still in the room. I ended my impromptu concert with "Turkey in the Straw," my tribute to Sarge.

As I lowered the bow, applause broke out from behind me. The entire music faculty stood in the open doorway.

The college string instructor rushed to my side. "Please tell me that you are here to audition for admission to our program next fall."

I laughed and shook my head. "Sorry, sir, I'm a little long in the tooth for that. I'm just visiting your campus from New Mexico."

"Ah—" He waved his hand in the air dramatically. "—what a waste! I am crushed. Nevertheless, thank you for allowing me a moment of hope."

After all the music faculty had left, Dr. Rayburn suggested we drive to the restaurant in his sporty yellow Dusenburg. We walked to the opposite side of the campus from where Phoebe lived. I loved the art-deco look of the stark white mansion he called home.

"My car's parked around back. I'll go get it."

"It's beautiful," I whispered as I gazed up at the building's clean, simple lines.

"Excuse me?"

"The house, it's beautiful."

"Would you like to see inside?"

"Oh no. It wouldn't be proper, what with your wife away and all."

"No problem." He gestured toward the house. "The presence of Myrna and Franz, our cook and butler, will dispel any naughty rumors that might arise."

"I don't know." An uneasy feeling welled up inside me.

"Aw, come on. You know you want to."

I admit that it didn't take much to convince me to give in to my curiosity. And I wasn't disappointed. The lofty ceilings, the black-and-white tile, the sleek, modern furniture that looked more pleasing to the eye than to the human anatomy all produced enthusiastic responses from me. I followed Dr. Rayburn from room to room, never realizing that I hadn't once seen Myrna or Franz.

Suddenly, I found myself standing in the middle of the master bedroom, feeling terribly uncomfortable. I turned to leave and found Dr. Rayburn standing in front of the closed door, smiling and holding two glasses of champagne. "For you, my dear."

My mouth dropped open. I wagged my head vigorously and stuttered, "N-n-n-n-no! Thank you, but no. I-I-I think we'd better leave for the restaurant now, don't you?" I rubbed my stomach and involuntarily moistened my lips. "Suddenly, I'm feeling very hungry."

"O-o-o-h, I knew you would be once I got you away from society's peering eyes. You and that fiery red hair of yours."

"No, you misunderstood. I'm hungry for food. Lunch!" I fingered the ruffled neckline of my dress nervously, my gaze darting about the room, searching for an escape. *Oh, dear God, Daddy was right about this man's motives all along. How could I have been so foolish?*

He smiled, his eyes partially shaded by the tilt of his head. "A little champagne will help you shed that Victorian reserve of yours." He sauntered across the room toward me. "Here, try some. It's a very good year, I assure you."

"I, uh, am sure it is." I backed away from his approaching figure. "Please, if I unknowingly led you to think that I would—" I couldn't bring myself to even use the term for what he had in mind. "—then I am sorry."

"CeeCee, my dear, it is natural for you to be timid, especially if this is your first assignation. Trust yourself in my experienced hands."

"Dr. Rayburn, I love my husband."

He set the wine glasses down on a library table behind the sofa. "And I love my wife. But let's be realistic, my dear. My wife's basking in the Mediterranean sunshine with who knows whom, and your Thaddeus is preaching to a bunch of jack rabbits and coyotes in New Mexico. That leaves you and me, here, together, to comfort one another in our lonely state."

The aspersions he cast on Thad filled me with fury, and I dashed for the door. "I don't know what kind of women you're accustomed to bringing into your home for your afternoon trysts, but I won't be one of them," I gasped as he stood staring at me in disbelief. "And just so you know, my Thaddeus is twice the man you will ever be. I feel sorry for your wife, Dr. Rayburn. If I were she, I'd spend the rest of the year on the Riviera too."

I ran down the stairs and out the front door. Pausing at the sidewalk, I glanced up at the huge floor-to-ceiling window in the master bedroom, through which Dr. Rayburn was smiling down at me. When he saw me looking up at him, he lifted his wine glass in a toast.

Irritated even more at my own naiveté than at the man's advances, I marched across campus to my stepsister's home and drove home without stopping to tell her I was back from my adventure. As I drove up Russian Hill, I caught the reflection of myself in the Packard's side window and noted the high color blazing in my cheeks. *How could I be so stupid? Of all the dumb things I've done in my life! How will I ever face Thad again?* My guilt overwhelmed me. *I can't go home now. I need to be alone.* I did a U-turn and drove north to the Presidio and back before I felt composed enough to meet my parents' intuitive gazes. *Chloe Celeste, it's time to go home! Really home! To Thaddeus!*

New Beginnings, New Horizons

"Hello. Mama?" I called as I stepped into the cool interior of my parents' home. Sundance bounded down the hall and skidded to a stop by my feet, and I bent down to pat his head. "Oh, you big old baby. Of course, I'll pet you. Where's Mama, anyway?"

"Excuse me, ma'am." Hilda, the cook, stepped into the hallway from the kitchen. "If you are looking for the missis, she said to tell you that she would be at the clinic all afternoon."

"Thank you, Hilda." I felt an overwhelming need to talk with Thad, but under the circumstances, the letter I had received that morning would have to do.

I gave Sundance an extra pat and hurried toward the stairs.

Hilda followed me. "Excuse me, but your mother told me to remind you about the art-gallery opening she and your father planned to attend this evening. She hopes you will go with them."

I groaned but continued walking. "Thank you, Hilda, for reminding me. I had forgotten." Still shaken from my encounter with Dr. Rayburn, I didn't want to see anyone or be with anyone, let alone stroll through an art gallery, holding a glass of seltzer water, smiling, and nodding at people I didn't know and didn't really want to know. Startled, I recognized my problem. *I am homesick! I've had more than enough of the "good life" for a while. Dear God, take me back to the simple, open people of New Mexico.*

The memory of the morning phone call surfaced in my mind. I could hear the haunting loneliness in my husband's voice—

like a little boy lost. *Mama's right—I've been here long enough. I'm going home!*

In a surge of energy, I bounded up the stairs with Sundance at my heels. Hauling my luggage out from under the bed, I began packing my clothes. When the dog realized that my flight up the stairs wasn't for his entertainment, he sprawled on the floor in front of the open window and went to sleep.

If I catch the morning train, maybe I can beat Thad home. Won't he be surprised to walk into the house and find fresh flowers, a pot of lentil stew bubbling on the stove, and me wearing the mandarin wedding dress? I hugged myself and danced a little jig in the middle of the floor. *I'd like to take him a present of some kind. Let's see. A fountain pen? A book? A new suit? A set of pastels? Why not buy all of it? Everything!*

Abandoning my partially filled luggage, I hurried to the trolley stop. I decided against taking the Packard, since I knew my folks would need the car that evening, and I didn't want to be rushed.

My first stop was at an art supplies store, followed by a gentlemen's clothier; then I pressed on to a number of bookstores. I felt like my Grandma McCall on one of her shopping forays in Boston. Like her, I requested that the merchandise be delivered to my parents' home. On my way back to the house, I paused in front of a small shop specializing in ladies' sleeping apparel. *I haven't bought any frilly or lacy things since before our wedding. I deserve some—and so does Thad!* My last stop was for a box of bonbons and a molded-chocolate rosebud.

By the time I arrived home, many of my purchases had proceeded me. As I raced up the stairs with the parcels, I caught my reflection in the mirror. Pleased with the color and vitality evident in my face, I whirled about the room, singing, "How ya gonna keep 'em down on the farm, after they've seen Paree?"

"My, my!" My father peered into my room through the open door. "Aren't you feeling frisky!"

"Oh, Daddy, I've had the most, the most—" I thought for a moment. "—the most revealing day."

He glanced at my luggage spread out across the bed. "Going somewhere?"

"Oh yes." I cast him a devilish grin. "I'm going home to Thad."

His eyebrows approached his hairline. "Oh, really?"

"Yep." I removed the box of chocolates from the shopping bag. "Tomorrow morning, in fact. I've lain around long enough, don't you think?"

My father grinned and shrugged. "We've enjoyed having you here, little one."

"I know, and don't think I haven't appreciated all you and Mama have done for me—but, well, as Mama said the other morning, a wife belongs by her husband's side. Thad needs me."

"I'm sure he does."

"And I miss him too."

"So I take it you won't be attending the gallery opening with us this evening?"

"Oh no. I have too much to do. I just wish I could see Granddaddy before I leave, but I guess that can't be helped."

"Suppose not," he added. "Don't work too hard tonight. You don't want to have a relapse."

"Oh, I won't. I promise."

"Oh, your mother's home." He spoke to someone in the hall. "Chloe, CeeCee's decided to go home to Thad." There was a slight pause. "Tomorrow."

My mother peeked around the edge of the door. "That's wonderful, darling. We'll miss you, of course."

"I know. I understand. Go get ready for your party; I'll be fine."

"Are you sure?" She turned to my father. "Maybe we should stay home with CeeCee, this being her last night with us and all."

"Nonsense!" I waved her away. "I'll be just fine. Go out and have fun together."

Mama laughed as her head disappeared around the edge of the door. "By the way," my father explained, "your mother and I will be out till quite late. We'll ask Hilda to prepare a light supper for you and leave it in the icebox."

"Thanks, Dad. You two have fun at your party."

The house quieted down quickly after my parents left. For a few minutes, I could hear Hilda puttering around downstairs in the kitchen; then I heard the kitchen door close and knew I was finally alone. I dug my shoes out of the closet and returned to the luggage, only to find Meeker sleeping on top of my clothes. I clapped my hands and cried, "Scat! You naughty cat!"

She turned and gave me her famous Meeker stare, as if to say, "How dare you disturb me!"

Picking up her limp body, I placed her on the afghan at the foot of the bed. "Now stay there! You shed hair all over my favorite dress!" Meeker just ignored me and licked her paws.

Once my cases were packed and lined up at the foot of my bed, I wandered down to the kitchen and ate the salad and sandwich Hilda had fixed for me. Grabbing a few carrot sticks to chew on, I ambled out to the gazebo to watch the sun set over the city. As darkness enveloped the world around us, the lights of the city blinked on one by one.

I sat hugging my knees and wondering what Thad might be doing. *Probably attending some stuffy meeting on the chronology of the Chronicles!* My hair fluttered in the breeze blowing off the ocean, and I could smell the salt in the air.

I've strayed, Lord, from trusting You, from praising You. Forgive me. I want to go back to Thaddeus clean and renewed in You. I want to be the helpmate You fashioned for him. The words of Psalm 42:8 came out of nowhere as I gazed on the peaceful nightscape. "Yet the Lord will command his lovingkindness in the daytime, and in the night his song shall be with me, and my prayer unto the God of my life."

Lovingkindness? Your lovingkindness is in the death of my baby? I can't feel it, Lord; please help me to trust You to keep Your promises.

Feeling a chill from the breeze, I returned to the house with Sundance tailing me. *Maybe I'll read a good book to pass the time.*

In the library, I decided to listen to my father's radio, and I fiddled with the knobs until I located a local concert through the static. Thad and I didn't have much use for a radio out on the high desert. *Remarkable*, I thought, *not as pleasurable as listening to the Victrola, but at least I don't have to jump up and change the record every few minutes.*

I curled up on the sofa with my mother's newest volume of Emily Dickinson's posthumously published poems. Sundance stretched out on the floor beside the sofa, and Meeker slept on my feet.

Around eleven o'clock, I put Sundance and Meeker outside for the night, then padded up the stairs to my bedroom. *I guess Daddy wasn't kidding when he said they'd be out late this evening.*

After a half-hour in a bathtub filled with hot water and orange-blossom bath salts, I scrubbed myself pink, dried off, and wandered back to my bedroom. I couldn't resist wearing one of my day's purchases, a petal-pink silk nightgown. "Not bad for a married woman, Mrs. Adams," I told my reflection in the mirror. "What will Pastor Adams think when he sees you in this?" Thinking pleasant thoughts of Thaddeus and the comfortable little adobe hacienda awaiting my return, I drifted off to sleep.

I remember dreaming that I was chasing waves on the beach by my parents' summer place on Cape Cod. I could feel the cool Atlantic surf wash across my bare toes before I stumbled to the dry sand and collapsed in a heap beside Thad, who'd been sketching the gulls on the nearby rocks. I watched Sundance bark and chase a pesky gull up the beach, then bound back to me. I laughed and tried to push the dog away as he licked my face. "Quit it, Sundance," I cried.

"Sundance?" A familiar voice jarred me to semiconsciousness. The voice laughed; then I felt the pressure of lips touching mine.

"Wake up, darling. Wake up."

My eyes blinked open, and in the moonlight, I found myself staring into Thad's smiling face.

"Oh, oh." I struggled to wake up. "Thad, it's you. It's really you." I burst into tears, and Thad gathered me into his arms and rocked me back and forth.

"I missed you too, darling. I missed you too." As he showered my neck and bare shoulders with tiny kisses, all I could do was cry.

"I'm so glad you're here," I hiccuped. "I love you, Thaddeus Adams. And I never want to be apart from you again!"

"Nor I, you. You are so precious to me. I was afraid I'd lost you forever."

"What?" I stared at his face shrouded in the shadows.

"Well, we didn't exactly part on loving terms. And, well, it's been a rough first two years of marriage." My heart, more than my ears, heard the incredible sadness in his voice. We spent the next several hours honestly discussing some of the issues that had driven us apart—something we should have done months before.

We arose late the next morning, after my parents had already left for the day. The spring day was warm enough for Hilda to serve us breakfast on the patio. As I gazed across the breakfast table at my husband, I kept thinking, *I still can't believe you're here.*

"What?" He frowned, his grapefruit spoon poised in his hand. "Is something wrong?"

"Hardly. Everything's so right. But what in the world made you decide to come for me and miss the rest of your meetings?"

He grinned sheepishly. "Well, yesterday, when I called from the conference, your mother advised me to come for you right away. She didn't say much, and I didn't ask any questions. She just said, 'Your wife needs you.'

"I told her that I'd try to catch the next train north and be in Oakland late that night. I caught a cab across town and boarded the train just as it was ready to pull out of the station. I even had to buy my ticket on board from the conductor!"

"I can't believe it."

He reached across the table and took my hand. "Your parents met my train after their party and brought me home to you."

"I'm so glad. And—" I swallowed hard, praying Thad wouldn't ask any questions. *Maybe someday, God, but not now. Please not now.* "—my mother was right. I did need you."

Tears glistened in his eyes. "I needed you too."

Later, as we lounged in the afternoon sunshine, Thad announced, "There's something I wanted to talk over with you. I don't know if this is a good time or not. And perhaps the whole thing is irrelevant after I left the meetings."

"What's irrelevant?"

"I met a Dr. George Gibson. He and his wife are missionaries in China. At the first meeting, he gave a talk on mission service."

"China? How interesting. Did I ever tell you that Mama once wanted to go to China as a missionary?"

"Yes. After the meeting, I told Dr. Gibson about Elder and Mrs. Van Dorn's influence on your mother. It was the Van Dorns who recruited him and his wife, Eve, twenty years ago."

"What a coincidence! Did you tell my mother?" I leaned back in the rattan patio chair.

Thad nodded. "She couldn't believe it either. He said the couple retired in Ohio after Elder Van Dorn had a stroke a few years back." He paused a moment, then continued. "But the part you and I need to talk about is this: when Dr. Gibson learned of your nursing skills and, of course, my experience as a traveling evangelist, he became very excited." Thad cleared his throat. "He's asked us to join him and his wife at their fifteen-bed clinic in northern China. The pastor's family we'd be replacing is transferring to Burma."

I lifted my eyebrows in dismay.

"Now, I know this is sudden and probably out of the question with your being ill and all, but I wanted to talk it over with you before I turned him down."

"Talk it over with me?" I asked cautiously.

"Of course. You're my wife, aren't you? My life partner? What affects you affects me." Thad took a deep breath. "Perhaps if we'd been in one accord on our previous two appointments, we would both have been a lot happier. That's the advice Genevieve gave me before we left her and Gideon in Oklahoma."

"She was probably right. But China?" I thought of Au Sam and the quaint stories she had told of China, of dragons and full moons, princesses and emperors.

"We don't have to decide today, but I should send the man a telegram to see if the position is still available. He might not want to hire a man who would go running off to his wife's side in the middle of a Bible conference."

"Well!" I huffed. "If he has any sense, that's the kind of man he should be looking for, one who cares enough to put his wife before his job."

He chuckled at my vehemence. "Would you be willing to work in a primitive clinic?"

"Maybe. Surely it can't be more primitive than the one in Chamonix!" I laughed at the surprise on his face. "I'd like to use my training somewhere."

"But China?"

"Hey, what's going on here? I thought you were trying to convince me, not the other way around."

He grinned and shook his head. "Seriously, before we make any decisions, we need to pray about it together."

"Let's walk out to the gazebo, where we won't be interrupted," I suggested, rising from my patio chair.

Thad took my hand tenderly and placed it on his as we strolled to the gazebo amid the aroma of Mama's prize roses.

"I wish we'd had more time for this before we were married." He caressed my hand.

"It was kind of rushed there at the end, wasn't it?"

The California sun warmed my shoulders and back as we gazed at the diaphanous haze over the city. "You don't know how many times I prayed for us from this spot."

"That's another thing. We haven't developed the habit of praying together, except at meals, of course. It's my fault, but I'd like to begin having some kind of worship together each evening," Thad suggested.

"I'd like that." I smiled to myself.

He studied the cityscape for several seconds. "I think that you and I need to begin behaving like a real family instead of two people trapped in the same house, for better or for worse."

I gazed at his profile. "I'd like that too. Where do we begin?"

He turned slowly toward me. "Right here, right now." He led me to a bench. There, we knelt, face to face, clutching each other's hands, while Thad poured out his heart to God and to me. He asked forgiveness for the times he'd neglected his responsibilities as a husband, for the times he disregarded my will in preference to his own and failed to consult God for His will for us. By the time Thad said Amen, we were both teary.

My husband's honesty in confessing his faults demanded the

same from me. "Dear heavenly Father, I don't know where to begin. I've made so many mistakes as Thad's wife and as Your daughter." I enumerated the times I'd purposely made it difficult for Thad to do the Lord's work, the times I'd hated God and Thad for the death of our child, the times I'd nursed the idea that maybe I'd married the wrong man. "I was wrong; I know that now." I peeked at Thad. Though his eyes were squeezed shut, a tear trickled down his cheek.

I gulped back my own tears and continued. "But most of all, Father, I confess to You and to my husband that yesterday, when I toured the university campus with Dr. Rayburn, I secretly welcomed the man's flattery and praise. I realize now that my foolish ego could have cost me my marriage. Thank You, Lord, for protecting me from myself." My voice faltered.

"Since we're making confessions," Thad began to pray again, "I, too, must confess that I found Miss Masters's attention more flattering than is wise for a married man, especially for one who desperately loves his wife. Please forgive me." Thad squeezed my hands tightly.

Feeling a strange heaviness in my heart, I opened my eyes to find Thad searching my face. A silent healing passed between us as he lifted my hands to his lips and tenderly kissed my fingertips. We continued to look into each other's eyes as he prayed, "Thank You, Father, for giving me this beautiful woman to love and to walk by my side. Help me never to take her love for granted again. And now, Lord, we stand before You clean, forgiven, and eager to serve You. Please guide us; make us wise and willing. Amen."

Our answer came that evening in a telegram. "China position filled—STOP. May God bless your ministry in New Mexico—STOP."

Two days later, Thad and I kissed my parents goodbye and boarded the train for Grants via Springville. However, this time when I visited Jamie, I eagerly held my nephew. I was no longer afraid that I might expose JC to some terrible lung disease or that he would expose me to a love I couldn't handle.

Warm feelings spread through me when I caught sight of our adobe hacienda. While I felt a bit disappointed that the China appointment didn't work out, I was eager to make up for all the time Thad and I had missed in New Mexico. My husband must have been thinking similar thoughts, because at the threshold, he lifted me into his arms and carried me into the house. As he set me down, he said, "Welcome home, Mrs. Adams."

I planted a kiss on his lips. "It's good to be home, Mr. Adams."

"By the way, Mrs. Adams." He removed my bonnet and tossed it on the sofa, then slowly removed my hairpins, allowing my hair to tumble down to my shoulders. "Did I tell you that I like your new hairstyle?" His eyes twinkled with deviltry as he ran his fingers through the mass of curls and chuckled. "Easier to undo."

"Oh, really?" I gave him a teasing grin and stretched on tiptoe to kiss him again. We pulled apart when we heard a polite cough at the open door.

"Excuse me, but Emily, er, Mrs. Bowman suggested I welcome you home with these."

Thad strode to the door while I turned my back on the intruder. I knew without looking that the owner of the cloying simper would be none other than perky little Miss Elizabeth Masters.

"Oh, Miss Masters, what a surprise. The flowers are beautiful. Aren't they, darling?"

I curled my lip in disgust.

"Miss Masters, you haven't met my wife yet, have you? Honey, this is Miss Masters from Atlanta, Georgia."

Before turning around, I pasted on my "pastor's wife" smile. "How do you do, Miss Masters." I extended my hand to greet her. The impact of this diminutive woman left me breathless for a moment—corn-silk-blond curls, distinct curves beneath the ecru lace chemise, delicate pointed toes on her matching shoes. Her natural blush would have made my cousin Ashley jealous, as would the tilt of her nose and her pouty red lips.

"No, no, please call me Elizabeth," she simpered, ignoring my hand. "It's so good to meet you too, CeeCee. What a strange little name." She wrinkled her nose and giggled delicately. "Thad has told me so much about you." She rolled her blue eyes toward my husband. I clasped my hands behind my back to control the urge to scratch them out.

"And me, you, Miss Masters." I strolled to my husband's side and slipped my arm around his waist, snuggling close to his chest. "I want to thank you, and Mrs. Bowman, of course, for taking such good care of Thaddeus while I was recuperating at my parents' home. We women need to tend to our men, don't we?"

Her face darkened for a moment; then she recovered. "Absolutely. A southern woman learns at her mama's knee how to spoil her man." She gazed adoringly into Thad's face and giggled once more.

"CeeCee, why don't you put Miss Masters's flowers in water before they wilt." A frowning Thad disentangled himself from my arms, took the flowers from the woman's hand, and shoved them into mine. Then, escorting the frothy Georgia peach to the door, he said, "And thank you, again, for welcoming us home. Please tell Mrs. Bowman how much my wife and I appreciate the gesture."

The moment I was certain the woman had left, I threw the gladioluses out the front door onto the walkway.

"CeeCee!" Thad couldn't conceal the twinkle in his eyes when he shook his head and clicked his tongue. "That reaction is hardly suitable for a minister's wife."

I slammed the door behind me and planted my hands on my hips. "It is precisely a suitable reaction for a minister's wife who loves her husband and can spot a home-wrecker five miles down the road!"

He laughed, wrapped his arms about me, and twirled me about. "What a lion of a woman I married!"

Before classes commenced in the fall, Miss Elizabeth Masters decided she wasn't cut out for frontier living and returned to her beloved plantation. And new peace settled over our little home.

Though Thad was immediately engulfed in his pastorate and I eagerly resumed my schedule of assisting at the reservation clinic, we were careful to set aside time for each other. My worship turned to praise as I grew stronger, hiking the barren hills outside of town several times a week.

Whenever possible, I went along on Thad's pastoral visits. The long drives to his parishioners' homes gave us time to talk and to enjoy one another in new, exciting ways.

After church one week, Mrs. Bowman asked if I could teach her eight-year-old daughter, Cecilia, to play the piano. Before I realized what was happening, I had fourteen children coming to the church for piano lessons and three others starting the violin.

The only discordant note in our lives was my inability to become pregnant. Every baby I treated at the reservation made me long for one of my own. A week before Christmas, we drove to Albuquerque to get a second medical opinion on my condition. We returned home the next morning with little hope that we'd ever have children of our own.

As I cleaned potatoes to boil for supper that evening and Thad sat reading in our only easy chair, I asked, "What would you say to bringing up other people's children, Thad?"

He glanced up from his book. "You mean adopting?"

I shrugged. "That's one possibility. Another is to open our home to children needing a temporary home for one reason or another. We could convert your office into a nursery, since you do all your desk work next door at the church."

He ignored my reference to his office space. "Do you have a specific child in mind?"

I dried my hands and placed the kettle on the stove. "Not really. But there must be agencies we could contact to let them know we're available."

"Hmm. Would you want to bring someone into our home to love, then have to give him or her back to the parents?"

The profound sadness in his eyes tore at my heart. I walked behind his chair and massaged his tired shoulders. "Remember what Tennyson said, 'Tis better to have loved and lost / Than never to have loved at all.' All I know is, my arms ache to hold a little one of my own."

Thad looked sad for a moment, then chuckled. "I don't think the bard was talking about parenting when he wrote those lines."

I circled the chair and plopped myself into his lap, trailing kisses along his strong jawline. "Are you sure?" I teased.

"M-m-m, pretty sure." His smile tightened into a scowl of concentration. "Perhaps we should consider all possibilities and, of course, ask God to lead us."

I tickled his ear with a strand of my hair. "You're so cute when you get serious."

Preparations for the children's Christmas program at the church on Christmas Eve pushed the subject of babies, adoption, and child care from my mind. As church pianist and director of the children's choir, I ran from task to task like a base runner trying to steal second.

Christmas morning, Thad and I opened the presents our families had sent us, opened each other's gifts that had arrived weeks earlier from the Montgomery Ward catalog, then relaxed in front of the fire. Thad seemed so relaxed and happy, much like I'd felt ever since returning from San Francisco. *Newlyweds*, I mused. *If only we could have found this kind of happiness in the first few months of our marriage instead of two years later.*

After the holidays, the community settled down to the cold winds of winter. We tucked away our thoughts of adoption or caring for children in our home until spring. I still bundled up and went along with Thad on his visits whenever possible. And my visits to the reservation became more important, because the circuit-riding doctor couldn't always make it over the snow-blocked passes. It was only when I cared for a tiny newborn at the reservation that my twinges of emptiness resurfaced.

Toward the end of February, a young mother in town died in childbirth. Running from his grief, the husband and father left town, leaving his newborn son and two-year-old daughter in my care until his mother-in-law could come for the children.

The evening after I saw the three of them off on the train heading east, I wrote in my diary. *April 29, 1926. I said goodbye to Harold and Deborah today. I don't think I can stand to do that again. It sounded so easy to care for two children until their grandma came west from Ohio. But I never realized how strong the cords of love could grow in two months' time. I miss them terribly.*

I cried for a week after they left. Thad didn't fare much better, I could tell, especially after supper. That was the time when little Deborah would climb up on his lap and request her favorite bedtime story—"Davy and the Naughty Giant."

For my birthday, Thad promised to take me to Albuquerque for a shopping trip. "I don't understand what women find exciting about shopping, but since it's your day, I promise to do whatever you want to do."

On the morning of our drive to the city, I was making sandwiches for our picnic lunch when Thad burst through the front door. "CeeCee, you're not going to believe it."

I wiped my hands on my apron. "Believe what?"

He stuffed an envelope into my hands. I glanced down at the unfamiliar handwriting, then back at him. "Who is it from?"

"Open it. Just open it," he urged, his face glowing with excitement.

Lifting the envelope's torn flap, I removed the letter and read the salutation aloud. " 'Dear Elder Adams.' " I glanced at Thad once again.

"Read it! Read it!"

I mumbled through the first paragraph. " 'You might not remember me, but we met and conversed at the Bible Conference in Los Angeles last summer. At that time we talked of the possibility that you and your good wife—' What?" My eyes widened. My mouth dropped open. "But I thought—"

"Read the rest of the letter!"

"—Elder Johnson—consumption. He and his wife—returned to America. If you and your wife are still interested—China before autumn." The paper rattled as my hands shook. "Before autumn? That's only four months away!"

"I know. I know. So, what do you say?" The look on Thad's face reminded me of a boy of ten requesting a new bicycle for Christmas.

"I think we'd better do a whole lot of praying before we send our reply to Dr. Gibson."

"You're right. Of course, you're right." Without warning, he swept me off my feet and whirled me around the large open kitchen.

I laughed and begged him to put me down. "This is hardly respectable behavior for a married woman of twenty-six."

Thad gently lowered me to my feet once more, his eyes glistening with excitement. "Oh, CeeCee, imagine—China! I was so afraid that when the door for us closed last spring, we'd never again have a chance. Do we dare hope this time?"

Treasures That Never Fade

The freighter, *City of Tokyo*, loomed like a harbinger of doom over San Francisco's Pier 27. I gazed up at the scarred black hull and grimaced. "Well, the S.S. *Amsterdam*, it's not."

"The ticket agent said the accommodations would be spartan," Thad reminded. "The ship's not designed for passengers."

My father examined the hull of the ship with a critical eye. "Are you sure the vessel is seaworthy?"

"For the moment, at least," my mother joked nervously. She peered over the edge of the pier into the oil-slick water, where two sea gulls fought over a partially devoured fish. "Whew!" She pinched her nostrils closed. The foul odors from the decaying garbage unsettled even the most sturdy of stomachs.

"I can't believe how warm it is today." Mama turned away and fanned herself. "Today feels more like the beginning of August than the end of September."

The month we had spent in San Francisco preparing to leave for the Orient sped by much faster than any of us imagined possible—except, perhaps, for Thad. No amount of self-control could hide his eagerness to be underway on our great adventure—China.

My mother, on the other hand, grew increasingly disenchanted with our appointment as the time for us to leave drew near. One evening a week before we left, she and I stood beside the wooden packing crates that would carry Thad's and my personal possessions across the Pacific Ocean. She was carefully wrapping a crystal bud vase, a wedding present to Thad and

101

me, when she stopped and shook her head sadly. "The thought of your going so far away and being gone for so long tears at my soul."

"But, Mama, going to China was always your dream. Aren't you thrilled that your daughter will finally live out your dream?"

She smiled sadly. "I'm beginning to wonder if it takes more commitment to go into mission service or to send a loved one." She closed her eyes and massaged her left temple. "I'm sorry, CeeCee, for my moment of weakness. I am so proud of you, darling. It won't be easy living, as you know, but you are more than enough woman to meet the job's demands."

Tears glistened in my eyes as I stared unseeing down at the box of Thad's belongings that I was sorting. "Thanks, Mama. I needed that." I took an old work shirt from the box and held it up to examine it. "This looks more like a dust rag than a garment to wear!" I tossed the shirt on the discard pile. "He said to throw away anything I thought he wouldn't need, and he definitely won't need that." As I rummaged through the odds and ends he'd stuffed into the box before we left New Mexico, my hand brushed across a stack of letters tied together with string. Curious, I opened the top letter and began to read aloud.

"Dear CeeCee and Thad, Recently I learned, from Thad's father, of the loss of your infant son. I don't have the words to tell you how sorry I am—" I scanned the rest of the letter, then the next and the next. I looked at my mother in surprise. "These are the letters of sympathy we received after—after—" My words stuck in my throat. I swallowed hard. "He saved every one of them."

The wrinkled, tear-stained outpourings of love and sympathy obviously had been read many times. I choked back my tears. *How many times, when I rejected him, did he seek solace from these letters? How often during the months that he needed comfort and strength did he read them?* My heart ached as I traced over the splotches of tears on one letter, then the next. *Oh, dear God, I thought Thad didn't need anyone or anything. He seemed so busy with his church work. He acted as if our baby's death barely touched him.* I'd been so absorbed in my own suffering that I hadn't taken the time to recognize Thad's.

During the days immediately before we sailed for China, my eyes remained constantly at flood stage, as did the rest of the family's. If I wasn't crying with my father in the library, it was with Granddaddy Spencer in the gazebo or with Thad when he and I took our last drive in our little Ford before we sold it.

The evening before we sailed, the entire family met at Uncle Phillip and Aunt Jenny's house for a farewell dinner. Determined to have a good time and not become overemotional, I did remarkably well until after dessert, when Uncle Phillip handed an envelope to Thad. "This is in case you need emergency passage home," he explained. Inside the envelope was a money order.

"You will find that it's good in any port in the world; I guarantee."

Stunned by my uncle's uncharacteristically thoughtful gift, I stared at the document. "Uncle Phillip, I don't know what to say."

"Just take care and come home to us." He cleared his throat, eyed my mother for a moment, then turned away.

When the evening ended and we returned to my parents' home, Mama called me to her room. As I stepped inside the confines of the soft, willow-green walls, she handed me a dilapidated Bible. I remembered it immediately. *Au Sam!*

"Remember Au Sam's request that should I ever get to China, I try to look up her surviving family and tell them what happened to her? It looks like the responsibility has fallen on you. She would have liked that."

I shook my head vigorously. "I can't take this. I know how much it means to you."

"Please take it. It has the names of her family members as she remembered them."

I opened the book carefully to the pages where she had listed the names of her family members. "Instead of taking the entire Bible, to China, why don't I remove the pages of the family register and leave the rest for you? Her family might resent the Bible as it is unlikely they're Christian."

"Are you sure?"

"I'm sure."

My mother thought for a moment, then agreed. Then she opened the top drawer of her bureau and removed a brooch and three photographs, each of Au Sam. "Take these with you. If you find her relatives, they will appreciate seeing her as the lovely woman she became."

I gazed lovingly at the photographs of the solemn-faced woman, her hair drawn tightly back from her face, her eyes revealing the joy that her dour expression often hid from the camera.

Carefully, I removed the treasured pages from the tattered Bible. And along with the photographs and my grandfather's twenty-dollar gold piece, I slipped them in the tooled-leather box Calvin Blair made for Thad and me as a wedding gift. I then placed the large family Bible Nina had given us in the box. These items were the last to go in my steamer trunk.

The next morning a leaden ball settled in the pit of my stomach as my parents and my brother Rusty gathered around Thad and me on Pier 27. The rest of the family, including my grandfather, had agreed the evening before that my immediate family members would be the only ones to accompany us to the pier. As I gazed at the subdued faces of the people whom I loved most in this world, I felt overwhelmingly rich and overwhelmingly homesick.

"I don't know what to say," I sniffled. "I am so—"

Suddenly, a loud growl erupted from my stomach. Everyone looked at me and my offending body part in surprise. I grinned sheepishly. "—famished?"

Everyone laughed. We hadn't eaten since before dawn. For some unexplained reason, the boarding of the passengers had been delayed.

"I would sure enjoy one of Hilda's oatmeal cookies!" Daddy looked longingly at the basket of goodies Hilda had packed for our journey. Except for two portmanteaus and the basket of food, our shipping crates and our luggage had been loaded hours before.

"Never you mind, Mr. Chamberlain. Those are for CeeCee and Thad to eat!" Mama's schoolmarm tone and my father's little-boy look sent the rest of us into fits of laughter.

Yet the higher the sun rose in the sky, the more other stomachs growled in protest until, in desperation, I unlatched the basket and supplied each of us with cookies.

As the delay lengthened, I secretly rejoiced, while the other passengers grew fretful. Twenty or so in number, they looked shabby and ill-fitted for the journey.

Finally, high above our heads, the ship's bell gonged. The travelers around us pointed at the tall, gaunt seaman striding down the gangplank, a sheaf of papers clutched in his hands. All the passengers except Thad and me raced to line up at the base of the gangplank as the steward untied the hemp cord across the entrance and began the boarding process.

My father gathered us together for prayer, closing his tearful supplication with the mizpah. Tears flowed as we kissed one another goodbye. As I took one last look at each person's face, I tried to memorize every line, for I realized that I had no guarantee when or if I'd ever see them again on this earth. In front of us, the boarding went quickly. Mama and I held each other's hands until the last possible moment. Finally, Thad took my hand and gently led me to the gangplank.

"Name?" the steward asked.

"Adams, Thaddeus and Chloe Celeste." Thad sent me a reassuring glance.

The man checked us off the passenger list, then waved us on board. As I stepped onto the gangplank, I stumbled. Thad grabbed my arm and supported me the rest of the way up to the ship.

"May God go with you, darling," Mama called.

I waved and blew her a kiss.

The tugboat horns tooted, and the anchor chain clanked against the side of the ship. *We're moving.* Thad and I lingered on deck until the ship headed through the Golden Gate and out to sea.

"We'd better locate our stateroom before lunch," Thad reminded. The ticket stated that a noontime repast would be served a half-hour after sailing.

I glanced down at my wristwatch and grimaced. "It's already past two." He shrugged and urged me toward the staircase.

We found our way to our stateroom, if one can call a closet with two fold-down berths a stateroom. Thad dumped our portmanteaus on our trunks at the far end, under a porthole.

A wave of claustrophobia swept over me as I stared in horror at the space that would be our home for the next thirty days.

"I suppose this is the bathroom." Thad opened the door at the head of his berth. "Yep, the essentials are all here." He chuckled.

I joined him. I knew that if I didn't laugh, I'd cry. And I had no more tears to shed. We both laughed until we wilted onto the berth in hysteria. "I can only imagine what the cuisine is going to be like!" I croaked between bouts of laughter.

Although the freighter advertised "excellent and nutritious food," our lunch consisted of potato soup, platters of fried fish, and sourdough rolls. When Thad asked for a glass of water, the steward told him that it was available for a price. "I'm sure thankful that Hilda insisted on packing us a basket full of goodies," I hissed, hoping the steward would overhear my remark. "We'd starve if we had to depend strictly on the ship's kitchen!"

Since we were traveling by freighter, there was no evening entertainment other than what the passengers and crew provided for themselves on deck. That first evening, Thad let it be known that I'd brought along my violin. I fiddled until my fingers threatened mutiny.

We stumbled back to our stateroom around midnight. The two-inch mattress on the berth did little to cushion my elbows and hips. Around three in the morning, a storm struck, causing the *City of Tokyo* to roll and pitch violently. I lay awake wondering if we'd survive to see dawn. Even flat on my back, I thought I'd lose the slice of Hilda's German chocolate cake that I'd eaten earlier.

Thad slept through it all, at least until one roll of the ship tossed him onto the floor. Crunched in the narrow space between the berths, he struggled to his feet, accompanied by my smothered laughter. "Laugh, will you!" he muttered as he crawled onto his berth and faced the wall. "You have a sadistic sense of humor, woman!" And within minutes, his heavy snore resumed.

Rain lashed against the porthole for several hours. Over and over, I repeated the promise of Micah 7:19 about casting our sins into the depths of the sea. When one particularly violent wave hurled the ship almost on its side, I cried aloud, "Thank You, Lord, that my sins are cast into the bottom of the sea."

In the darkness, from my husband's berth, I heard, "But if it's OK with You, Lord, I'd prefer not to join them right yet!"

Fair weather and a calm sea returned soon after dawn the next morning. For the next two days, Thad and I spent as much time as possible on deck to escape our cramped stateroom.

On the fourth day, the weather changed again. The cold fog and rough seas forced us to take refuge in our stateroom. There, we sat on Thad's berth, playing Monopoly by the light from one wall sconce, balancing our pieces on the board and our money on our laps.

"Thank you, Rusty, for giving us such a 'frivolous' bon voyage gift!" I announced as I mortgaged my last property to pay rent at Thad's hotel on St. Charles Place. I tossed the last of my money into the box. "I don't understand why this game has become such a fad!"

Thad chuckled under his breath.

"I heard that, Mr. Adams! What if I show you who's boss on the Chinese checker board?" Thanks to my younger brother, I could level the playing field with Chinese checkers and mah-jongg—two other fads currently popular with America's young people.

The crossing to Japan took a month, including a weekend stopover on the island of Oahu. We docked in Tokyo amid intermittent rain squalls. Despite the thunderclaps and wind gusts, the other passengers, smelling of sweat and garlic, crowded onto the deck, eager to go ashore. A wave of nausea swept over me, and I clamped my hand over my mouth and nose. Focusing my eyes on the city's skyline, I repeated to myself, *You are not going to be sick. You are not going to be sick.*

A trim cutter bearing Japan's official insignia pulled alongside the freighter. The *City of Tokyo* lowered a midship gangplank, allowing three men in snappy white uniforms to board. "Immigration officials"—the words skittered through the anxious crowd. After going through customs, we rented a room in a boardinghouse near the pier. While Thad slept, I spent the night executing bedbugs with the heel of my best leather walking shoe.

The next morning we rushed to the pier to board the side-wheeler *Nantien Tao* that would take us to Shanghai, only to find the gangplank barred. When we inquired as to the reason, a government official told us that there'd been a fourteen-day delay due to an outbreak of cholera in Shanghai.

"Cholera!" We exchanged worried glances.

"Now what?" I whispered.

"Good question!" Thad stared at our tickets.

The day grew hotter as we wandered the waterfront. "Thad," I suggested, "maybe I should stay here with our luggage while you try to find out what we're supposed to do for the next fourteen days."

I sat on our luggage in the shade of a warehouse wall and watched my husband stride away. *Lord, You know that we must get to Shanghai to meet the representative from the local mission board. Dr. Gibson is expecting us at the clinic; he needs us as soon as possible.*

I'd been guarding the luggage for more than an hour when two sandy-haired sailors strode by, looking me over as they passed. I studied the horizon to avoid making eye contact. Seconds later, they returned and spoke to me in what sounded like German.

I shook my head. "Sorry, no. I don't understand you."

"Ah, you speak English?" the taller man with the scraggly beard inquired.

"Yes." I nervously looked away.

"Are you alone? Do you need a place to stay?" The men inched closer.

"No, my husband is just up the way, trying to get us passage to Shanghai. We're missionaries, you see."

"A missionary! Leave it to you, Jorge, to find us a woman. She's married!" The shorter man jabbed his friend in the ribs. "Next, you'll proposition a nun!"

"You have to admit she's a mighty pretty piece, though, married or not." The man's leer infuriated me.

I frowned, arched one eyebrow, and gave him my best Meeker stare.

"A schoolteacher too, I bet." The shorter man's laughter died. "You say you're looking for passage to Shanghai?"

"We were supposed to sail on the *Nantien Tao*, but the Japanese officials say it won't sail for fourteen days due to the cholera outbreak in Shanghai."

The two men exchanged knowing glances. "We've signed on to the side-wheeler *Sanchow Wan*. She's sailing at eighteen hundred hours for Shanghai."

I eyed the men critically. "But the officials said—"

"Hey, lady, we're just a couple of salts heading for the South Sea Islands. We want no trouble."

The bearded man turned and strode away. The other paused before joining his friend. "If you and your husband are at Pier 4 an hour before sailing, maybe I can get you on board."

"Tha—thank you." I waved at the men's receding figures, certain they couldn't hear my reply. I stood and gazed up and down the docks, my stomach lurching with fear for my safety. *Maybe staying here alone wasn't such a good idea, Lord.*

Finally, from between two of the warehouses, Thad appeared and hurried to me. "Am I glad to see you! I couldn't tell which warehouse was which. I thought I'd never find you."

I told him about my encounter with the two sailors and their offer to help us get to Shanghai.

Thad's eyes lighted up with hope. "Really? I didn't have any luck at all. The only thing I did accomplish was to wire the mission board headquarters in Hong Kong."

"Did they reply?"

He stuffed his hands in his pants pockets. "They said to come through as soon as possible, that Dr. Gibson desperately needs our help at the clinic."

I folded my arms and squinted up at him. "But what about the outbreak of cholera?"

He shrugged. "At the cable office, I spoke with a British missionary from another denomination who is returning to western Manchuria. He believes that this delay is a Japanese ploy to delay a few more Westerners from invading the Orient."

"So, what do you want to do?"

Thad paced back and forth in the building's shadow. "Do you think we should risk traveling on this side-wheeler—what did you say its name is?"

"The *Sanchow Wan* or something. What about our crates?"

"They're already on board the other side-wheeler. They'll be delivered at the mission—hopefully."

"You mean there's a chance that—"

"There's always a chance that our belongings will be stolen, no matter which boat we take."

All our wedding gifts, stolen? A cold chill skittered up my spine. "I think we should pray about this."

Thad responded quickly, "You're right. It's not my mission; it's God's mission. I keep forgetting that."

There beside a dilapidated warehouse, we took each other's hands and asked for God's guidance.

Thad had barely said Amen, when I knew what we should do. "Honey, I think we should leave for China today."

He studied my face for an instant. "We don't know anything about this other side-wheeler," he warned.

"What do we know about either boat?"

"And the cholera epidemic?"

I could tell by his tone that he wanted to leave as badly as I. "Cholera is but one of many life-threatening diseases we can expect to encounter here in the Far East. We knew that before we accepted the call from the mission board."

"You're right. If we let fear control us now, it will control our entire ministry here."

Once we made our decision, we hired a man with a cart to haul our luggage to Pier 4. There, on the dock, I spread a red-and-white gingham tablecloth over my suitcase, and we dined on our dwindling fare of dried fruit and bread sticks. An hour before we were supposed to purchase our tickets, the activity around the vessel intensified. The British missionary Thad had spoken with earlier arrived at the pier, bearing his luggage and a large satchel of books. It seems Elder Brewster had also learned of the side-wheeler's destination and departure time and had decided to take the risk.

Elder Brewster watched over our belongings while Thad and I hurried to the nearest open-air market and bought a supply of foodstuffs for us to eat until we landed in Shanghai. When he returned, I stayed with all the luggage while he and the missionary went to secure our passage.

Though I trembled with anticipation, I had many questions. *How can the ship leave without reporting its destination? And if the Japanese officials know its destination, why are they allowing the captain to ignore the ban? Father,* I prayed, *as we embark on this leg of our journey, I claim Your promise to never leave or forsake us. Thank You, Father, for always keeping Your promises. Amen.*

Relief swept through me when I saw the two grinning preachers coming down the gangplank toward me. Thad broke into a run when his feet hit the pier. "We're on our way to China, honey!"

As Thad took my arm and led me up the gangplank, he explained what had happened aboard the ship. "At first, the captain denied that his craft was sailing for Shanghai. I guess he thought we might be spies for the Japanese authorities. But when Elder Brewster spoke to him in Cantonese, then in Mandarin, the man was convinced we sincerely desire passage to Shanghai." My husband added, "You'll be glad to know that there are two other missionary couples on board, one from Canada and the other from Germany. They're both returning after taking short leaves in Honolulu."

The sleeping accommodations aboard the *Sanchow Wan* made our earlier accommodations aboard the *City of Tokyo* seem almost elegant. As I examined our cabin, I wondered if steerage could be much worse. Canvas sheets draped from the ceiling divided one room into six compartments. Two cots, two pillows, and two blankets were the room's amenities. There was only enough floor space between the cots to squeeze past one another. As to the necessary conveniences, there was but one facility.

I stashed as many of our belongings as possible beneath the cots while Thad jockeyed our luggage to the head of the cots. When we heard the ship's whistle blow and the anchor chain clang against the side of the boat, we rushed up the stairs to the deck for a last look at the Japanese skyline.

As Thad introduced me to the other missionaries, I scrutinized each face, searching for outward evidence of unusual nobility and dedication. But instead, I found good, plain people, wearing clothing that was a little out of date, but otherwise they were people like I would have found in Oregon or Texas or New Mexico. I could feel the other women studying the cut of my traveling costume and the style of my hair. Their questions centered around life in the United States, while I was eager to learn everything I could about China.

We sailed for several perfect days along the craggy Japanese shoreline. Then the captain set a course due west, and our side-wheeler plied the notoriously wild waters of the China Sea for five rough days and nights. Even the seasoned travelers in our group spent most of their waking moments lying on their cots, nursing queasy stomachs. I was thankful for the packets of herbal teas my mother had insisted I take with us. As a result, Thad and I experienced very little seasickness.

My favorite memories aboard the little boat were the morning and evening worships the men in our little group conducted aboard the rickety vessel. Each family represented a different denomination. Like too many roosters in a hen yard, the missionaries' fervent sermons took on an evangelistic quality. No one could miss the tension behind our benign and sanctimonious smiles.

I quickly became the official accompanist, while the men took turns leading the services. Our singing attracted many of the sailors. Finally one evening, after we'd finished the last verse of "Day Is Dying in the West," the timid German woman did the unthinkable. She took the makeshift pulpit. The entire trip, I'd admired the shy, rotund little woman for her ability to give comfort and encouragement without saying a word, whenever and wherever needed.

She looked at each of us with compassion-filled, soft brown eyes. In broken English, she said, "Before my husband speaks tonight, I want to say something that's been burdening my heart since the first night we worshiped together. We are all here, far from our homes and family, to witness to the Chinese for our wonderful Lord, Jesus Christ. Though we represent different denominations, we represent only one God." She paused and moistened her lips. "I think it's time we demonstrate that fact to one another and to the sailors who join us for worship." Her eyes darted toward her frowning husband, then down at her hands. "Thank you," she concluded simply.

We sat silenced and shamefaced while she took her seat, no one quite knowing what to do next. As I looked at the faces of the sailors lounging on the fringes of our group, the words of 1 John 4:20 popped into my mind. "If a man say, I love God, and hateth his brother, he is a liar."

Without hesitation, I lifted my violin and played the first two measures of "Blest Be the Tie That Binds." On the third measure, the Canadian woman started singing. The others quickly joined in, the women and the two children first, then the men. I will never hear that old hymn without remembering the courageous German woman who taught us what it means to be true missionaries for our Saviour. It was a lesson I knew would affect Thad's and my entire service in China.

When our ship approached land, I looked eagerly for the picturesque coastline we'd enjoyed in Japan but saw, instead, the yellow, muddy waters of the Yangtze River flowing into the sea. We sailed through low mud flats before we finally docked at the busy port of Shanghai.

As the passengers prepared to disembark, we women vowed to keep in touch with one another. Our husbands and the sailors who had attended our meetings joined us in our last gesture of friendship. We linked hands and formed a circle on the deck of the side-wheeler. The sweet, four-part harmony blocked out the sounds of shrill whistles, the shouts from shore, and the engines' roar as we sang the first verse of "God Be With You Till We Meet Again."

While we women wept openly, more than one stalwart preacher and one crusty sailor surreptitiously removed his handkerchief from his pocket and blew his nose or wiped a tear from his eye before we finished the song.

At the dock, Elder and Mrs. Roscoe greeted us. We soon

learned that the Roscoes, a warmhearted, dedicated couple, had refused to retire at home in England. Instead, though retired, they continued their ministry by meeting and caring for incoming mission families who arrived in Shanghai, the largest Chinese port.

We spent the evening asking questions and sharing the latest news from America. When I asked Mrs. Roscoe about the cholera outbreak, she laughed. "That's the Japanese government's way of trying to discourage us 'foreign devils' from entering the Orient. They do everything they can, short of violence, to keep out Westerners."

I shuddered. "Is that why there are so many soldiers in the streets? To protect from a possible Japanese invasion?"

"Oh no. Japan might rattle a few sabers or shout empty threats, but they'll never risk invading a country as large as China." Mrs. Roscoe waved her hand to dismiss my concern. "Pay them no mind, my dear. Everywhere you go in China, you will see soldiers. Over the centuries, warlords, invaders, and, now, the Nationalists have maintained armies to protect their territories—hence, the soldiers."

"By the way," Mr. Roscoe asked, "did you encounter any, er, threat or violence on your trip from Tokyo?"

Thad looked at him in surprise. "No, other than the primitive accommodations, we had a pleasant journey."

"Then the Lord obviously was with you. You had no way of knowing that the *Sanchow Wan* crew have a reputation for committing piracy against their own passengers."

"Really?" Thad and I exchanged glances.

"I've heard that some of their passengers have actually disappeared, never to be heard from again."

My husband assured the white-haired gentleman that we had no problem at all. "Everyone was cordial. Many of the sailors even attended our morning and evening worship services."

Since Shanghai was one of the few places where we could purchase foreign goods, we stayed with the Roscoes for two weeks while they helped us purchase the supplies we needed for winter. Dr. and Mrs. Gibson had sent a list of medical supplies to the Roscoes for us to purchase and transport to the clinic. "Before you leave Shanghai, buy something frivolous for your home, dear," Mrs. Roscoe advised on one of our excursions to the markets. "Something bright and pretty. It will encourage you on the cold, dreary winter days. And it does grow cold in northern China, my dear, much different from Shanghai's warm climate."

I took her advice, much to Thad's chagrin, by purchasing ten yards of pink-lavender-and-red-flowered muslin. How I would use the splashy fabric in my home, I had no idea.

It did disturb me that everywhere we went people followed us and stared at my red hair, my light eyes, and my taller stature. I didn't like it! At one point, while I waited for Mrs. Roscoe to bargain with a shop clerk for some blankets, I paused to stare back at my observers. *These are the people for whom I gave up my family and my country. Will I ever truly love them as Jesus loves them? They look so cruel and so coldly curious.*

When I mentioned my thoughts to Mrs. Roscoe, she laughed. "They think you are a devil. You know, I think it would be good for you to see a bit of the countryside before you head north. It will give you a better feel for the people."

That evening, I wrote the following in a letter home to Mama. "Wonderful! I travel halfway around the world to care for people who imagine me to be a devil because of my red hair! How can I possibly do the Lord's work under these circumstances?"

The next morning the Roscoes invited us to take a ride with them on a junk. When Thad asked me if I'd like to go, I demurred. "You'd really like to get underway, wouldn't you?"

"Well, we do still have a long way to go to reach the mission," he reminded. "And so much to do—"

"You're working too hard, darling. A day to relax before we head north might be something we both could use." Actually, I was worried by the heightened color in Thad's face. I touched his cheek with the back of my hand. "We're not accustomed to this tropical sun, you know."

"Maybe you're right. I am a little tired."

"Be sure to wear a hat. You look like you might be getting too much sun."

The next morning we were up early, eager to enjoy our outing into the countryside. As the boatmen poled our junk through the canals of Shanghai, curious people crowded the canal banks to see the foreign woman with hair like fire. We glided past houses crowded so close together they spilled out over the canal itself on poles sunk into the muddy canal bottom.

The canal ran smooth and still once we left the city. I sat on the prow of the junk, enthralled by the clear blue sky, the graceful willow trees, and the crops ripe for harvest. Inhaling the sweet autumn air, I watched the bank as we glided past feathery bamboo, fields of heavy-headed rice, and brown villages of thatched houses. The sun-browned people in the villages smiled more readily than did the city people in Shanghai. As I looked into their curious faces, I realized that there were so many things I could do to make their lives more comfortable.

Fortunately, our shipping crates holding most of our earthly possessions arrived on the *Nantien Tao* two days before we were to head north. Thad and Mr. Roscoe arranged to have them delivered to the train station in time for our departure. That evening we praised God again for His protection and goodness to us.

By sunrise the next morning, Thad and Mr. Roscoe were at the train station, purchasing our tickets and overseeing the loading of our goods for the next leg of our journey. At her home, Mrs. Roscoe and I were preparing enough food to satisfy Thad's and my hunger for the first few days of the trip. We rushed to finish before the two rickshaws arrived that would take us to meet our husbands at the depot. Before we left the house, Mrs. Roscoe pressed a small blue-and-white tin into my hand. "Some peppermint candies for your journey."

I looked at her in surprise. "Why, thank you." After all the shopping I'd done in Shanghai, I knew how costly such delicacies as candy of any kind were.

She laughed. "Remember me each time you eat one."

"I will. And thank you again."

As I leaned back against the seat for my first rickshaw ride, I anticipated a leisurely trip to the depot. But from the moment the driver took his first step, I realized the ride would be anything but leisurely. I pressed my straw hat firmly against the top of my head as the driver wove his rickshaw through the narrow and crowded streets. I knew that my hostess was some-where behind me in a second chair, and I prayed that we'd end up together again at the depot and not in the city morgue.

At the railway station, Thad introduced me to Mr. Lin, a convert to Christianity whom the mission board had hired to be our guide and interpreter. When the three of us finally boarded the train, tears glistened in my eyes as I waved goodbye to the Roscoes. Once again I was leaving people I'd come to love.

The opulence of the train's private compartment pleased me. I ran my hand over the dark green felt-covered walls decorated with gold-leaf medallions. As he finished loading our suitcases onto the overhead shelves, Thad asked, "Will you be all right here alone while Mr. Lin and I go to the dining car to work on our itinerary?"

I eyed the plush seats and grinned. "You go right ahead, dear. I'll be just fine, I'm sure." The train had barely pulled out of the station before I pulled the shades on the window and door, then curled up on one of the benches and made up for the sleep I'd lost the previous night.

When the train stopped at the first station, I awoke with a start at the shadows of people dropping off the roof of the railway car. I raised the shade and watched as more people jumped to the ground and scampered clear of the tracks and others clambered up the sides of the car before the train pulled out of the station. *That's one way to get to where you're going*, I thought. *Not the safest way, but it is a way, I suppose.*

Far Beyond the Horizon

Dressing quickly, I brushed my hair until it shone. Then I poured a splash of water from the pitcher into the washbasin, moistened the bar of soap, and scrubbed my face vigorously, bracing myself for the day ahead. I eyed myself in the tiny round travel mirror perched against the kerosene lantern. My hair caught a ray of sunlight from the narrow slat of a window beside me. I smiled. *Stop looking so eager*, I scolded, my stomach quivering with excitement. *You have no idea how these people will react to your popping into their lives with news of their long-lost sister, Au Sam.*

In a small city a few miles outside the port city of Tientsin, Mr. Lin had located Au Sam's family from the sketchy information my mother had shared before we sailed from America and from the page of information I'd torn from Au Sam's Bible. Because Au Sam's family were influential members in their community, our search was simplified. Mr. Lin first contacted Au Sam's older brother, a local warlord, and made the appropriate arrangements for Thad and me to meet with the family.

Thad and I followed Mr. Lin away from the congested city street, through a low gateway that opened into a courtyard paved with rough-hewn slabs of stone. Two stone lions guarded the entrance. At the base of a flight of stone stairs, a male servant, armed with a British saber and garbed in splendid ceremonial clothing, spoke momentarily with Mr. Lin, then gestured for us to proceed up the steps.

At the top of the steps, a second servant, similar to an

English butler but also dressed in splendid ceremonial clothing, spoke briefly to our interpreter and guide, then gestured for us to follow him through a spacious salon. The heels of my dress shoes clicked on the mosaic tile floor, echoing off the high ceilings and stone arches. Luxurious draperies bordered the lattice-covered windows high over our heads. In the center of the room, a spectacular vase of silver, embossed and burnished, stood on a mahogany table inlaid with mother-of-pearl and chased with silver. Bouquets of flowers filled the room with a heady fragrance. On every side were displayed rare vases, jeweled cups, and statuettes, in an unusual blend of antique and modern, Oriental and European craftsmanship.

Our guide halted before a massive set of carved wooden doors as a plainly dressed male servant, wearing an impressive Mongol sword, unlatched the door's brass handles. The doors opened silently into an equally impressive audience chamber, where a party of servant girls waited. The male servant gestured for us to enter the room.

A similar combination of Oriental and European artifacts decorated the room, along with a number of highly polished wooden screens that had been carved with scenes of horses and men and landscapes. A grouping of four heavily carved dark wooden chairs circled a low tea table in the center of the room. Heavy midnight blue velvet draperies hung floor to ceiling at the far end of the room. Thad and I huddled closer to one another, suddenly apprehensive and bewildered by the magnificence and strangeness surrounding us. I clutched the pages from Au Sam's Bible, her brooch, and the three photographs tightly.

Silently, the curtains parted, and a tall, pale man with a mustache that drooped at the corners swept into the room. His wide-sleeved scarlet silk robe fell smoothly to his pointed shoes, and a long, glossy queue hung down the middle of his back. Three attendants scurried into the room behind him. When his eyes caught mine, I bowed, as Mr. Lin had instructed.

As Mr. Lin introduced Thad and me and the warlord responded, I found that I could understand a word here and there.

Being female, I stood in the background while my husband and Mr. Lin addressed Au Sam's brother with the ceremonial bows and courtesies, obeying the ancient ritual of a person of medium rank addressing the high and mighty.

Thaddeus, with Mr. Lin interpreting, said, "Sir, are you well?"

"Yes, I am well. You are well?"

"Yes, I am well. Have you eaten your food?"

"Thank you, yes, I have eaten my food. Sir, are your old relations well?"

"Yes, my old ones are quite well."

The exchange continued for a while longer. Then, with the courtesies over, the warlord asked the purpose of our visit. Mr. Lin interpreted the request, and I extended my treasures toward the man. The nearby servants gasped, and Mr. Lin intercepted my gesture. "You are female," Mr. Lin explained, his voice low and ominous. "You cannot approach the gentleman directly. Hand what you have to your husband, and allow him to present them."

I obeyed. "May I explain these things?" I hissed.

"Sh!" Mr. Lin replied, his voice filled with concern. "You may speak only if spoken to."

Thad presented the pages from Au Sam's Bible to the man. "My wife can explain better than I, since your sister lived for many years at her house, not at mine."

Before Mr. Lin had finished interpreting Thad's words, the warlord's eyes flickered toward my face, then back to the objects in his hands. *He understood Thad. The man understands English!*

The warlord studied the pages from the Bible for some time. When he looked up, Thad handed him the porcelain brooch. The warlord gasped. As he released the tiny silver latch hidden among the silver filigree surrounding the porcelain, the brooch popped open to reveal a photograph of a family. By the look on his face, I knew he recognized the photo of his family.

Suddenly, he glared at me and shouted a volley of Chinese at me. Mr. Lin, looking far more nervous than I ever remembered seeing him, quickly interpreted. "Where did you get this piece of jewelry?"

"From your sister, Au Sam. She was my governess for many years and my mother's best friend."

Mr. Lin turned to interpret, but the warlord interrupted. "It is impossible. My favorite sister died at the hands of Mongolian raiders!"

Thad and Mr. Lin stared at the man's sudden revelation. I smiled and bowed. "She did not perish, sir, but was sold to slavers and transported to California on a slave ship."

"And your family bought her?" The hard glint in the man's eyes sent an icy chill up my spine.

I shook my head. "No, sir. Another family purchased her, and she lived with them many years before I knew her. Your sister met my mother immediately after the giant earthquake that rocked our city." I hastened on. "They worked side by side, caring for the Chinese earthquake victims. When your sister discovered that her owners had disappeared after the quake, my mother invited her to live with us. She agreed if my mother allowed her to earn her keep as my governess. I was six at the time."

The warlord studied the photograph inside the brooch for a long time without speaking. "Do you have other evidence that your story is true?"

I turned to hand the three photographs to Thad so he could give them to the warlord. "No," he commanded, a little smile teasing the corners of his mouth. "I will take them from you." Placing them in his hand, I bowed. "These photographs were taken during the years your sister lived with our family. The first one is of her and me when I was a child of eight."

He compared the photograph with the one in the brooch. When he looked up, I continued. "The second photograph is of your sister and my mother. It was taken at a place called Cape Cod, where my parents own a summer home."

"Ah." He nodded. "And the third?"

"As you can see, it is also of Au Sam and me, taken at Boston Symphony Hall after a chamber-music concert."

Suddenly, he grunted a few words to one of his aides. The aide clapped his hands, and the curtains behind us parted. An elderly woman, flanked by three younger women, entered the room. By the agitation on the older woman's face, I knew she'd been listening to our every word from behind the curtain.

In a flurry of Chinese, the warlord spoke to the women. "Honorable Mother, may I present to you Chloe Celeste Chamberlain Adams, from America."

Patiently, the woman who'd mothered my precious Au Sam and I observed the rules of proper Chinese etiquette. Then her clawlike fingers, the nails on each one at least eight inches long, eagerly grasped the photographs of her daughter. Tears glistened in her eyes when she glanced up at me, then back at the photographs. Over and over, she mumbled Au Sam's name as her eyes devoured the images in her hands.

The warlord's voice was husky with emotion when he spoke. "You have brought unbelievable joy to our household today, Mrs. Adams. My mother can now die in peace, knowing that her daughter was not killed by the raiders. We are eternally grateful to you for this gift."

The warlord signaled for us to be seated in the chairs provided. Mr. Lin had previously explained that it would be an unusual honor if the man allowed us to sit in his presence. A female servant appeared carrying a silver tea service and placed it on the low table in the center of the cluster of chairs. While the warlord's mother assumed the duties as hostess, he urged, "I would be honored if you would tell my mother more about her favorite daughter, Au Sam."

I told them the stories Au Sam had related about the day she was kidnapped, about the first family who owned her, and about the earthquake. "She never tried to contact you because she thought she was the only survivor of the raid," I explained.

I told them about how much Au Sam had loved my little brother Rusty and about how she'd chase me around the kitchen with a wooden spoon whenever I'd snitch a cookie, still warm from the oven. "She was much loved by my entire family. I miss her terribly."

The afternoon sun teased the horizon by the time I finished answering all their questions about their lost sister and daughter, ending with a description of the neat little grave site overlooking the ocean.

The warlord interpreted my words for his mother. When I told how Au Sam had died, the man's eyes grew sad, and he shook his head. "We, too, lost many due to plagues such as you describe. But thanks to your family, my sister lived a good life, so it seems. Her mother wishes to keep one memento of her daughter's life, to place at the altar of our ancestors. What can I offer you in payment?" The man's eyes pleaded, though his body and the tilt of his chin still exuded arrogance.

"I would be most honored for her to keep these humble mementos. I know she will treasure them always, as I have." I bowed, hoping that my sadness over losing the mementos of Au Sam didn't show. "And, please, your sister gave me far more during her lifetime than I could ever ask. And far more than I could possibly repay."

When the ruler expressed his gratitude, Au Sam's mother whispered to her son and handed him the pages from the Bible and the photograph of Au Sam and me at the concert hall. He listened, then turned toward me. "My honored mother has observed the love in your eyes for her daughter and wishes you to keep these as remembrance of her and of us, her family."

I struggled to control my tears as the warlord placed the pages from Au Sam's Bible and the photo taken in front of the concert hall in my hands, but a tear slipped down my cheek unbidden. As I lifted my gaze to meet the old woman's, she smiled shyly, a tear trickling down her cheek also.

When Mr. Lin indicated that we'd overstayed our welcome and should be heading back to the small inn run by the mission board, the warlord frowned. "Do not be ridiculous! You will stay here, of course, in honor of my sister."

I glanced at Thad, then at Mr. Lin, and shrugged. The warlord continued. "I have already retrieved your belongings from the inn where you were staying. We dress for dinner, European style, you know. If you would like to rest before dinner, your rooms are ready." He stood. We leapt to our feet and bowed as he exited the room.

When the servant led us to the room where we would spend the night, I felt as if I'd stepped into one of Au Sam's fairy tales about princes and princesses and fire-breathing dragons. Now I knew where she'd gotten her inspiration. Silk curtains draped from the ceiling added a dreamlike softness to the room. As I lounged up to my neck in bubbles in the sunken marble pool, I decided I was as close to heaven as I could get on this side of eternity. Thick Turkish towels awaited me after my bath, as well as a wide array of crystal bottles with perfumes from around the world. *Au Sam lost all of this to become a laundry servant, then a governess? How homesick she must have been.*

After an evening of exotic foods and continuous entertainment, we returned to the sumptuous room to sleep for the night. Early the next morning, we bade the warlord and his mother goodbye. He had arranged to have his personal carriers transport us to the railway station in his private sedan chairs. The warlord's parting remarks were, "Remember, Mrs. Adams, my family is eternally in your debt. You have made my mother very happy. Now, she can die in peace. My home, my wealth, my influence is available to you as long as I have breath in my body."

By late afternoon, my back ached, my head throbbed, and the soles of my feet burned. For after the train had arrived in Peking, Mr. Lin insisted that we tour his beloved city. While I found the tour fascinating, my body could only take so much. It screamed for a hot soak in the marble tub at the warlord's home.

I found it difficult to comprehend the idea that I was touring a city that had been in existence centuries before Jesus was born in Bethlehem. Archaeologists believe that city after city has been built on that same spot since as early as 723 B.C.

We tramped about the outer city, or "Chinese City," most of the morning. From the look on Thad's face, I knew he was as exhausted as I. Though I enjoyed seeing the ruins of Kublai Khan's capital, Cambaluc, in the heart of Peking, I knew I'd appreciate everything more if I could get a little rest.

"This is the southern boundary of the 'Forbidden City.' " Mr. Lin swept his hand dramatically toward the towering thirty-five-foot wall that, from where I stood, stretched unendingly in both directions. "This is where our young emperor and his bride reside, courtesy of the republic, of course, and our president, Chiang Kai-shek."

"Is it true that until recently your emperor could never leave the Forbidden City?" I asked, my interest piqued. "What about his wife? Could she leave, to go shopping or to visit her family?"

"I'm afraid not." He shook his head. "Once she agreed to marry the emperor, she, too, became imprisoned within those walls."

"How sad. So there was probably no way either of them could have heard the beautiful story of Jesus, was there?"

"Not unless one of their servants who lived in the Imperial City— But, then, who would have dared?"

Out of the corner of my eye, I saw Thad stagger, then grab hold of a nearby lamppost. I rushed to his side.

"Are you all right, honey?" I touched his brow and realized that he had a slight fever.

"My head aches. Too much sun, I guess." Thad licked his dry lips.

I called to our guide, "Mr. Lin, my husband isn't feeling well. Can you help me get him back to the mission house?"

"I'm fine. I just need a good night's sleep," Thad protested. "I didn't sleep well last night."

I slipped under his right arm to support him while Mr. Lin supported him on the left. "And you've hardly eaten a thing all day," I scolded. "That's probably why you feel so weak."

Back at the inn, Mrs. Cross, who operated the establishment for missionaries passing through the city, managed to force a bowl of vegetable soup into my husband; then Mr. Lin and I hustled him into bed. As a last ministration before letting Thad rest, I insisted he drink a cup of tea my mother had blended with equal parts chamomile, mint, and catnip. "Mama says that a cup of this is guaranteed—"

"—is guaranteed to cure any headache. I've heard all of this before, remember?" He grimaced as he obediently drank his portion of the hot mixture. I made extra since I personally enjoyed the tea's brisk, minty flavor.

I slept only intermittently that night as Thad tossed restlessly. Since he didn't feel much better in the morning, we boarded the train for the next leg of our journey instead of sightseeing. The *click-click* of the train passing over the tracks lulled Thad into a deeper sleep than he'd gotten for quite some time.

Our guide used the time on the train to review the common words I'd already memorized in the dialect of the northern province where we'd be living. I was surprised at how much of the basic language came back to me from childhood. *Thank you, Au Sam; once again you are here for me.*

When the train stopped at a station, I glanced out the window at a young Chinese woman nursing her infant and decided to try my new vocabulary on Mr. Lin. "She is a mother, yes?"

His eyes sparkled as he grinned and shook his head. "You just called her a horse."

"A horse? But I thought *ma* meant 'mother.' "

"It's how you pronounce the word that determines whether you are calling her a mother or a horse."

I giggled. "I'll never get the hang of this!"

He smiled patiently. "Yes, you will. Try again. *Mother* is spoken like this, 'ma'—short *a*. With *horse*, you hold onto the *a* little longer, like this—'ma.' "

Whatever difference there was in his inflection was lost on me. I rolled my eyes toward the ceiling. "Oh, that makes it easy."

"Be patient. You are in too much of a rush. When you learn to think like the Chinese, the language will come—you will see." He stood and stretched. "Perhaps you have learned enough for today."

"I agree. We can work at this again tomorrow."

He smiled and bowed. "Now, if the lady will excuse me, I have arrangements to make for us. I will return."

After he left the compartment, I leaned my head back against the cushioned seat and gazed at the scenery flashing by. It was hard to imagine that within a few hours I would find myself on the outer fringes of the world's civilization. The villages we sped by were noticeably poorer the farther we traveled from Peking. By the amount of clothing the villagers wore, I could tell that the warm temperatures we had enjoyed in Shanghai had dropped to the late-autumn temperatures of Cape Cod. Soon, along the western horizon, an immense semicircle of purple mountains rose against the sky.

The train chugged past fields and mud-walled villages, past cemeteries with gray stone walls and intricately carved ornamental gates. On the road beside the railroad track, pigtailed peasants drove heavy, two-wheeled carts, pulled by shaggy

Mongolian ponies.

"Those poor animals," I mused aloud.

Mr. Lin smiled indulgently. "It was on just such beasts that the horde of Genghis Khan rode south to extend their empire. It was against the successive waves of similar invaders that the Great Wall of China had been built. Men might scale a wall, but horses, never."

"Those little animals don't appear strong enough for battle."

Mr. Lin added, "Mounted on those horses, the Tartars could raid as swiftly and devastatingly as an infestation of locusts. The horses were their only edge over the Chinese."

My first glimpse of the Great Wall of China was from the buckboard of a covered wagon, much like the covered wagons that had carried pioneering Americans across the plains to California, except that instead of canvas, the wagon was covered with mats of woven straw.

Once the railroad ended and our belongings were loaded onto four horse-drawn vehicles, it was as if we'd stepped back eighty years in time. The roads, the vehicles, the horses, all spoke of another era. The evening before we left the train, Mr. Lin advised both Thad and me to change out of our Western garb into the peasant clothing we had purchased before leaving Shanghai. "For your own protection," he said. "There are bandits in the mountains who would assume you must be rich because you are a foreigner."

"No one is going to think I am Chinese." My fiery red hair contrasted sharply with the dark blue jacket and trousers, commonly worn by the local population.

"It would be best if you covered your hair with a scarf," he advised solemnly, himself dressed in a dark Chinese robe. "These are a simple, primitive people; they think all foreigners are devils! It's better not to draw too much attention to yourself."

The next morning, as we set out on our journey, I did have to admit that fewer people stared at us as our caravan passed through the tiny villages. The *clip-clop* of the horses' hooves echoed in the cool morning air. High overhead, eagles soared lazily. Several hours later, the driver of our cart halted at a bend in the trail and pointed with a grimy finger.

"He's pointing out the Great Wall," Mr. Lin informed me.

I gazed in amazement as the structure zigzagged across the landscape and disappeared beyond the horizon. "Fifteen hundred miles! That's halfway across the United States! What an incredible feat."

"Some say," Mr. Lin added, "that it's also the world's longest graveyard."

"Graveyard?"

He nodded, his face inscrutable. "It's believed that one man died for every yard of the wall."

One glance over my shoulder at the two uniformed men who were watching every move I made, and I hugged my purse possessively to my chest. "More soldiers. It's rather frightening, you know, seeing them everywhere we go."

Mr. Lin nodded politely. "Soldiers have been part of the landscape since before the arrival of Marco Polo. With fifty-four different nationality groups living in China, each with its own language, customs, and laws, it has always been a country of unrest."

Thad, who'd been listening, added, "No wonder governing the people is so difficult."

Mr. Lin frowned. "Skirmishes between Nationalist troops and local warlords break out regularly, especially in the area of China where you'll be living."

"Oh!" I groaned and rolled my eyes toward the overcast skies. "That's nice to know."

"And the governor over our province?" Thad asked.

"Mandarin Ho Feng is a progressive man," Mr. Lin replied. "He has been good to Dr. Gibson and the clinic."

When I climbed into the front wagon to continue our journey, Thad followed. "My head is aching again, honey," he said. "I'm going to lie down on the quilts in the back of the wagon for a while."

"You do look a little flushed." I noted the unnatural brightness of his eyes. The fact that his head still pained him worried me. When I voiced my concern to Mr. Lin, he reminded me that we would be stopping at an inn, safe within the walls of a small outpost town, since no one in the region dared travel at night.

"The paths are too steep and dangerous to travel at night, and the thieves—too vicious."

As we bounced over the ruts on the narrow track hacked from the mountainside, I looped the gold chain attached to my purse over my wrist and gripped the wooden seat beneath me to keep from being thrown from the wagon. I decided I'd never been so uncomfortable in my life. That thought lasted until it started to rain. Soon, the rain turned into a downpour. That's when I found out how much more uncomfortable my life could become. Immediately, the drivers halted the wagons and began shouting and scurrying around the wagons.

"Mrs. Adams!" Mr. Lin shouted above the storm. "It would be best if you would go sit under that tree while we cover these wagons."

Stinging, icy bullets pelted my head and body as I stood shivering while the men spread patched canvases over the straw roof of each of the four wagons. I watched Thad as he helped with the canvases. *He's going to take a chill from this.*

Once the canvases were secured, we climbed back into the wagon. While we rode in back, under the protection of the wagon's canvas roof, our stalwart driver sat out in the deluge, wrestling to control the frightened horses. I was cushioning Thad's head on my lap when a loud crack sounded, followed by an earthshaking thud. I peered out the canvas flap at the rear of our cart. "Oh, dear God," I cried. "Thank You!"

A massive limb had fallen directly behind our cart, separating us from the rest of the carts. Steam hissed from the tree trunk at the spot where the lightning had struck and severed the limb.

"God is very good to us today," Mr. Lin said. Mere inches had separated us from sure injury and possible death.

Again, the men were forced to climb out of the wagons, this time to clear the branch from the roadway. And, of course, Thad insisted on helping, heedless of the downpour. Irritated with my stubborn husband, I listened to the steady chopping of the axes as the team of workers cut the branch enough to allow the rest of our wagons to pass. After a few minutes, I opened the canvas flap at the back of the wagon to be certain Thad was all right. He was far from all right. Between each stroke, he had to pause and massage the back of his neck, swinging his head from side to side as if to dislodge a kink in his neck.

"Thad, wouldn't it be best if you came in out of the rain?"

He waved, casting me a weak smile, coughed, then resumed chopping at the tree limb. I dropped the flap and sat back against the wagon's rough boards. *Thaddeus Adams! You make me furious! Why are you so stubborn?*

A few minutes later, the drivers guided the wagons through the opening, and we resumed our journey. When Thad climbed back into the wagon, I resisted the urge to tell him to change into a dry shirt. *If you want to catch your death, go ahead. I can't stop you.* Thad scowled at me as he dried himself off but said nothing. Finally, after fifteen minutes had passed in silence, he said, "Don't worry, Mommy Hen. I refuse to arrive sick at the clinic."

"You may not have a choice on that." My mouth settled into a tight little pout. I reached across the wagon and rested the back of my hand on his cheek. "Just as I thought. You have a fever! If we have to stop again, for whatever reason, you are staying put, do you hear?"

I'd barely finished my command when the cart jostled from side to side, and all its contents—including us—shifted forward. I struggled to my knees and peered out of the canvas. "What's wrong?"

"A river, Mrs. Adams, we must ford a river."

I rose to my feet to see our latest obstacle and gasped. "Oh, dear heavenly Father!" Runoff from the sudden storm had turned what had been a quiet, shallow river into a raging torrent. "We'll never make it across in this wagon!"

Behind me, Thad lifted his head. "Huh? What's that?"

"Nothing dear," I cooed, clutching my purse to my chest. "Mr. Lin and our driver have everything under control."

Mr. Lin smiled and nodded. The driver, who understood no English, did the same as he flicked the reins over the back of the sturdy little horses, urging them into the maelstrom.

Heavenly Father, if ever I've prayed to You for help before, I pray to You now. You promised to be with us through the raging

*storm. Well, here it is, Lord, about as raging a storm as I've ever
seen.*

"It's going to be a bit bum-py." A jolt of the wagon added em-
phasis to my warning. "So you'd bet-ter hold on to something."

Without warning, the horse on the right stepped into a hole,
tipping the wagon forward. The driver shouted and snapped
the whip over the terrified animals' heads, trying to right the
wagon. Too late! Suddenly, I was falling, tumbling, bouncing
around inside the wagon as the icy water rushed in around me.
I remember shouting at Thaddeus, but amid the frightened
neighs of horses and the cries of the startled drivers, I doubted
that he heard me.

My breath caught as I plunged beneath the water. Coughing
and sputtering, I fought my way to the surface. I found myself
twenty to thirty feet downstream from where the other carts
waited on the bank of the river, and I was being swept farther
and farther downstream in the raging current. Memories of trying to rescue my little brother from the riptides in the Atlantic
Ocean flashed through my mind as the waters tumbled me over
rocks and around snags.

At one point, I caught a glimpse of three Chinese drivers running along the bank, but I couldn't hear their calls. And if I had,
I still wouldn't have understood their words. Unaware of my
own peril, I searched the area for signs of Thad. It wasn't until
I heard the loud roar of a waterfall that I realized I was in serious danger.

As the current propelled me beneath an overhanging tree
branch, I grabbed for it and held on until two of the drivers
running along the bank extended a broken branch and hauled
me to shore.

My hair hung in strings about my face as I crawled out of the
water. I shivered despite the blanket the men threw about my
shoulders. "My husband? He is safe?" I cried, my purse still
dangling from my wrist. Not comprehending my question, the
men grinned and nodded enthusiastically, their hands reaching
out to help me scale the muddy bank of the river. I shook them
off.

"Mr. Adams! Thaddeus! Is Mr. Adams all right?" I shouted,

frantic to be understood. Their indecipherable babble irritated me. "Mr. Lin! Where is Mr. Lin?"

The name Lin they understood. They repeated his name and pointed upstream to the cluster of wagons on the opposite side of the river. Still clinging to the gold chain on my purse, I clawed my way unaided up the muddy riverbank. Mud squished from my shoes, and muddy water dripped from my dress as I stumbled to the spot directly across from the wagons.

With every step I took, the drivers tried to take my arms, but I continued shaking myself free of their grasp. "Thaddeus! I just want to know where my husband is!" The raging waters drowned out my shrill voice. Being a nurse, I sensed I was riding the ragged edge of shock. I reached the spot opposite the wagons that held our personal possessions. Mr. Lin shouted and waved, but the water's roar drowned out his words.

"My husband!" I shouted again. "Where is he?" By now, tears mingled with the rivulets of water streaming down my face. Jumping up and down in frustration, I shouted toward the heavens, "Oh, dear God! Make someone understand me."

Winter's Chill

I looked across the river and burst into a new round of tears—this time, tears of relief. Mr. Lin and one of the drivers stood on the bank with Thaddeus between them. *He's alive. Oh, dear God, he's alive!* I pushed the dripping strands of hair away from my face as I half crawled and half slid down the bank toward him.

"Stay where you are, Mrs. Adams," Mr. Lin shouted. He shouted again to the drivers, and immediately they grabbed my arms and held me fast. I watched helplessly as the three men, holding on to each other, entered the raging river. Digging my fingernails into my palms, I prayed while slowly, carefully, they inched their way through the swirling waters to the shallows where I stood.

The moment Thad stepped onto the rocks on the riverbank, I threw myself into his arms. "Darling, I thought you had drowned," I sobbed. "I couldn't see you anywhere." We laughed and cried together in relief.

"I'm so grateful that you're safe. I saw the river sweep you downstream."

"I know. I know. I thought everything was lost." Gently I caressed Thad's shoulders and arms. I didn't care that we'd lost the wagon in which we'd been riding. Thad was alive and unhurt; that's what counted. We clung to each other for a moment, each praising God and thanking Him for protecting us from possible death.

After Thad's amen, Mr. Lin urged us to climb the bank to

solid ground. "Come. Hep Chaing will stay behind to tend the wagons while we take Pastor Adams to a village across the valley. Hep Chaing is a good man—and a Christian," he added.

I was so relieved my husband was safe that I nodded without comprehending what our guide was trying to tell me. "Come. Pastor Adams needs to get out of this heavy rain," Mr. Lin urged.

"Wait, I have some herbal—oh, my supply of medicine was in the wagon we lost!" Resigned to the loss, I glanced at the smoke ascending from the chimneys on the small cluster of cottages across the valley. Then I turned toward Thad and noticed his drawn, flushed face. "It's at least two miles to the village, Thad. Do you think you can make it?"

A wan smile crossed his face. "What other options do I have?"

Mr. Lin chose one driver to accompany us and ordered the others to help Hep Chaing protect our belongings until the floodwaters subsided and the wagons could safely ford the river. Supporting Thad, we plodded through the downpour toward the tiny hamlet. As daylight faded, it became more difficult to avoid tripping over rocks.

When we were within a hundred feet of the community, Mr. Lin paused, rainwater streaming down his face. "Wait here. I will go ahead and make certain it is safe for you to enter the village. We might have stumbled upon a town of bandits."

"Bandits!" I shouted. "I don't care what they do for a living. My husband needs a place to dry off and to rest. He needs medical attention, and he's going to get it!"

Mr. Lin waved his hands, trying to quiet me. "I will do the best I can." He bowed several times, then ran toward the nearest cottage.

He'd been gone less than five minutes when several men rounded the corner of the building, carrying lanterns and running toward us. *Oh no! Bandits! Robbers! Mr. Lin was right. We're all going to be killed; I just know it.* Clutching my soggy purse, I cast about for somewhere to hide. But where does one hide in a harvested grainfield? So I just stood there, clinging to Thad for the little support he could supply.

As the bobbing lights drew closer, I recognized Mr. Lin's voice. "It is all right, Pastor Adams. These people have agreed to help us. It is all right."

Kind hands helped Thad to the nearest house. Inside the cottage, Mr. Lin introduced us to a cluster of women and children while the men helped Thad onto a mat along the wall. After an excited exchange between our guide and the women, two of the women led me behind a curtain. Using sign language, they told me to remove my wet clothing. Laying my purse on the small wooden table, I obeyed.

Shivering, I struggled into the trousers and knee-length shirt they handed me. As I eased the shirt over my head, the women laughed and pointed toward my feet. Being six to eight inches taller than my hostess, the trousers revealed a generous portion of ankle and calf. The shirt came to four inches above my knees. The women exchanged a flurry of Chinese; then the younger of the two slipped away and after five minutes returned with another pair of trousers, those owned by the tallest man in the village. These cleared my ankles by only two inches. Judging by the nods and grunts of my hostesses, I assumed that I must now be more presentable. Longingly, I eyed my own clothing spread out before the fire.

The women motioned for me to follow them across the room to the corner where they had placed Thad. His flushed face and glassy eyes revealed that he was seriously ill. As I felt his hot forehead, he looked up at me and tried to smile.

A young girl brought me a pan of cool water, and I bathed his forehead with a gauzelike cloth.

"Thank you." Thad smiled weakly.

I rose slowly to my feet. "Mr. Lin, my husband needs Dr. Gibson and his medicine. How far is it from here to the mission?"

"Seven hours in daylight and on horseback," he replied. "At dawn, I will ask one of the men to fetch the doctor."

"Until then?" My hand wringing belied my calm tone of voice.

"We turn to the Great Physician," Mr. Lin reminded. "That was Mr. Wong's suggestion." He gestured toward our host. "Mr. Wong says that Dr. Gibson's God saved his wife's life during her last pregnancy. Dr. Gibson is the reason Mr. Wong and his wife opened their home to us."

My face reddened at the peasant's simple faith. I'd been praying ever since I realized Thad was ill, but I'd been expecting God to answer my prayers through me. After all, I had the medical training and the medications.

While Mr. Lin offered a prayer, I silently begged God to heal Thad. *You can't leave me here in China without him, God. You can't!* At the end of Mr. Lin's prayer, I paused beside Thad to collect my thoughts. First, I needed to step back from Thad emotionally. *OK, Nurse Adams, let's review the patient's symptoms. He complained of feeling overtired and weak, of a chronic headache, and of cramps in his back, legs, and arms. His appetite has been poor. He's running a fever that has to be well over a hundred degrees, has severe diarrhea, and has been coughing a lot.*

He groaned when I gently touched his distended abdomen. My husband was growing weaker, and I could do little to help him. I knew that without further tests, the symptoms could indicate any number of problems or maybe a combination of diseases. *Look, CeeCee, you don't have your medications, so forget about them. Do the next thing. As Mama says, "Take it one step at a time." Keep his fever down; keep him warm and filled with fluids.*

As I considered the course of treatment, Thad's arms and legs jerked. He thrashed about and threw off his blanket. *Convulsions too? What's next, Lord? Delirium?*

I was just pulling the blanket over Thad once more when Thad shouted, "CeeCee, the Communists are coming! Hurry, we need to run—run—run—" His words faded into a mumble.

My voice trembled. "Excuse me, Mr. Lin, but could you ask Mrs. Wong if she has any herbal teas on hand?"

He asked and she shook her head. Mr. Lin turned to me and shrugged. "There has been a drought."

Hearing the rain pattering on the roof, I thought, *Obviously, that's not a problem any longer!* I made a second request. "If nothing else, could she heat a kettle of water? Even plain hot water will keep him from dehydrating."

Plain water! Wait a minute! The peppermints in my purse! I leapt to my feet and ran across the room, flinging back the curtain. My sudden movement startled the people gathered in the small, drafty house. I grabbed my purse from the table and rushed back to Thad's side.

"The water, is it hot yet?" Around me, I could hear a hostile murmur as I opened the soggy leather pocketbook and removed the tin of mints. I glanced at Mr. Lin in triumph. "They're still here! I'd forgotten them entirely."

He nodded, his face drawn with worry.

I frowned. "What's the matter?" I glanced about the room at all the scowling faces.

"They think you were afraid they would steal your purse, and that's why you ran to rescue it," he explained.

"Huh?" My jaw dropped open in surprise. I shook my head vigorously. "No, no. I hurried to get my purse because I remembered the mints that Mrs. Roscoe gave me in Shanghai." While I spoke, our hostess, now sullen, handed me a cup of steaming hot water. I thanked her and dropped one of the candy mints into the cup. "See? Mint tea!" I held the cup up for all to see. Then, lifting Thad's head, I urged him to drink the hot liquid. "Please assure them that I did not suspect anyone of stealing from me. I only wanted to prepare a cup of hot mint tea for my husband."

Mr. Lin's face relaxed. He smiled as he interpreted my message in a flood of Chinese words. The sullen faces instantly broke into grins, and they nodded and chatted among themselves.

I held the tin out for them to see. "Mints! See? Candy."

He shook his head. "They have no idea what candy is."

I looked questioningly at him, then at the little children peering from behind the adults. "They've never had a piece of candy?"

He shook his head again.

Of course, I couldn't help but give each child one mint apiece; they rewarded me with wide grins.

Mr. Lin and I took turns caring for Thad that night. His fever spiked, then plummeted. Though our host and his family slept on mats in the same room, they didn't complain when Thad's convulsions and the accompanying delirium awakened them from their slumber.

The next morning, our host and another man from the village set out on horseback for the mission. Mr. Lin and I considered making a bed for Thad on one of the wagons and driving to the mission, but as a nurse, I knew that Thad was too sick to make the seven-hour journey.

Because the water level had dropped overnight, Mr. Lin oversaw the drivers as they maneuvered the supply wagons across the river. Later in the day, one of the drivers found our belongings downstream—the medicines were spoiled, but many other things were salvageable.

Thad's temperature hovered around one hundred degrees throughout the day. I still had no idea what disease he'd contracted. While I couldn't understand her, nor she, me, Mrs. Wong left her three-year-old son in the care of her eldest daughter and remained constantly by my side, eager and willing to help however she could. Uncomplainingly, Mrs. Wong's mother scrubbed the soiled bedding and clothing on a washboard, outside in the cold. She draped the wet clothing over bushes that grew near the house, hoping the wash would dry in the overcast weather before it was needed again.

Toward evening, Thad's fever spiked again, bringing on delirium. Mrs. Wong and I bathed his torso and face with cool water. When he slipped into a deep sleep, I buried my face in his chest and cried out loud. "Oh, dear God! I've done everything I know. Please save my husband! I love him so much, Lord."

A gentle singsong voice broke through my grief. I lifted my head to find my hostess, with her hands folded and her head bowed, chanting a prayer. A wave of peace washed over me as behind me, the woman's seven children, clustered in the far corner of the room, joined in singing. I folded my hands and bowed my head. After the prayer, Mrs. Wong, in a high, trebly voice, began singing the melody of "What a Friend We Have in Jesus."

Our voices, theirs high and reedy, mine low and emotion filled, wouldn't have won applause in any congregations I'd visited, but somehow I knew all of heaven was singing with us. I prayed that the tune would bring Thad peace, even through his delirium. They sang for more than an hour, and I joined whenever I recognized a melody.

That evening Mr. Lin entered the curtained-off area where

Thad lay and studied my face for a moment as he stood beside Thad's mat. "How are you doing, Mrs. Adams?"

I looked up at him. "Fine, just fine."

"And Pastor Adams? He is better?"

"It's touch and go."

"Touch and go? I don't understand."

I thought for a moment. "Sometimes he seems better and other times, well, not so good."

"Has Mrs. Wong been able to understand you enough to meet your needs?"

I smiled and nodded. "We understand one another very well, Mr. Lin, at least about the important things."

"I'm glad. I was afraid the two of you would have difficulties."

"The woman has been most gracious, a real sister in Christ. Isn't it remarkable how God led us to a Christian home?"

Mr. Lin looked surprised. "You must have misunderstood. The Wongs aren't Christian; they are Buddhists. See the candles over there on the shelf?"

I laughed nervously. "But we sang hymns together and prayed together."

Mr. Lin raised one eyebrow and shrugged. "Interesting. Very interesting."

That night, I insisted on caring for Thaddeus myself because his fluctuating temperature continued to worry me. I sat by his head and repeatedly bathed his face and chest with cool water.

The sound of galloping hooves outside the Wong's one-room house awakened me with a start. I was surprised to discover I'd been dozing and that I was in China. My dream had transported me to Cape Cod and my summer there with Au Sam. I lifted my head and yawned, still far from alert, as Mr. Lin and Mr. Wong rushed to the door and peered out into the night. A bass voice boomed the traditional Chinese greeting through the darkness.

"It's Dr. Gibson," Mr. Lin called to me.

"Dr. Gibson? Here? Already?" I slipped into my shoes and dashed to the door, where I peered over Mr. Lin's shoulder. The illumination from the one candle inside the house lighted only a few feet beyond the open door. In the blackness of the night, a horse whinnied as a lantern bobbed toward the house.

As Thaddeus began to babble in delirium again, I returned to his side and felt his forehead. His temperature had stayed near normal since Mrs. Wong and I had prayed together earlier, but now it had shot back up.

I felt, rather than saw, the giant of a man standing over me, holding a black medicine bag in one hand and a bowler hat in the other. "Mrs. Adams, I presume."

"Dr. Gibson." I struggled to my feet.

Towering over me by almost a foot, the giant of a man brushed past my extended hand and knelt beside Thad. I watched silently as he measured Thad's pulse, then took his temperature.

Without turning his heavily bearded face toward me, the doctor boomed, "I need a basin of cold water. We must break this man's fever."

Dr. Gibson ripped open Thad's shirt and sucked in his breath sharply. I, along with everyone else in the room, gasped at the sight of the angry red spots spread across Thad's stomach and chest.

"Typhus! That's what I was afraid of." The doctor pounded his fist on the floor. His Scottish burr accented each word. "What have you been doing for your husband, Nurse Adams?"

This is the man I will be working with for who knows how long? I cringed at the unmistakable censure in his voice. "Cool baths to keep the fever down and peppermint tea to replace the fluid he lost with diarrhea. The spots weren't there when I last checked him, Doctor."

"Hmmph!" The man glanced at me over the gold rim of his spectacles. "If this man is to have the least chance of survival, he must be moved to the British hospital in Peking. I've lost three good workers to this nasty disease over the last ten years, and I don't intend to lose another!"

I bit my lip and closed my eyes. *No, Lord, please, no. I can't lose him. Not here. Not now!*

Dr. Gibson eyed me over his shoulder. "I suppose you'll insist upon accompanying him."

His question took me by surprise. "Of course."

"Hmmph! And I suppose I'll have to accompany him as well!

Where's that basin of water?"

Mr. Lin translated the doctor's orders to Mrs. Wong. The woman disappeared and returned immediately with a basin of water and a clean cloth. "If you're returning with us to Peking, Nurse Adams, you'll be required to attend to your nursing duties and not play the role of the overwrought wife!"

Overwrought wife? Of all the— It's not as if I haven't been caring for the man for more than twenty-four hours straight. I stared at the man in disbelief.

He whirled about to face me. "Don't just stand there. Take your post, woman. Begin cooling his brow and chest!"

I opened my mouth to speak but couldn't. I looked over at Mr. Lin, but I couldn't read the expression on his face. I glanced toward our host and his family. They hadn't understood the exchange.

"Nurse Adams? When I give you a command, I expect an instant response."

Suppressing the urge to snap back at the man, I knelt beside Thad and dipped a clean cloth into the cold water. Anyone who knew me would have seen the fire in my eyes as I glared at the doctor. Of course, I waited until he was listening to Thad's heart before I shot my hateful daggers his way.

The next morning, Thad seemed to be resting a little better. Dr. Gibson decided that Mr. Lin would guide the carts on to the mission while he and I took Thad by cart, then by rail, to the hospital. Throughout the long trip, I avoided speaking to the doctor any more than necessary. Of course, I followed his orders precisely but all the while fighting the urge to scream in his face. Dr. Gibson appeared totally unaware of my fury.

Two bearers met the train in Peking and transported Thad to the British hospital on a litter. Dr. Gibson and I followed in rickshaws. The moment the doctor's feet hit the dirt in front of the hospital door, he began shouting commands. And people scurried to obey.

In minutes Thad was situated in the hospital matron's private room. "We wanted the pastor to have a bright, airy room in which to recuperate," she explained when I thanked her. "Doctor Gibson says we are to fix up a bed for him in the sitting room next door. He wants you to sleep on a cot in the room with your husband."

"Oh, he does, does he?"

The nurse started at my tone of voice. "That will be acceptable to you, won't it, Mrs. Adams?"

I struggled for self-control. "It will be just fine. Thank you."

For thirteen days, Thad's wasted body failed to respond to the hospital's best efforts and medication. The cold sweats continued. Once during those two weeks, I came upon the doctor kneeling beside Thad's bed, with his head bent and his hands folded on Thad's chest. "—all go sometime. But this young man has a mission to fulfill before You call him to rest. By the stripes on the back of Your Son, Jesus Christ, by the blood shed at Calvary, spare him. Do not let the evil one consume him with the fires of typhus!"

I stood, silent with astonishment, in the doorway. I'd never heard anyone be so demanding of God—except perhaps me— yet instinctively, I knew not to be afraid. Dr. Gibson, for all his brashness, loved his God—that I could not question.

On our fourteenth night in Peking, I sat in a straight-backed chair at the foot of Thad's bed and wrote in my journal.

Dear Emily. I smiled to myself and nibbled on the cap of my fountain pen. When I first started addressing my diary entries to Emily Dickinson as a girl of thirteen, I never expected to be writing from Peking, China, nor under such circumstances. Paris or Munich, perhaps, but never Peking. I poised my pen to write. *So much has happened since I last wrote in this journal. Too much. I've never known such pain as I felt these last days, watching Thad waste away. One attack of delirium after another. He's imagined himself back in Paris. He's imagined himself at college and shouting at his father on the Cape. And, sometimes, his babble makes no sense at all.*

I looked at Thad lying limply under the sheet, then returned to my notebook. *Dr. Gibson has been constantly at Thad's side, doing everything known to modern science to save his life. I couldn't ask for better medical care. As to his attitude toward me—* Again, I paused and turned at the sound of the door opening. The doctor strode across the carpet.

"Any changes?"

I shook my head. "Not really." I took a deep breath.

"It's my turn to take over." Dr. Gibson placed his hands on the back of my chair. "You need to get some sleep. A martyred wife won't help our patient, will she? The hospital matron has another bed ready for you down the hall."

"I'd feel better, Doctor, if—"

His voice boomed in my ear. "And I'll feel better if you'll get yourself out of here and rest!" He grasped my elbow and lifted me to my feet. "I thought you knew by now that I don't make suggestions; I give orders!"

"I really would prefer to—"

"Nurse Adams! Do not thwart me on this."

I could feel the steam building within me. "Dr. Gibson, at this moment, I am not your nurse to be ordered about at will. I am Thaddeus's wife, and I want to stay with him."

"What you want, at this point, is neither here nor there. As Thaddeus's doctor, I order you to give your husband a break, or I will leave orders to restrict you from his room entirely. Do I make myself clear, Mrs. Adams?"

I stiffened. "You wouldn't dare!"

"Oh, wouldn't I? Try me!" He narrowed his gaze as we stared nose to nose. "Now, have I made myself clear, Mrs. Adams?"

Glaring unflinchingly in his face, I snarled, "Perfectly clear, Dr. Gibson!"

My back ramrod straight and my head held high, I clenched my fists and stormed from the room. I refrained from slamming the door for Thad's sake, not for proper protocol. Outside in the hallway, my chin began to quiver, and my eyes watered. From the sympathetic looks on the faces of the nearby hospital staff, I knew they'd heard every word. I marched over to the nurses' desk. "Dr. Gibson told me that Mrs.—"

"We've fixed you a bed in room 37, Mrs. Adams," the young nurse interrupted. "I know you'll be comfortable there. If you'd like a hot drink before you go to bed, I can—"

"No! Thank you," I snapped and strode down the hall to the room I'd been assigned.

My anger burned too brightly for me to fall asleep quickly. Slipping out of my dress, I slid between the cool, clean sheets. I didn't plan to sleep. I had too much to say to my heavenly Father about Dr. George Gibson and his arrogance.

"The man's absolutely incorrigible! He has the sensitivity of a rhino!"

I awoke fourteen hours later to someone shaking my shoulder. "Go away!" I mumbled and tried to roll over to face the wall.

"Mrs. Adams, Mrs. Adams!" The voice belonged to Nurse Sarah Whitington, one of the nurses on the day shift. "Dr. Gibson told me to bring you to your husband's bedside immediately!"

The urgency in her voice broke through my semiconsciousness. I sprang from the bed, wrestled my dress over my head, and, while fastening the buttons, bounded out of the room and down the hall to Thad's room. Nurse Whitington raced to keep up with me.

When I burst into Thad's room, Dr. Gibson straightened and turned, a smile wreathing his face. "We did it, Mrs. Adams!" His bass voice filled the room. "You, me, Thad, and God—we did it!"

I shot a glance at the doctor, then at Thad, then back at the doctor. "He's—he's?"

"He's going to make it!" The man took a deep breath and ran his fingers through his shock of red hair. "There for a while, it was touch and go, I can tell you."

For a moment, I froze as I digested the doctor's words. Then, as if my feet had been released from a prisoner's shackles, I ran to Thad's bed and dropped to my knees beside him. My husband opened his eyes slowly and smiled. "Hi, honey. You look tired. Are you all right?"

"Am I all right? Thaddeus, I love you." My eyes filled with tears. "Do you know how much I love you?"

Thad lifted his gaze to the tall, imposing man behind me. "Dr. Gibson, I presume? Where am I? Is this the mission?"

"Hardly! I wish it were." The big man chortled.

I kissed Thad's cheek and brushed a strand of hair from his cool, dry forehead. "You're at the British hospital in Peking."

"Peking? But didn't we—"

I laughed. "It's a long story, darling."

"One that can be told and retold on long winter nights at the mission clinic. But for now, I think it's best if you sleep for a few hours. Nurse Strickland—" Dr. Gibson gestured to the gray-haired woman who'd come into the room a few moments before. "—will stay with you while this young wife of yours gets a few more hours of sleep. She's been caring for you almost around the clock." The doctor took me by the shoulders and drew me to my feet. I kissed Thad good night and allowed Dr. Gibson to lead me from the room.

In the hallway, I waited while the doctor stopped at the nurses' station to record his instructions for caring for Thad. I expected the man to elaborate on his findings and the events of the night. But when he finished writing, he straightened, placed the chart on the desk, and shook a finger at me. "One more thing, Nurse Adams—in case I don't see you before I leave for home in the morning, I'll expect to see you in two weeks to assume your duties at the clinic. Is that clear?"

"T-t-two weeks?"

"Is there a problem?"

I blinked twice. "And Thaddeus?"

"After a week of egg-drop soup and a few of the Brits' heavy cream dishes, your husband will be ready to travel. I'll send Mr. Lin to guide you, of course." His thoughtful look disappeared into a scowl. "In the meantime, you get as much rest as you can. You'll need it when you start working at the mission." He strode two steps down the hall, then whipped about. "Did I commend you for your excellent nursing techniques? Your instructors should be proud!"

Managing to stammer a thank-you, I stared after the man until he turned the corner at the end of the hallway and disappeared from view. I slowly turned to see the hospital matron standing behind me. In her eyes, I could detect a distinct air of hero worship, the same look of awe I'd seen in most of the other nurses' faces whenever Dr. Gibson strode onto the floor. I couldn't understand it. While I would be eternally grateful for the care he gave Thaddeus, I dreaded being at his beck and call for the next who-knew-how-many years of my life.

Two weeks later, on the evening of the 15th of November,

Thad and I arrived at our new post. The winds whipped the fragile canvas top on our wagon as we raced against the sun to make it inside the city gates before dark. We had spent the previous night with the Wongs and had gotten a late start that last morning of our journey. I'd brought with me gifts I'd purchased in Peking to repay them for opening their home to us during Thad's illness. Mr. Lin instructed me on the proper way to offer these gifts without offending their hospitality. Along with two large boxes of foodstuff for winter, I gave Mrs. Wong a red woolen shawl and a Chinese Bible. I knew she couldn't read, but by the smile on her face, I had no doubt that she'd treasure it always. I grinned at Mr. Lin when the woman placed the Bible reverently in the midst of her religious candles and used the shawl to cover her scarred kitchen table.

The dread I'd acquired regarding working at the clinic abated when I met Mrs. Gibson. Eve was the kind of genteel, middle-aged woman one finds in teahouses in Bath or Canterbury. Her soft brown hair, kept in place by a silk net, and eyes that could melt the hardest of hearts gave her an air of delicacy. But quickly I detected a competent woman who operated the clinic and mission with extreme efficiency and grace. *She needs it to live with Dr. Gibson*, I thought as she served me a cup of hot tea while the men sequestered themselves in the doctor's study.

Within minutes, I discovered Eve was a woman gifted in languages, especially Mandarin Chinese and the local dialect. She peered at me through her silver-rimmed spectacles.

"My dear, the first thing we must do is take you to your little home behind the clinic. It is a trifle drab, I suppose, for an American, but I am sure that as soon as you unpack your personal belongings, it will be a cozy love nest for the two of you." She paused a moment and frowned. "Second, I must teach you the local dialect."

"I admit that I am eager to see my new home, Mrs. Gibson."

"Eve, call me Eve. While I was born and raised in proper Old England, I've been here in China too long to go by proper protocol." She smiled. "I'd like to suggest that you and Pastor Adams sleep in our guest room tonight. Tomorrow will be soon enough for you to begin unpacking. Would I be presumptuous to call you Chloe?"

I laughed. "I would prefer that you call me CeeCee, short for Chloe Celeste."

"All right, CeeCee. That's a friendly name. In the morning I will introduce you to your cook and servant girl, Jian Mei."

"I don't feel comfortable—"

Eve continued speaking. "Ten years ago, Jian Mei was left at the clinic. After beating her, her father threw the seven-year-old in the town dump for dead. One of our hospital workers found her and brought her to the clinic." She paused to study my reaction. "Girl children are of little value in the Orient. I trained Jian Mei myself, and she is now ready for regular employment."

Oh no! The last thing I want is to have a servant hovering while I unpack our crates! I cleared my throat. "Would it be inconvenient if she waited to begin working for us until I get our place organized?"

The woman smiled. "I think that can be arranged."

The Adventure Begins

I surveyed the stone cottage, one room at a time. Running my hand across the scratched tables and shabby green brocade sofa, I laughed to myself. "Ugly, but sturdy!"

Once I'd completed my initial inspection, I unpacked the shipping crate that held our kitchen supplies. What didn't fit in the wooden kitchen cabinet I stacked under the gray metal sink and promised myself I'd sew a skirt for it. The second crate sat in the center of the living room. After eyeing the stained wallpaper, I vowed I'd ask the Gibsons for a can of white paint and a brush.

I placed the silver tray and the sterling silver tea service we'd received as wedding gifts on the mantel above the massive stone fireplace, alongside Thad's and my favorite books and a cluster of silver-framed family photographs. On the wall beside the fireplace, I grouped Thad's framed sketches, then stepped back to admire the effect. *Something's missing. The natural rattan rocker!* I dashed into the tiny bedroom and dragged the rocker out to the parlor. *It overpowered the small bedroom anyway. Now I need a lamp stand.* I grabbed the smallest wooden crate and dumped its contents onto the sofa. Turning the crate on its side, I placed it between the wall and the rocker. *Once I add a lamp and a lace doily—* I visualized the setting before me. *—we'll have a delightful place to sit and read on cold winter evenings.*

From another crate, I unpacked the bolt of the brightly colored fabric I'd purchased in Shanghai and held up a portion of the fabric to one of the windows. *Yes! Thank you, Mrs. Roscoe, for your suggestion.* In the bottom of the crate, I found my sewing box and set about to fashion curtains for the living-room and kitchen windows and a sink skirt. Hours later, I hung my masterpieces in place, then stepped back to admire the results. *I think I have enough leftover fabric for a tablecloth—maybe enough to make a couple of sofa pillows.*

Humming to myself, I cut and stitched the sofa pillows. *All I need now is a basket of dried weeds for the living room and some herbs to hang from the open beams in the kitchen, and* voilà*! A house becomes a home.*

As I hurried to unpack the last of the crates before Thad returned home, I felt like a bride decorating her first home. The bedroom was my last project. Unpacking in this tiny room was more difficult. After I stashed what didn't fit in the closet under the bed and into our two trunks, I slid my humpbacked steamer trunk to the foot of the bed and shoved Thad's trunk under the windowsill, where it would serve as a tabletop. Then, on the straw-tick mattress, I placed my best percale sheets and my favorite quilt, a melange of red, blue, white, and yellow calico.

I straightened and sighed. *It's still too crowded in here. If we ever have a baby, there'd be no room for his crad—* I brushed the thought from my mind and continued unpacking.

To soften the rough, unpainted sills, I draped one of my white lace shawls over the window. *Hmm, I like that.* On the floor beside the bed, I spread the Native American rug I'd purchased in Albuquerque. A multicolored, handwoven blanket placed across the trunk at the foot of our bed added to the riotous color of the room, giving it a warm and friendly atmosphere.

What I liked best about the tiny bungalow was the veranda off the kitchen. Taking a short break from my work, I fixed myself a cup of hot mint tea and strolled out onto the covered area overlooking a small, dormant garden. *I could plant my herb seeds over there along the west wall. That would give them the maximum sunlight for growing,* I planned. In my unpacking, I'd run across the collection of tiny white packets my mother had meticulously filled, sealed, and labeled for me before I left San Francisco. *Leave it to Mama—*

Ambling along the narrow stone walkway that some missionary wife many years before me had created, I tried to imagine the scraggly rosebushes blossoming along the mission compound's brick wall. When the thought of my mother's rose garden overlooking the city of San Francisco came to mind, a wave of homesickness washed over me. For a moment, I again saw the grieving faces of my mother and father as I waved goodbye to them from the deck of the *City of Tokyo.*

Melancholy would have set in if it hadn't been for the incredible panorama of the mountains beyond the brick wall surrounding the mission.

"I will lift up mine eyes unto the hills . . ." The words comforted me as I stared at the unfamiliar landscape. The rumble of wagon wheels, the shouts of street vendors, and the *clip-clop* of plodding horses beyond the mission wall reminded me that I was surrounded by a small city, a city whose gates were closed each night and opened each morning. Instead of comforting me with a sense of security, this fact greatly disturbed me. I tried to describe my feelings in my diary entry.

Knowing I am trapped behind locked gates and cannot come and go freely fills me with an unreasonable fear, a claustrophobia that is new to me. What if I should have to leave quickly? What if I need to escape?

When Thaddeus arrived home that evening, I greeted him at the door with a kiss and welcomed him into our newly furnished cottage. We giggled and laughed like honeymooners as we ate a simple meal together, then strolled arm in arm out onto the veranda. That evening, as Thad told me about his new post, I rejoiced at the glint of excitement I saw in his eyes once again. Yet I worried that, in his enthusiasm, he might overdo. He'd lost so much weight during his illness that when I wrapped my arms around him, I could count his ribs. "You need some of Hilda's rich German cooking to fatten you up," I teased.

I stood for some time on the veranda, watching the bright moon sailing against the wash of the clear night sky and listening to my husband's dreams and plans. "Look, honey—" I pointed to the pagodas above the city walls. "—look how the moonlight edges the roof tiles with silver."

I shifted my gaze from the pagoda to the mountains beyond, the moonlight highlighting the jagged ridges. When I began to shiver in the nippy autumn breeze, Thad wrapped his arms around me and held me close. Reassurance swept through me as I listened to the steady beat of his heart. My world felt whole and complete, safe in his arms.

Thad's thoughts must have paralleled mine. "Go ye therefore, and teach all nations—" His voice faded into a whisper.

I finished the quote. "And, lo, I am with you alway, even unto the end of the world."

He sighed. "This certainly is the end of the world, isn't it, darling?"

I snuggled closer. "Are you sorry we came?"

He shook his head. "No, are you?"

"Not really." When I yawned and rubbed my eyes, Thad kissed the top of my head.

"It's been a long day, and tomorrow won't be any shorter. We'd better get some sleep."

I spent the next morning tagging after Dr. Gibson as he oriented me to the operation of the clinic. When he finished the tour, he asked me if I had any questions. When I didn't, he disappeared into his office to begin seeing the day's patients. Midmorning, Eve arrived with a pot of hot tea and a tray of English biscuits.

"Now, don't let that husband of mine throw you into a tizzy," she cautioned. "Some people find him to be rather intimidating, but I assure you, he's really a pussycat."

I choked on a biscuit crumb. *Oh yes, a pussycat? One with claws and sharp teeth!*

Eve repeated her visits each morning. Over crumpets and tea, she told me what to expect from our patients. "Feelings regarding the invasion of 'foreign devils' are still strong in these parts because the Boxers originated here in northern China. In 1899 and 1900, the Boxers killed many missionaries and Chinese converts to Christianity, whom they considered to be traitors. Hence, the work of the Lord has grown slowly over the last twenty-seven years." She sipped her hot tea.

"Even Dr. Sun, China's George Washington, couldn't eliminate the strong anti-Western sentiment. He led eleven revolutions against the Manchu Dynasty, before the emperor abdicated and a republic was proclaimed in 1912. And while he and his ministers were Western-thinking people, the old grudges remain firmly entrenched in the minds of the citizens."

By the end of the first week, I decided that if *Eve* means "life" or "mother of life," Eve Gibson was aptly named. Her gentle demeanor notwithstanding, the woman was a powerful combination of Au Sam, Nurse Bouchard, Grandma McCall, and my own mother rolled into one. I couldn't help but love her. When she was around, even Dr. Gibson grew less irascible. Obviously, the man adored her. *Maybe he has more than one redeeming virtue, after all.*

Between my work at the clinic and Thad's determination to scrub the chapel from the pitched ceiling to the wide plank floor before the weekend services, we saw little of each other that first week. He worked his crew from dawn to dusk. And my hours at the clinic weren't much better. I didn't really mind, because exhaustion kept me from dwelling on my family so many thousands of miles away. In the evenings, by the time I made supper, ate, and cleaned up, I had little energy left to write letters home or to even jot a few lines in my diary. And no time to think.

I quickly learned not to leave the mission compound without the company of Eve Gibson. The first excursion that Thad and I attempted on our own a few weeks after our arrival ended with a crowd of children screaming, "Foreign devil!" and throwing dirt clods at us.

In tears, I poured out my tale to Eve when we returned to the clinic. She patted my arm soothingly. "Don't worry. They used to do the same to my husband and me. But now, they tolerate us. We've bandaged too many of their bruises for them to maintain their hostilities. Antiforeign sentiment has gotten a little worse, I must admit, since last July, when the Nationalist army and Generalissimo Chiang Kai-shek started defeating the warlords of the northern provinces."

From then on, whenever I ventured out of the compound, it was with Eve. After those excursions, I would return angry and frustrated at the way children were treated, especially female children. "That's the custom in China. Girl babies quickly grow up, marry, and leave their parents for their husbands' household—not much profit to be made of girls, the fathers figure."

She told me about often finding little girls of three or four years old abandoned on the clinic steps and infants, some alive, some dead, left in garbage dumps. "We have an agreement with the mission orphanage in Peking. They take any child we deliver safely at their gates."

"Well, if I ever get to speak with the mandarin," I vowed, "I'll demand that something be done about this atrocity!"

Eve would silently smile and allow me to vent my anger at the government that allowed men to beat and to kill their wives and daughters at will.

A week before Thanksgiving Day, the weather turned brutally cold. Winter swept through the valleys and down the mountainsides. The wind howled around the corners of our little house in spite of the high mission walls. It seemed I was always cold—my hands, my nose, my feet, my toes—no matter how much clothing I wore.

Each morning I reluctantly crawled out of my toasty warm bed before the sun rose bright in the east. And each evening, I fell into our bed exhausted, grateful for Thad's warm body next to mine and for the short respite of sleep I would enjoy. Occasionally, after a day at the clinic caring for an infant, I would snuggle down under the blankets and wonder what it would be like to have a baby of my own to love. But most of the time, I was too busy to yearn for the things I did not have.

During whatever free time Thad and I had together, we worked on improving our language skills. Thanks to the background in the classic Chinese language that I'd received from my mother and her work at her women's clinic and Au Sam's attempts to interest me in the Chinese language, my speaking vocabulary increased rapidly. I quickly learned how to ask some basic medical questions in the mountain dialect of the district in which we lived.

Thad, however, found learning Chinese extremely difficult. "It's like I have to turn my tongue upside down to say the simplest of sentences. Sometimes I think I'll be ready for retirement before I can preach my first sermon without an interpreter!"

I laughed and caressed his arm. "Don't worry, honey. You'll soon catch on."

"Easy for you to say," he retorted, "Your nanny spoke fluent Mandarin." Thad shook his head. "Poor Mr. Lin. He's so patient with me."

"I wish I could say the same for Dr. Gibson."

"I thought you said it was getting easier since you've learned the routine of the clinic."

"It is, but at least once a day, the man charges through the building like a rampaging bull elephant. He explodes over tiny details that hardly seem worth his time." I pinched the bridge of my nose and squeezed my eyes shut. "I am looking forward to next week, when he and Eve will be gone for the holidays."

"That should give you a short break." Thad laughed, then quickly sobered. "I do hope the two of you can build a working relationship."

I leaned my head against the back of the sofa. "I think we will—if I can last long enough, that is."

When the doctor had announced to his staff his and Eve's planned journey to Peking, I swallowed the urge to cheer. The clinic ran so much smoother whenever he left for a few hours. As head nurse, or I should say, the only registered nurse at the clinic, I found it difficult to temper both the physician's mood swings and the native staff members' injured feelings. I know that we all respected him, but we didn't like him. The result was, we all breathed easier in his absence.

He and Eve had been gone three days of their two-week holiday, and except for a few minor injuries, I had little to keep me busy. Since the clinic was operating so smoothly, I decided it would be a good time to inventory the supply room.

Jian Mei, the young woman whom I was training to work as my assistant, counted the number of clean sheets on the shelf while I recorded it on my check sheet. A loud commotion in the courtyard interrupted us. Voices were shouting excitedly, "The mandarin's coming! The mandarin's coming!" I walked out the storage-room door into the clinic's waiting area in time to see Yang, one of the clinic's orderlies, running toward the gate, his queue bouncing to the rhythmic pounding of his feet.

"The mandarin?" I turned to look at Jian Mei, but she was nowhere to be found. Neither were any of the rest of the clinic staff. *What am I supposed to do? What am I supposed to say?*

The mandarin ruled his district by decree from the governor of the province. The governor owed nominal allegiance to the Nationalist Republic, but many mountain ranges rose between our remote province and the capital city. Life and death, freedom and imprisonment, lay in the mandarin's hands.

In Chinese society, the mandarin was an absolute ruler, to be treated with obeisance. From his yamen, he ruled in much the same way as in the time of Confucius. He had earned his position through many years of education and through passing civil service exams, not through heredity, like the European aristocracy. Coolies and government officials alike knew the correct protocol for their station in life—so many bows when greeting a mandarin. I had no idea what was considered appropriate for a foreign devil like me, especially a female foreign devil.

Mr. Lin? Thad? Where are you when I need you? I'm really not prepared for this! I took a deep breath. *I guess it's just You and me, Father.*

Straightening my back, I marched down the corridor to the front door of the clinic, where I stood awestruck by the magnificent entourage. Coolies bore a sedan chair, curtained against prying eyes. Around it were grouped the mandarin's clerks in robes of dark blue. At a respectful distance, a backdrop of deferential learned men with pale faces, tight skull caps, and black almond eyes waited.

After a clerk carefully opened the door of the sedan chair, a well-built servant stepped forward and took the limp body of a child from inside the sedan chair, then turned and looked expectantly at me.

"Bring the child into the clinic immediately," I ordered in the local dialect. The servant glanced at the person hidden behind the curtains of the sedan chair, then back at me.

I turned and strode into the clinic, hoping the servant would follow with my patient. He did.

Spotting Jian Mei peeking out from behind the shrubbery, I called, "Jian Mei, I need your assistance."

The frightened young woman followed me into the examination room.

"Place the child on the table, please." I poured clean water into the basin and washed my hands before checking the comatose child's eyes. "What happened to the boy?"

The servant babbled a frightened response and darted from the room.

"Jian Mei, you are no help, cowering in the corner like that. Please assist me on the other side of the table."

Once Jian Mei stood opposite me, I rolled the boy onto his side and found a large bump on the back of his head. "You really gave yourself a goose egg, young man."

"He fell from a tree."

I examined the wound more closely. "How high is the branch?"

"Twenty feet." I turned to identify the source of the information and found myself face to face with the mandarin.

The man's face radiated the arrogance of power. His red satin brocade robe swept the floor behind him as he approached the table. He watched as I bowed; then he turned his attention to my patient.

"This is my only son. He cannot die."

"I will do what I can for your son. First, I need to cleanse the wound."

"No!" The mandarin slammed his hand down on the end of the examination table. "You are but a woman. Where is the doctor?"

"Dr. Gibson should be arriving in Peking this afternoon. He will not be returning until the evening of the second."

Though I read only concern in his expression, his retainers retreated to the doorway of the examination room, as if waiting for him to explode in anger. Instead, in a controlled voice, he asked, "There is no man available to help my son?"

"The minister and Mr. Lin are at the chapel if you would prefer. As to the medical clinic, I am in charge during the doctor's absence." I cringed at the sharp edge I heard in my voice. I only hoped the mandarin wouldn't detect it as well. "Do you or do you not want me to care for your son?"

The mandarin's eyes flickered with a moment of indecision. "Proceed, woman."

I bowed, then resumed my examination of the boy.

"You have children of your own?" the mandarin inquired.

I hesitated, then answered. "No, sir, unfortunately, I do not."

"Then you cannot know how I feel about this child."

My heart softened, and I glanced up into the man's inscrutable face. "I do not need to be a parent to care about my patients, sir. I promise you that I will give him the very best of care." I requested Jian Mei to prepare a cold compress for the boy's injury while I settled him in a quiet patient room at the end of the hall.

When I asked the burley servant to wait outside, he refused. "Let him stay," the mandarin ordered.

"I really think—"

"Chin Shui is my son's protector. From the moment of my son's birth, the man has never left the child." The mandarin's face hardened; his eyes grew cold as steel. "If my son dies, Chin Shui will accompany him to the land of my ancestors."

"You'll execute him?"

"Of course not." The mandarin grew indignant. "He will willingly fall on his sword."

I gulped in surprise, then cast a quick glance at Chin Shui's stoic face. Clearly, he understood his fate.

The child looked tiny and fragile against the starched white sheets. In spite of my bravado, I had no idea how or when he would awaken from the coma. But I did know that I'd done all I could for the boy, short of surgery. And that was Dr. Gibson's forte, not mine. From here on out, the fate of the mandarin's son was in God's hands, though I doubted I would receive much more mercy than Chin Shui if the boy didn't regain consciousness.

"Perhaps you would be more comfortable in the waiting room, mandarin." I bowed again, hoping the man would take my suggestion, thus making care of the boy less stressful.

"I shall stay beside my son." The man snapped his fingers,

and two of the retainers standing in the doorway disappeared and returned with the upholstered chair from Dr. Gibson's office. The mandarin gestured toward me as he made himself comfortable in the procured chair. The rest of his staff, including the doomed servant, fell to the floor in obeisance. "You and your assistant may remain standing while you care for my son."

"Thank you, Mandarin." I ordered Jian Mei to open the window. "We need fresh air."

A skirmish broke out in the hallway, and the mandarin's servants unsheathed their swords and positioned themselves to defend their master's life. I took a cloth from Jian Mei's hand and in a low voice said, "Please find out what the problem might be."

She scurried from the room but returned almost instantly. "It is the pastor and Mr. Lin asking about your safety. The mandarin's guards refuse to allow them to enter the room."

So that's where Yang disappeared to. I thought for a moment. "Jian Mei, please assure Pastor Adams and Mr. Lin that they can best assist me by gathering the workers into the chapel and conducting the midday prayer meeting."

She looked at me quizzically. We had no midday prayer meeting. I smiled at her confidently. "Please hurry back. I need your assistance."

Oh, dear Father, help them get the message to begin praying for this child's life. You've promised that where two or three are gathered in Your name, You will be with them. Then ten or fifteen praying believers should increase the odds, right?

Five minutes later, the familiar strains of "Father, Lead Me Day by Day" drifted through the open window. I smiled across the bed at Jian Mei, hoping to encourage her. Though fear filled her eyes, she returned my smile with one of her own.

As we ministered to the unconscious child, I mouthed the words along with the singers. "When in danger make me brave."

"What is that tune you sing?" the mandarin demanded.

"A hymn to God."

He thought a moment. "When will you demand that your God heal my son?"

"I beg your pardon?"

"If Dr. Gibson were here, he would shout at his God, demanding His attention. But, of course, I expect too much from you." The mandarin's voice held a tinge of sarcasm. "You are but a woman."

But a woman. For once, I had the sense not to protest. I wanted to assure the heathen ruler that God is no respecter of gender. *Show him, CeeCee,* the voice within me whispered, *show him how God's healing power is available to all who love and worship Him, regardless of their sex.*

"Jian Mei, I think we should pray for the young child." I stretched my hands across the bed and clasped Jian Mei's hands in mine. In a quiet voice, I began to pray, "Dear heavenly Father—"

"Dr. Gibson always kneels."

Resisting the urge to glare at the man, I began again. "Dear heavenly Father—"

"You must speak louder. Dr. Gibson shouts. He demonstrates his authority to his god."

"It is not necessary—"

"Ah!" The mandarin arched one eyebrow. "What god will respond to the voice of a weak woman?"

I turned toward my antagonizer and managed to smile. "My God responds. He hears my prayer, even when I do not put my requests into words. He does so because He loves even me, a mere woman." My left eyebrow arched despite my efforts to conceal my irritation. "And, now, Mandarin, if you will excuse me—" I bowed slightly, then, in a soft, gentle voice prayed, "Dear heavenly Father."

I paused, expecting the mandarin to interrupt again. A tremor of fear coursed through me with the realization that probably a woman had never spoken to him with such force. When he remained silent, I continued, my voice barely above a whisper. "In Your Word, You promised to hear the prayers of Your children. You said, 'Ask, and it shall be given.' I am asking, Lord, that You heal this child. I have done all I can do medically for him." I paused, then added, "I come to You as Your faithful daughter, trusting this child's life in Your capable, life-giving hands. If healing the child will magnify Your holy name, let it be so. If not, I rest his fate in Your hands. Amen."

Jian Mei squeezed my hand and opened her eyes to meet mine. The hymns drifting through the open window reminded me that she and I weren't alone. I had no doubt that Thad and the others would continue praying throughout the ordeal.

" 'I have called upon thee, for thou wilt hear me, O God: incline thine ear unto me, and hear my speech.' " The familiar words of Psalm 17 comforted me as I waited beside the child's bed. " 'Shew thy marvellous lovingkindness, O thou that savest by thy right hand them which put their trust in thee from those that rise up against them.' " I glanced meaningfully at the mandarin, who sat staring at the open window. " 'Keep me as the apple of the eye, hide me under the shadow of thy wings.' "

Hours passed. I sent Jian Mei to my house to fix a plate of shortbread cookies I'd made for our Christmas celebration and a pot of chamomile tea. *Mama swears by the calming properties of chamomile tea. This time, I guess I'm putting her theory to the test.*

When Jian Mei returned carrying my silver tea service and English bone china teacups on a tray, I smiled at the surprised look on the mandarin's face. *What did you expect? Earthenware?*

Acting as hostess, I poured the hot tea into a cup and offered it to the mandarin. Instantly, one of his servants snatched the cup from my hand and lifted it to his lips. With a nod, he returned the cup to the mandarin; then the servant tested the corner of one cookie and gave his approval.

The evening passed slowly. Clouds rolled in from the west and with them a brisk wind. The drop in temperature forced me to close the open window, making it more difficult to hear the music still coming from the chapel. I resisted the urge to pace. Instead, I recited to myself the names of the bones of the body, then the muscles and nerves. When I ran out of medically related mental gymnastics, I wrote to my mother, in my imagination, of course.

"You will never believe the situation I find myself in at this moment," I began. I thought of all the frightening escapades my mother had experienced over the years—the time she delivered the child of a bandit, the time she shot an elk to feed herself,

me, and my older brother, the time she faced down my real father's murderer, the time she faced down a couple of drunken sailors to protect a little girl's life. *"On second thought, yes, you would. I wish you were here right now, helping me to know what to do. Is there anything more I can do for the mandarin's son than what I've already done? Barring brain surgery, of course!"* I chuckled to myself. *"Even you wouldn't go that far, or would you?"*

A shadow passed through my mind as I remembered the times when, as a teenager, I'd resented my mother's courage and her faith in God. *Measuring myself against a woman like you was difficult. I always seemed to fall pitifully short.* I stared at the flame in the kerosene lantern on the table across the room. *How appropriate that I would think of you and find strength in your example at such a time as this.*

A groan from the patient beside me snapped me from my reverie.

The child whimpered, "Father? My head hurts."

I shot a glance at the mandarin, and for the first time, I saw a worried father instead of the most powerful man in the province. I stared at him in surprise, then down at the child, whose face broke into a smile at the sight of his father. "I'm sorry I climbed the tree, Honorable Father. Chin Shui told me not to, but I disobeyed."

I struggled to hide my grin. The pitiful look on the child's face would have melted any parent's heart, mandarin or not.

The father, trying to conceal his emotion, turned toward the child. "Have you learned a lesson, my son?"

"Yes, Father." The boy heaved a ragged sigh.

"And what is that lesson, my son?"

"Not to trust a branch that is dead."

I choked and coughed to cover my giggle. "Mandarin, it seems that the God in heaven, who answers the most humble of prayers, restored your son to you."

Solemnly, the mandarin bowed in acknowledgment. As he did, I caught a twinkle of humor in his eyes. I bowed in return.

Once I had examined the boy and was certain he was out of danger, I gave him a cup of chamomile tea to ease his headache.

Then I suggested that a mat be prepared beside the bed for Chin Shui and that the rest of us vacate the room so the child could get some sleep. This time, the mandarin agreed, though he left two of his armed guards in the hall outside the room as added protection.

"I will return tomorrow for my son," the mandarin said in parting.

I shook my head. "I will need to keep him here at the clinic for another twenty-four hours for observation."

The mandarin studied my face for a second. Then a hint of a smile formed at the corners of his mouth. "You do not trust that your God completely answered a mere woman's prayer?"

Instinctively, I knew that a bond of friendship had formed between me and the imposing ruler. I shot him an "I will not be goaded" stare. "Good medical practice, Mandarin." I bowed respectfully.

He returned my gesture. "I will accept your skilled advice, Nurse Adams."

Nurse Adams? How did he discover my name? He hadn't used my name previously.

He obviously could read the question on my face. "The fame of the foreign devil woman with hair the color of burnished gold is known throughout the province."

"Likewise, the fame of the powerful mandarin is known from the east to the west, from the north to the south."

His retinue of servants gasped as the mandarin and I bowed simultaneously. With a wave of his hand, the great man and his entourage departed from the clinic. His sedan chair had barely left the grounds when Thad burst into the clinic, with Mr. Lin in tow. Seeing the child's protector bristle, I ran into the hall to stop my husband from dashing into the child's room uninvited.

I fell into Thad's arms.

"Oh, darling." He showered my face with tiny kisses. "I was so frightened. What happened in here? Tell me all about it."

"I hardly know where to start." I giggled from relief. "It's almost too fantastic to be believed."

Little and Not So Little Surprises

Two days before Christmas, the mandarin sent his sedan chair to transport his son home. He also sent a retinue of servants carrying ten freshly killed and plucked turkeys. The men laid the plump dead birds at my feet.

"Partial payment," the mandarin's ambassador informed me, "for your service to his son. Being a wise, all-knowing ruler, he knew you would celebrate the birth of your God in two days. These are for your feast."

Oh, dear, what am I going to do with all these turkeys? I bowed to mask my distress. "Tell the honorable mandarin I am most grateful for his generous gift."

The ambassador clapped his hands twice. A second wave of servants came forward, bearing baskets of candied and dried fruit. When they laid their gifts at my feet, they stepped back to make room for a third wave of servants, bearing trays of freshly baked pastries.

My mouth dropped open in surprise. "I can't accept all this."

The man frowned and shot an angry glance toward Yang, who'd walked out of the clinic during the delivery of the turkeys. Yang rushed to my side. "Nurse Adams, you must accept the mandarin's gifts. If you returned them, it would be a great insult."

The last thing I wanted to do was anger the man whose goodwill allowed the mission to exist in the city, so I smiled and bowed before the ambassador. "Please tell the mandarin that I accept his generous gifts on behalf of Dr. Gibson and the mission clinic. His magnanimous gesture will feed many hungry people in the city."

Pleased with my speech, the mandarin's ambassador bowed and departed. I ordered the clinic staff to carry the gifts to the clinic's small kitchen; then I turned to Yang. "Can we gather the town beggars tomorrow at noon?"

The man grinned with pleasure. "I will take care of everything, Mrs. Adams, everything."

Freed of having to attend to the mandarin's son and with the other demands of the clinic met, I turned my attention to the upcoming holiday. *We need a tree, or it won't feel much like Christmas*, I decided. The day I unpacked and settled into our cottage, I'd run across a box of Christmas decorations my mother had stuck in the bottom of one of my household crates. I'd laughed at her when she insisted I take them with me.

After instructing Jian Mei to call me should any emergencies arise, I checked on Su Lee, the Gibsons' cook and housekeeper.

"Do you mind preparing the food for the people of the streets?" I asked.

She grinned with delight and bowed several times. "I am most honored to be able to feed the people as my Master did. Tonight, I will make many loaves of bread to serve also."

"The staff and I will help you as much as possible," I assured her. "I appreciate everything you are doing. Is there anything I can get you that you need?"

Again, she bowed respectfully. "Oh no." She glanced shyly away. "Ru-Mai, er, Yang, has said he will take care of everything."

Ru-Mai? Yang's first name? For some reason, I'd never thought about Yang having a first name. "Well, if you're sure I can't do anything right now—"

"I am sure. I am sure."

Hurrying home from the clinic, I tossed my cape onto the sofa, ran into the bedroom, and threw open Thad's trunk. As I lifted the gray cardboard box containing the hand-painted glass baubles from the trunk, I felt an overwhelming gratitude for my mother's good sense. I removed a second cardboard box from the trunk, one containing the tiny white candles that sat on the end of each bow. Grabbing my cape once more, I picked up Thad's ax from the toolbox on my way to the church, where Thad said he'd be working on his Christmas sermon.

"Thad," I called as I peered into the quiet little chapel.

"Here, honey, in the side room."

I hurried down the aisle and through the open door. Thad sat at a scarred desk, pen in hand, a score of papers and books stacked around him. "Here," I said, thrusting the ax toward him. "We need a Christmas tree."

He looked down at the ax, then at me. "A Christmas tree?"

"Absolutely. Not too big, about this tall." I indicated one about my eye level.

"All right. Are you coming with me to find this tree?"

I hung my head. "I can't leave the clinic for that long. What if—"

He lifted his hands in defense. "I know! I know! What if there were another emergency? OK, when Mr. Lin returns from the railway with the mission's mail tomorrow evening, I'll ask him to go with me."

Two days earlier, after the mandarin's unexpected visit, Mr. Lin had harnessed the mission horses and had started over the mountain trail to the railroad to pick up the mail pouch for the mission.

"Do we have to wait that long? Can't Yang go with you?"

"All right. Yang and I will go fetch your Christmas tree." Thad grinned at my eagerness.

"My Christmas tree! If it's my tree and not yours, I don't want to catch you enjoying it for one minute, do you hear?" We both knew which of us was more sentimental about holidays, especially Christmas. Beauty and nostalgia always stirred Thad's artistic soul.

Thad stood and reached for his heavy woolen jacket. "Woman, you will be the death of me yet."

"Huh!" I helped him into his jacket. "I am the one who keeps you alive and healthy! And don't you forget it!"

With Thad's arm around my shoulder, we strolled back to the clinic to locate Yang. Minutes later, I waved goodbye to them from the front gate. "Hurry home," I called, then returned to the clinic.

A few hours later, Thad and Yang dragged a five-foot spruce tree into our parlor, where I had the bucket of sand ready in the corner by the fireplace. While Thad and I adjusted the tree, Yang watched, observing my excitement. When I invited him to join us, he helped me place the baubles onto the branches while Thad fastened the brass candle holders in place. One by one, I secured the candles into the holders, then lighted them.

The three of us stared at the tree with wonder.

"Nurse Adams," Yang asked, "why do you drag a dead tree into your house and decorate it like a bride, then put candles on it?"

"Oh, Yang, it's part of our holiday celebrations. You know, Christmas and the birth of Jesus Christ."

"But what does a tree have to do with that?"

"I don't know. It's just something we do—kind of like fire-crackers and almond cookies at your New Year's celebration."

"Oh." He gazed at the tree without speaking.

"What did he say?" Thad asked.

After I explained, Thad admitted, "It is a strange custom, when you think about it."

I made both men cups of hot chocolate, reluctantly parting with four of the oatmeal cookies I'd secretly baked for the holidays. Standing to leave, Yang, who could speak broken English, asked, "Pastor Adams, when you tell about—"

Thad's finger flew to his lips. "Sh, it's a surprise."

"Ah!" The man's face broke into a wide grin. "I understand *surprise*."

I looked from one man to the other. "Surprise? What surprise?"

Thad slipped his arm around my waist. "I'll tell you about it in a few minutes, when we're alone."

The moment Yang closed the door behind him, I whirled to face Thad. "OK, what's the surprise?"

He ambled over to the tree and began blowing out the candles. "I left it at the clinic on the way home. We need to go over there to pick it up."

Grabbing the cape I'd worn earlier, I threw it around my shoulders and urged my husband toward the door. Thad chuckled at my intense curiosity. I couldn't imagine what the two men could have brought back from the forest, other than another tree. As I burst into the clinic ahead of Thad, I called over my shoulder, "Did you leave it with Jian Mei?"

Hearing a soft cry coming from my office, I threw open the door and froze. Seated in the chair behind my desk was Jian Mei, holding a newborn baby wrapped in white flannel. A young woman I did not know sat in the other chair.

"Oh, excuse me. My husband said—" My voice trailed off as one tiny fist appeared from beneath the blanket. "Oh, how darling." I completely forgot my mission. "May I hold your baby?" I asked the young woman. Her eyes filled with question. Without waiting for the mother's permission, I circled the desk and gently took the child from Jian Mei's arms. "Oh, you precious little thing," I cooed. "Aren't you the most beautiful little—" I glanced toward Jian Mei.

"Girl, she's a little girl, only a couple of days old, I would guess."

I shot a surprised look at the young woman whom I believed to be the child's mother. *She's doing well for having given birth only a few days ago.*

Jian Mei started to speak, but Thad silenced her. "CeeCee, this woman is not the child's mother. She's the wet nurse Jian Mei found for the baby."

"But, but, where is the baby's mother? Did she—" I couldn't bring myself to say it. "Did she die in childbirth?"

Thad took a deep breath. "CeeCee, Yang and I found the child abandoned in the woods and brought her home with us. By nightfall the wolves would have devoured her."

Instinctively, I drew the tiny bundle closer to me. "But what kind of mother—" I'd heard the stories about the female children the mission rescued each year, treated, and sent to the mission orphanage in Peking, but I hadn't seen any or held any in my arms. As I gazed down into the tiny face, her eyes closed tightly, her lips forming a pink bow, a cry escaped my lips. "You beautiful creature. How can anyone give up such a lovely gift from God like you?"

Behind me, I felt Thad's hands on my shoulders. "The child needs a home until Dr. Gibson returns and can make the arrangements for transferring her to the orphanage." He cleared his throat. "I thought it might be fun to play Mommy and Daddy, considering the season and all. You don't have to if you don't want to," he hastened on. "Jian Mei has arranged for a wet nurse to care for the child if you're not com—"

"Nonsense!" I snapped. "As the acting head of the clinic, it is my job to care for the patients admitted here. And I will do so. However, if—" I looked at the young wet nurse.

"Hsi Kim," Jian Mei hastened to add.

"If Hsi Kim is willing, I will gladly hire her. She can stay here at the clinic."

"I have room in my quarters for her." Jian Mei's face broadened into a smile. "Hsi Kim is my cousin. Her baby died soon after birth. She has much milk—good, rich milk—for this baby."

I couldn't believe how conveniently this was working out. I turned toward Thad. "Are you comfortable with this?"

Tears glistened in his eyes as he looked down at the sleeping child and nodded.

My thoughts of decorating for Christmas, of the feast I was to throw tomorrow from the mandarin's largess, of the clinic, of the letters I was eagerly awaiting from America, of everything other than the beautiful child in my arms disappeared from my mind. "We'll need a few—"

"I have everything ready for you." Jian Mei gestured toward a stack of linen sitting on a table across the room.

"And Hsi Kim—"

Jian Mei interrupted. "The child has just eaten. Hsi Kim will come to your home in four hours for the next feeding."

"Perhaps it would be better if Hsi Kim slept on our sofa."

Jian Mei shook her head. "Hsi Kim would feel more comfortable sleeping at the clinic with me."

I sighed with relief. I wanted to keep Thad's and my moments together with the baby private. As I hurried home, clutching the infant under my cape, I refused to think of how I'd feel when Dr. Gibson returned and sent her to the orphanage.

"Where will she sleep?" Thad asked as he closed the door to

our cottage and helped me with my cape.

"You mean, when I'm not holding her?" I caressed the child's tiny fingers. "What's your name, little one? Did your mama give you a name before she left you to die on the mountain?"

"Chances are, she has no name." Thad gently brushed his fingers across her soft black hair. Probably it was her father, not her mother, who did the abandoning."

"What shall we call you, little one?"

Thad hesitated for a moment before answering. "Do you think we can name her Elizabeth?"

I looked up at my husband in dismay. "Wasn't that a certain Miss Master's first name?" I didn't try to mask my sarcasm, and I gave him my best Meeker stare.

"It was, wasn't it?" He looked surprised. "I'd forgotten her. My mother's name was Elizabeth."

My gaze softened. Thad had said so little about his mother since her death. "That would be nice. But can we call her Beth, for short?"

He grinned. "Sure, Beth it is."

I held the baby out to him. "Here, you hold her while I change out of my uniform into more comfortable clothing."

Gingerly, he took her in his arms.

"She's not crystal. She won't break." I chuckled.

I hurried to my room and changed into my light blue chenille housecoat. I could hear Thad in the other room singing an old familiar English lullaby. *He's missed being a parent as much as I.* The thought surprised me. In spite of evidence to the contrary, I'd continued to harbor the notion that my loss had been much greater than his.

He deserves equal time with her. I forced myself to take the time to brush my hair and to tie it away from my face with a blue satin ribbon. *Elizabeth? Elizabeth what? Elizabeth Anne? Elizabeth Mae? Elizabeth Elaine? Hmmm, yes, Beth Elaine.*

When I returned to the parlor, I found Thad rocking the baby in the rocking chair. During my absence, she had awakened and lay staring up at him through the biggest pair of almond eyes I'd ever seen. She'd also wrapped the fingers of one hand around his pinkie.

"I think Beth likes you." I kissed him on the neck and leaned over his shoulder.

"I think the feeling's mutual," he replied.

The next morning, the staff at the clinic insisted that I spend the day with Beth rather than help in the kitchen. I did entrust her to Hsi Kim while I helped serve the scores of hungry people who swarmed onto the mission grounds for the free food. Thad personally invited each one to the Christmas Eve service being held at the church that evening.

The Christmas service had never held such meaning for me as it did in 1926. Cradling little Beth in my arms and listening to the familiar story, I experienced for the first time Mary's pain, her fear, and her joy. The candles in the church windows flickered as Thad described the arrival of the wise men and Yang interpreted as best he could. I turned to learn the reason for a draft of cold air and saw Mr. Lin, dressed in his heavy travel gear, standing in the doorway. Over his shoulder he carried a large leather pouch of mail—Christmas mail.

After the last of the worshipers had filed out of the chapel, Mr. Lin and Thad sorted the mail while I stood by, soothing a hungry baby. "Just a minute, sweetie," I cooed to the infant's delicate whimper. "Mama will get you home and fed in just a minute, darling."

A few minutes later, Yang helped me carry our mail home from the church. Thad had stayed at the church to talk with Mr. Lin, I suspected about Beth. In both of our minds, there was no doubt; we wanted to keep the child. I placed the hungry baby in Hsi Kim's arms, then ran to the bedroom to sort through my personal mail—a letter and a package from Mama and Daddy, a letter from Ashley, another from Nina in Oregon, a small package from Aunt Jenny and Uncle Phillip, and a larger one from Grandma and Grandpa McCall in Boston.

My happiness couldn't have been more complete. The decorated tree, gifts from home, and the letters from loved ones increased my holiday joy, as did the first snowfall of the year, gently lazy flakes drifting to earth on the evening of the 25th. Carols played on our little phonograph as Thad and I exchanged the small gifts we'd both secretly purchased before leaving

Shanghai. But our greatest gift was definitely the one neither of us could leave alone—Beth.

Throughout the days following Christmas, a little voice inside my head warned me as I cared for the baby and as I performed my tasks at the clinic, "Don't get too attached, CeeCee. You won't want to give her up when the Gibsons return."

Thad arranged to do much of his work at home while I was at the clinic. Then, when we had a lull in the patient flow and I could get away, I would return to the cottage so that Thad and Mr. Lin could leave to visit the sick and the elderly of the mission's growing congregation.

It was during one of my breaks at home when Dr. and Mrs. Gibson returned home from Peking. Like a whirlwind, he stormed into the clinic, shouting orders and demands. Hsi Kim appeared at my front door, shaking with fright. "The big man is here. Jian Mei says for you to come! He is terribly angry."

"But Beth—"

"I will stay with the baby; you go, now!"

I grabbed my cape and dashed out of the house.

"What is the meaning of all this?" the doctor demanded, his face red, his eyes glaring.

"The meaning of what, sir?"

"Throwing a feast for the entire town while I was away. Do you think that the mission board is made of money?" His tirade continued. "There I was, begging additional funds from the mission board while you were here hosting a feast." He flung his hand dramatically into the air.

"Excuse me, sir, but doesn't the Good Book say to 'cast thy bread upon the waters: for thou shalt find it after many days'?"

"Don't be impudent, Nurse Adams. Imagine the humiliation I felt upon arriving home and being stopped every few feet throughout the city to have someone tell me about the marvelous holiday feast you threw at the mission's expense."

"I beg your pardon, sir. The only expense to the mission was the cost of the flour for the bread."

He paused. "Only the flour?"

"Only the flour. Everything else was supplied by the mandarin himself." When Dr. Gibson didn't respond, I continued. "It was his way of saying thank you for services rendered." I told him the rest of the story. "So you see, Dr. Gibson, the goodwill we created from our generosity will more than make up for the cost of a sack of flour."

"Hmmph! We'll see how you feel about that when we run low on flour this spring," he sputtered as he marched from his office. Frustrated, I made my way to my office at the end of the hallway. *Thad, wherever you are, please come home. I need your diplomatic skills when the man hears about Beth.*

But it wasn't to be. Less than five minutes later, the doctor stormed through my office door. "About the abandoned girl-child your husband found the other day—"

I looked up from the papers I was studying. "Yes?"

"When were you planning to tell me about her?"

"Sir, I didn't have a chance. You left your office immediately after our discussion of the mandarin's gift, remember?"

"Hmmph! Yes, well, thank you for caring for the child while Eve and I were away. I'm sure Eve will be glad to take her off your hands until we can transport her to the Peking orphanage."

I cringed at his use of the term *transport*. "Beth is not a parcel to be transported, sir."

"Beth?" The man's eyebrows shot up toward his hairline. "How did you learn the child's name?"

"We didn't. That's the name Thad and I chose for her."

"I see." He pursed his lips thoughtfully. "You realize it is against local government laws for a Westerner to adopt a Chinese child?"

"Yes, sir. I'm aware of that law." My words caught in my throat. I'd reminded myself of that fact every time I bathed Beth, every time I rocked her, cuddled her, comforted her. I knew the law, indeed.

"Just so you understand." He turned to leave.

"Doctor?" I hesitated. "Is there any possible way—" My voice trailed off wistfully.

As he turned and looked at me, I was surprised to see compassion in his eyes. "Eve and I have wished many times that there were."

Biting my lower lip, I nodded and stared at a speck on the ceiling.

"I suppose we cannot take the child to Peking for a few weeks anyway, her being so young and all." He touched my arm, giving me a glimpse into the man behind the doctor. "I'm sorry. I guess it's part of the sacrifice we must make in God's work."

Part of the sacrifice. Part of the sacrifice? Why, Lord, must an innocent child be part of some grand sacrifice? As a parent Yourself, You must understand. The mandarin's question "Do you have children?" flickered through my memory. *I think now I better understand his question.*

Baby Beth quickly became the darling of the clinic. Eve brought a cradle out of storage and insisted I bring the baby to work with me. I didn't ask the cradle's history, nor did she volunteer it. She gave me a box of infant clothing for the child. Again, nothing was said as to its origin.

Between the staff members dropping in to check on the baby and Thad's unscheduled visits during the day, Beth thrived from the attention.

When word reached the yamen that Dr. Gibson had returned home, the mandarin arrived at the clinic with his son. Nervously, I assisted the doctor during the examination of the child, afraid that the man would find something I'd done wrong. When the doctor finished, he smiled at the father. "Mandarin Ho Feng, your son seems to be in excellent health. I wish to thank you for your generous gifts and for your kind patronage of the mission clinic."

After they'd left, Dr. Gibson called me back into his office. "In case I failed to tell you, you did an excellent job with the boy. I couldn't have done any better."

"Thank you, sir." I smiled in surprise.

"By the way, I told Ho Feng about Beth and your desire to adopt the little girl. He, of course, reminded me that the law forbids Occidentals from adopting Chinese children."

My eyes misted at the doctor's gesture of kindness. "I understand, sir. Thank you for trying."

In a letter home, I told my parents, "Beth is growing more and more responsive every day. I know all parents think their baby is the most beautiful God ever created. But with her, I don't think it, I know it." I glanced over at the sleeping child and smiled, then returned to my letter writing. "She has the sweetest temperament. She seldom cries, just whimpers."

Whenever the subject of Beth's departure came up, Dr. Gibson said, "The child's too young to make the journey." As for Thad and me, we pushed all negative thoughts from our minds and praised God for every day the three of us had together. Days passed into weeks, weeks into months, and a harvest of happiness was ours each day. Finally, the melting snow turned the streets of the city into mires of mud, the frost rimming on the tiled pagoda roofs disappeared, and pink buds burst into blossoms on the cherry trees. Our "three-coat" winter was finally over.

Throughout the long winter, the land east of the mountains could have been as far away as the moon. But now with the thaw, mule trains arrived in the city weekly, the muleteers bringing news of unrest and skirmishes between soldiers of the Republic, led by Generalissimo Chiang Kai-shek, and the local warlords. Communist troops from the south, whom the commander-in-chief regarded as bandits, infiltrated the passes as far north as Yang-ch'uan, apparently on reconnaissance missions. The soldiers under the local warlords' control were kept busy chasing bandits in the mountains.

The distant clang of rattling sabers was little more than stimulating dinner conversation to me. My reality was that as Beth grew stronger, she became more a part of me than I'd ever imagined possible. The threat to my peace was the dread of being forced to say goodbye. Though Thad and I never mentioned it, I knew he, too, couldn't erase from his mind the reality that we couldn't keep her.

One day Dr. Gibson delivered the news. "Yang will take Beth and her wet nurse, Hsi Kim, to Peking a week from today."

I could see the pain in the doctor's eyes. "Please, let me accompany her to the orphanage. She'll be frightened. She'll need me to—" Dr. Gibson started shaking his head the moment I began my request. "But she's just a baby. She is ready to—" A sob welled up inside me. "Excuse me." I ran from his office and didn't stop running until I reached our little cottage, where Thad sat on our sofa, writing a sermon and patting Beth's back. He looked up in surprise.

"Sh! She's almost—"

I ignored his warning and snatched her into my arms. Crushing her close to me, I paced the room, with both of us crying. Thad didn't say anything. One look at my expression, and he knew what had happened. He rose to his feet and engulfed both the baby and me in his arms. We stood linked together by his arms and our grief for many moments.

By the time I got myself under control and returned to the clinic to complete my shift for the day, the word was out. Sympathy poured in from the staff members, for during her stay with us, Beth had become their baby too.

That night, I stayed awake and by the light of the kerosene lamp watched my child breathe—for she was my child, from her black silky hair to her curled-up pink toes. I watched her purse her tiny lips and blow bubbles in her sleep. I watched her scrunch up her little fist and rub it across her face. *What a blessing she's been to our home, dear Lord. Thank You so much for letting us have her for almost four months of her life.* I choked back my tears. *Beth Adams may never remember us, Father, but we will never forget her. May her life always glorify You and bring honor and praise to Your name.*

A comforting light flooded my soul when I realized that while Beth had been growing during those cold winter months, I'd been growing too. I recalled times past when at a moment like this I would be venting my fury at the world and at God. Yet here on the verge of such an emotion-wrenching event, I felt a peace like I'd never known. When Hsi Kim arrived for Beth's early-morning nursing, she found me leaning over the edge of the baby's cradle, asleep.

I went to the clinic that day with renewed strength, as if I'd had eight hours of sleep. The daily line of patients had grown since the snow had melted in the passes. Patients were coming from all over the mountains to have their winter ailments treated. Tooth extractions, digestive disorders, malnutrition—the list seemed endless.

Despite the added burden I carried that day, I enjoyed my work. I'd learned in the short time we'd been at the mission that the people were a simple mountain folk who rejected the invasion of a cold, structured religious creed as they had rejected all the military and political invasions over the years. I discovered that living rather than preaching the simple gospel of Jesus Christ was the only answer. The mountain people could appreciate a God who spoke of strength through humility, wisdom through love, and life eternal through faith. Dr. Gibson had finished lancing an infected big toe on his first patient of the day, an old man brought into the clinic by his relatives. "Nurse Adams will bandage your foot. Be sure to keep the wound clean and free from dirt." The doctor shook his finger in the old gentleman's face. "And no home remedies on it, do you understand?"

All three of us looked up, then at one another, when we heard a commotion in the waiting area. Yang burst into the room, gabbling at such a rate, none of us could understand him.

"Yang, slow down. What are you trying to tell us?"

The orderly bowed and gulped. "A messenger is in the courtyard asking for Missee, a messenger from the mandarin! He sent me to find you, chop-chop!"

Missee? Chop-chop? None of the workers at the mission ever reverted to pidgin English.

"Please, Yang, speak either in proper English or in Chinese, none of this other talk."

Yang took a deep breath. "A messenger from the mandarin is in the courtyard waiting to speak with Nurse Adams."

"Oh no!" I groaned and rolled my eyes. "I hope Mandarin Ho Feng isn't sending another load of turkeys."

Dr. Gibson scowled over the top of his gold-rimmed glasses. "Well, don't just stand there. See what the man wants."

"But the toe—" I glanced toward the patient.

"Yang, send in Jian Mei to assist, please. You—" He shot an impatient look my way. "—go! Go!"

I hurried into the courtyard. At the base of the steps, a bowing messenger held a sheet of scarlet paper. I returned his bow. Without a word, he placed the paper in my hands.

"What is this for?"

"It is an official summons from the yamen." I detected a nervous tremor in the messenger's voice. Behind him, I could see a sedan chair with four carriers. "When a piece of red paper arrives from the yamen, you must come immediately."

"I'm sorry, but I have a number of patients awaiting my attention. Please tell the mandarin that I will be happy to appear at the yamen when I get off work this afternoon."

The messenger shook his head vigorously. "No! No! You must come now. This is an official paper. You are ordered to come. Now! With me!" He shook a finger in my face. "If you refuse, you will get into big trouble!"

"All right! All right." I brushed my hands over my hair in frustration. "I'll come. I really don't know what can be so important that it can't wait a few hours. May I change out of my uniform into something more presentable?"

The round little man shook his head again. "You must come now!"

As I boarded the sedan chair, Thad called from the steps of the chapel, "CeeCee, where are you going?"

I gestured toward the messenger. "The mandarin wants to see me."

"What does he want? Do you want me to come with you?" he asked.

"I have no idea. And, no, I'll be fine."

"Can I do anything while you're gone?"

I thought for an instant. "You could stay with Beth once Hsi Kim is finished nursing her."

"OK, if you're sure you'll be all right."

"I'm sure." I waved. "I'll see you at supper."

I held onto the arms of the chair as the runners trotted along the city's busy street. The runners finally lowered the sedan chair in the palace courtyard. The beauty of the courtyard and the palace itself equaled that of Au Sam's brother's place. *All the starving people outside these privileged walls could be fed for many years from the sale of just one original painting hanging on one palace wall.*

Don't be judgmental, I reminded myself. *You and your family haven't exactly lived like paupers over the years.*

The head servant met me in the palace waiting room and immediately whisked me into the presence of Mandarin Ho Feng. The mandarin sat on an elevated gold chair upholstered in red velvet. His robe of red satin embroidered with blue, green, and gold scrollwork added to his regal bearing. He regarded me urbanely. His thin, fine face with the high cheekbones and dark almond eyes remained impassive, yet I could sense a note of irritation. About what, I could not imagine.

We performed the appropriate sequence of bows and obeisance, asking about each other's health and the health of our ancestors. Finally, the mandarin approached the reason for the summons. "I have recently learned that you and your husband have opened your home to an infant."

"Yes."

"And that you would have liked to adopt the girl?"

"Yes." My pulse raced. *Could he be offering to lift the adoption ban for me?* Eagerly, I moistened my lips.

He noted the gesture without response. "Such an adoption is against the law."

"Yes, Mandarin."

Ho Feng paused, touching the fingers of one hand to their mates on the opposite hand. "I am disappointed in you, Nurse Adams. I thought we were friends."

I bowed. "I have the utmost respect for you, Wise One."

"Then why didn't you come to me with your request for adoption?"

"I-I-I didn't want to impose," I said, barely above a whisper.

"Impose? I owe you the life of my son."

"No, Mandarin, you owe the life of your son to my God, not to me."

"I will not quibble over details." He brushed aside my explanation. "If you had only come to me immediately, I could possibly have worked things out for you and for this child. But, now, now, it is too late!"

Tearfully, I responded, "I am sorry, sir, that I didn't come to you with the request."

The mandarin stood and strode down the three steps from

his elevated chair and took my hands in his. "I only wish I could still do something, but alas—" His words failed. "If only you'd trusted me enough to ask me for my help."

The mandarin shook his head sadly and strode from the room. I felt a servant's hand on my elbow and allowed him to lead me from the room. He helped me into the sedan chair once more. As the silken curtains fell around me, hiding my face from curious onlookers, I leaned my head against the chair and sobbed.

And Life Goes On

The morning I kissed Beth goodbye, I thought my heart would break. But instead of watching the wagon leave the courtyard, I marched stalwartly back into the clinic and threw myself into a work frenzy. When Eve Gibson suggested I take time off to go with her to the market, I refused. "There's too much work to be done around here. I've been distracted the last few months and have let the paperwork slide. I need to get caught up."

Once I cleared my desk, I cleaned my office, then set to work on the clinic storeroom. Around seven in the evening, Thad found me on my hands and knees, scrubbing the examination-room floor. He knelt down beside me.

"The clinic has workers to do that."

"I want to be certain it's done well!" I yanked a handkerchief from my uniform pocket and blew my nose.

"Honey, please come home. You need your rest. You'll make yourself sick."

"I can't quit. I've got to keep busy!" I shook my head and averted my eyes.

"CeeCee, please." Thad lifted my chin until my eyes met his. "I miss her too."

We crumbled into each other's arms, sharing our pain and our tears. "If only," I wailed. "If only I had known that the mandarin could have—"

"You can't blame yourself. You had no way of knowing that he could have interceded for us."

Somehow, I managed to kneel beside my bed that night and

180

align my will with the command to praise God in all things. But my prayer ended with, "But, Lord, You'll have to take charge of my emotions and restore my peace. I can't do it without You."

I dragged myself out of bed the next morning to help Thad pack for a preaching tour that he and Dr. Gibson had arranged to take into a number of remote mountain villages. There, the doctor would minister to their bodies while Thad ministered to their souls.

"I wish you'd reconsider and go with me," Thad urged. "Dr. Gibson is willing to stay at the clinic. The break would do you good."

Everyone thinks they know what is best for me. I tightened my lips. "I'd really rather not right now. Maybe next month, if you go again."

Thad sighed with exasperation. "It would do you good to get out of here for a while."

When I wandered into the bedroom to make the bed, my gaze fell on the empty spot that the borrowed cradle had once occupied. *No. Lord, help me not to succumb to the sin of complaining. Restore the peace that You promised was mine. If I can no longer bestow my love on Beth, Father, send me someone else to love. Amen.*

"Please." Thad had followed me into the bedroom.

Reluctantly, I agreed. "I'll have to let Dr. Gibson know that I've decided to go."

Thad laughed. "Don't worry about that. Dr. Gibson is the one who insisted you go with me."

I placed my hands on my hips. "You two had this scheme all cooked up before I even—?"

Thad smiled softly. "We love you and are worried about you."

While Thad finished making arrangements with Dr. Gibson, I packed a few items of comfortable clothing. *Maybe Thad's right. Maybe it will be good for me to get away from here for a few days.*

We spent four days riding horseback on narrow mountain trails, visiting remote mountain villages to treat injuries, extract teeth, and hand out medicine. The mountain people were so grateful for the medical care that they stayed around to listen to the stories and the singing. They loved to sing. That they knew neither the melody I played on my violin nor the words to the hymns mattered little. They sang with exuberance.

By the time I rode my shaggy little horse back into the mission compound, I was overwhelmingly grateful to be home. It had been years since I'd ridden horses on my Uncle Joe's ranch in California. Limping into the house, I had to admit that the trip had accomplished its purpose. Seeing the incredible needs of so many people helped me refocus on my mission and less on myself and the loss of Beth.

The following morning when Thad and I gave Dr. Gibson our report of the trip, he commended us for our efforts. "Oh, by the way," he added, tossing a scarlet envelope across the desk, "this was delivered early this morning."

"Another appearance at the yamen?"

The doctor arched an eyebrow. "It looks that way. I've been summoned to the mandarin's court three times during the last twenty years. This is your second summons in six months. How do you do it?"

I shrugged my shoulders.

"Don't misunderstand me. Thanks to you, Nurse Adams, renewing our operating license should be much simpler this year."

I blushed. "I-I-I doubt that—"

"Spare me the false modesty, my dear," the doctor growled. "I believe in giving credit where credit is due."

I hung my head, uncertain of what to say.

"You seem to have the mandarin buffaloed. It's like he doesn't quite know what to do with you. You are an alien species."

"Excuse me, sir?"

"Think about it. You're a female, which in the eyes of his culture makes you socially and intellectually insignificant. Yet, as he tells it, you had the ear of the gods when healing his son." The doctor smiled. "What I'd give to be able to get into his mind."

"I wish you were the one summoned instead of me."

The man snorted. "Personally, I think he's captivated by your red hair and your sharp repartee."

I laughed nervously.

When I arrived at the palace, Mu Tong, the mandarin's head

servant, met me in the courtyard and, without explanation, spirited me away to the women's inner court. He left me in the care of Yu Li, the mandarin's number-one slave girl. Haltingly, she explained that the palace slave girls had contracted a despicable disease.

"Please, you and your god must do something to help them. If the mandarin learns of the plague sweeping the inner court of women, I cannot imagine what he might do." The woman trembled with fear.

Neither wives nor concubines, the slave girls were lovely and delightful creatures purchased by the mandarin for entertainment purposes only.

The woman took me to a small room where the infected women had been placed. I knelt and examined the first woman. After repeating the procedure with three more slave girls, I rocked back on my heels and smiled to myself. "It looks like you have an outbreak of chickenpox."

"Chickenpox?" the head slave exclaimed in horror. "But none of the women would have cause to come into contact with any chickens!"

I struggled to hide my grin. "It's not a disease transmitted by chickens, but by humans." I thought for a moment as to how the women might had been exposed. "Has the mandarin recently entertained any foreigners?"

The woman nodded. "The British ambassador and his entourage."

"About two weeks ago?"

She confirmed my suspicions.

"This is usually a child's disease," I told her. "However, young adults can contract it also."

"Will any of my girls die?"

"Fortunately, no. But there are a few precautions you must take to make the women comfortable until the disease runs its course." I wasn't certain that Li understood my words. "You must insist they not scratch the eruptions, because that could leave scars." I demonstrated. "When I get back to the clinic, I'll send a container of baking soda. Make a paste of the powder and water and apply it, repeatedly, to the itchiest rashes."

"Oh, thank you, thank you. I was afraid the mandarin might send us all away." Her dark eyes revealed the terror she felt. For a woman raised for the sole purpose of pleasing the mandarin and his honored guests, such a prospect would be tragic.

"Unfortunately, the rest of your girls might come down with chickenpox during the next ten to twenty days. Don't be alarmed. Just make sure they rest in a dark room and apply the baking-soda paste as needed." I slipped my arms into my jacket and prepared to leave. "If you have any further problems or complications, call me again."

The woman rapidly shook her head. "No, no. I didn't call for you. The mandarin called you. While in his presence, will you tell him about this chickenpox?"

I smiled at the woman's anxiety. "I'd probably better, since he has also been exposed."

She nodded, her forehead lined with worry.

After assuring her that everyone would recover, I stepped out of the inner court to find Mu Tong waiting. He took me to an anteroom, where I waited with a number of provincal officials for admission into the mandarin's chamber. I was the last to be called. And instead of being escorted into the official courtroom, Mu Tong hurried me past the entry and through the second set of carved wooden doors into the mandarin's private sleeping quarters.

If I hadn't first visited the women's inner court, I would have balked at entering the mandarin's bedroom. I found him propped up by brightly colored silk pillows. A purple satin coverlet draped the bed, while the matching draperies, along with white gauze curtains, were tied back at each of the four posts. Golden lions pursuing game decorated the headboard behind him.

Despite the unusual location and the mandarin's flushed face and glassy eyes, we performed the formal traditional greeting.

"Nurse Adams, I called you because I fear that I may have contracted the dread disease of smallpox."

"What symptoms have brought you to this conclusion?" I pursed my lips thoughtfully. "Perhaps you should have asked for Dr. Gibson. I am but a nurse and a woman."

"A woman whose God listens to her."

"My God listens to all who come to Him in faith."

"I do not feel much like quibbling, Nurse Adams." The mandarin paused a moment. "Do you not have a less formal name than 'Nurse Adams'?"

Where is this conversation going? I wondered. "Why, yes, my given name is Chloe Celeste."

He mouthed Chloe Celeste and frowned. I lowered my gaze, knowing that the *l* sound was difficult for the Asian tongue to pronounce.

"If you prefer, you may call me CeeCee."

Again, he frowned as if uncertain whether he should cross the distinct line between the ruler and the one ruled. I understood his reserve; I wasn't certain I wanted him to become too personal either. I'd been warned by Jian Mei that if the mandarin took a fancy to me, he could easily eliminate my husband and conscript me as one of his wives.

My apprehension must have been evident on my face. Ho Feng assured, "Nurse Adams, I am too sick for you to fear me."

I started to protest.

"Spare your breath. In my position, I see the look of fear on faces daily. I need a person trained in medicine, not another wife."

I blushed—he'd read my thoughts.

Ho Feng closed his eyes and leaned back against the pillows. "Only my personal physician and now you know of my illness. If my enemies should learn that I am ill, I would appear weak and vulnerable. That could prove disastrous for both me and the province." He recited his symptoms to me, then added, "My physician has already performed the traditional medicine of acupuncture." He opened the neck of his bed shirt to reveal angry red pustules. "What can I expect as I prepare myself for death?"

I stepped closer to the bed and studied the angry red eruptions. "There is little I can do, except relieve the itching. In a few days, the scabs will dry and fall off, leaving behind a slightly reddened area. But that will soon return to a normal color."

"And then?"

"And then, Mandarin, you will be ready to roll more heads again."

He looked puzzled. "Excuse me? What is this, roll more heads? I don't understand."

I laughed. "An American idiom, I fear. It means that you will be feeling well enough to return to the business of governing the province."

The man started. His dark eyes studied my face for several seconds. "You are saying this from fear."

I laughed again. "No, I am saying this from my formal medical training. You do not have smallpox, Honored One; you have chickenpox, a nonfatal disease, usually in children, that quickly subsides, leaving the patient with no side effects whatsoever."

"Nonfatal, you say?"

"I suspect that you and your court were infected when the British consulate last visited. Did he bring a child to court with him?"

"Yes." The man nodded. "His eleven-year-old son." The mandarin scratched his chest and growled. "I should have the man and his son expelled from my province for this. If he were Chinese, I would have him—" He stopped abruptly and shot me a sheepish look. "A child's disease?"

"A child's disease." I chuckled aloud. "I had the chickenpox when I was six."

"Six! Hmmph."

"I explained to Yu Li, your head slave woman, how to make the paste that will ease the irritation. I will send the ingredients back with your servant when I return home."

"So—" The mandarin eyed me cynically. "—your God cannot be bothered to deal with childhood illnesses?"

"My God, as you put it, is still the Healer. Sometimes He heals outright; other times, He uses His followers to do the healing—of which I am but one."

"We Chinese, too, have healing knowledge," he defended. "You Christians see us as a nation of heathen and barbarians, when our culture predates yours by many hundreds of years."

"I do not see your culture as either heathen or barbarian. My mother treats many of her patients with herbal medicines taught her by Au Sam, her longtime best friend."

"But you send your Christian missionaries to our land. My

people have developed art and culture far beyond any other in the world. Our poets wrote great poetry twenty or more centuries before your forefathers invaded the red man's continent. And you come to teach us to have faith in your new God?"

The gentle mockery in his voice was obvious. I considered arguing but instead bowed. "A very wise man, a ruler like yourself, once asked, 'What is truth?' Sadly, pride in his own heritage prevented him from seeing the Truth standing before him. Whether the man continued seeking, I don't know, but sometimes the God of the universe, whom I serve, uses the simple to confound the wise."

The mandarin gestured toward four immense volumes of Confucian philosophy sitting on a bookshelf to the side of his bed. "The words of Confucius contain truth; what is contrary to his teaching is false; what he does not teach is unnecessary."

I bowed respectfully. "I doubt that you truly believe that, Mandarin. The art objects and the tapestries decorating your walls represent the cultures of many countries of the world." I paused a moment. "As a student, did you not study mathematics? astronomy? botany? French?"

He removed a pale pink lotus blossom from a shallow vase on the ebony night stand. Silently, he studied the waxen petals while I prayed for wisdom. I took a deep breath and began.

"Long ago, in a far-off country, there lived a man named Jesus Christ." When the mandarin didn't stop me, I proceeded with the story. Ho Feng continued to gaze at the flower while I talked. By the time I described the scene in which Pilate asked, "What is truth?" the mandarin was leaning forward, his elbows on his knees, his hands cupping his chin, like a schoolboy listening to the tales of Rudyard Kipling or of Kublai Khan.

As I described Jesus' crucifixion, the ruler's eyes misted. He nodded sagely. "This Man, Jesus, was a good man. Martyrdom is often the way of truly good men."

"But wait. The story doesn't end there." I continued telling Jesus' story through His ascension. "His last words to His followers were, 'Go into all the world and preach My story. For I am with you always, even unto the ends of the earth.' That, your highness, includes China, and that is why I am here in your beautiful land."

In a quiet voice, the mandarin said, "I would like to read this story for myself."

A tremor of joy shot through me. "I will return with the baking soda and a Bible."

Every evening for the next six days, a sedan chair arrived at the mission and carried me to the palace, where I would first care for the women, then check on the mandarin's physical progress, and answer his questions regarding Jesus Christ. On the seventh evening, the mandarin, almost fully recovered, strolled out onto the balcony off his sleeping quarters. I paused in the archway, waiting for the word that would allow me to leave, while Ho Feng gazed in silence at the fiery sun disappearing behind the purple mountain peaks in the west.

Finally, he took a deep breath and straightened his shoulders. "The life I know will soon be as extinct as the dinosaur. All my years of intense study will be for naught. It's only a matter of time. I believe that the Communists will accomplish what the Japanese and the Mongols could not—the defeat of more than two thousand years of wisdom and culture."

I'd heard the rumors about the outbreak of Communist-instigated strikes and riots in the cities to the south. I had also heard tales of the Nationalist government's progress toward uniting the country under a conservative government. Ho Feng was right. The control of all China by either government would bring an end to his feudal way of life.

The mandarin shook his head thoughtfully. "If only a people could live out the principles of either a Confucius or a Christ, war would be a thing of the past."

"You are wise in your observation. However, because people cannot live by a set of rules, Jesus Christ needed to come here and die for us. Forgiveness for people's sins required a blood sacrifice."

The mandarin again nodded.

"Without the covenant God made with human beings, we would need to die for our own wrongs."

"But is death so terrible?"

I started at his calm acceptance of dying. "I believe that death is the ultimate insult to our Creator, who offers eternal life to His children."

After a pause, the mandarin requested, "I would like to keep the Book, if you don't mind. I find the portions written by the man called Paul fascinating."

Sending a silent prayer of thanksgiving heavenward, I bowed respectfully. "The Bible is my gift to you. It is not given to curry your favor, but it is a gift from one friend to another."

After he nodded his acceptance of my gift, the mandarin gazed silently into the distance. Finally, he announced, "I, too, have a gift for you. Mu Tong will give it to you on your way home."

"Please let me do this small thing for you without repayment."

"I appear to be returned to good health, Nurse Adams. I will not need your services regarding my illness." He dismissed me with the wave of a hand.

Mu Tong escorted me down the marble staircase to an ante-room off the main reception area. There, he opened the wide double doors and bade me enter. I stopped in the doorway and gasped. "Hsi Kim! What are you doing here? Surely Beth hasn't been weaned yet!"

The young woman led me behind a gilt screen, where a six-month-old baby grinned up at me and gurgled.

"Beth!" I sobbed, snatching up the child. "What are you doing here? What is going on?"

Mu Tong bowed, then handed me a sheaf of papers. "The mandarin has purchased Beth from the orphanage as a slave."

The word *slave* sent shivers of horror through me.

"These official papers grant the ownership of this child to one Chloe Celeste Adams."

"Slave? Beth, my slave?"

The head servant shrugged, a hint of a smile stretching the corners of his mouth. "If you will sign this paper to make it legal."

Sign? Of course, I'll sign. I grabbed the pen from the man's hand and scribbled my name on the place he indicated.

"Should you and your husband ever desire to leave China, this will allow you to file for adoption in whatever country you choose."

I hugged my child so tightly that she squirmed and whimpered. The warmth of her tiny body brought tears to my eyes. I turned to Mu Tong. "Please, take me back to the mandarin. I must thank him."

The man shook his head. "No! The mandarin does not wish to speak of this, either tonight or any time in the future." He emphasized each word. "Do you understand?"

"But why? I don't under—"

Mu Tong repeated, "Not now or in the future."

Holding my precious Beth close, I hurried outside, Hsi Kim right behind. As we climbed into the sedan chair, I glanced up at the second-story veranda. And for a moment I thought I saw a tiny ripple in the heavy velvet draperies, as if brushed aside by an unseen hand.

The mission compound erupted into chaos when I deboarded the sedan chair with Beth in my arms. Dr. and Mrs. Gibson burst from the clinic, followed by my husband. When Thad saw Beth in my arms, I feared he would pass out; his face grew so pale at the sight of her. They'd been afraid for my safety when I didn't return as soon as I had on the previous evenings. When I explained what had happened, Dr. Gibson insisted on reading the documents to be certain all the arrangements were legal.

"I still don't trust the man myself," the doctor muttered as he deciphered the splashes of Chinese script.

"And I know why. The man's brusque and demanding. The two of you are too much alike," Eve taunted.

Thad took Beth from my arms and tootsed her about the office. She responded with gurgles of delight.

"She remembers you!" I'd never been so happy in my life.

With Beth's return, our lives at the clinic settled into a peaceful routine. Whenever there was a medical problem at the palace, the mandarin sent for me, but neither of us ever mentioned his extraordinary gift to us. Instead, we discussed philosophy, politics, and religions of the world. I felt honored, since in his culture, men never spoke about serious things with a woman. While he never mentioned it, I knew the mandarin was still reading the Bible, because he would occasionally quote a Scripture text in passing.

In the meantime, Beth became everybody's baby. A mere whimper would send staff members scurrying to meet her every need. Eve appointed herself Beth's "grandma in residence." For Beth's first birthday, my mother and grandmothers bombarded the child with packages containing every kind of toy and outfit, so many that the muleteers complained at the size of the bundles they had to haul up the mountain. I would have worried that Beth might grow into a spoiled and self-centered little girl, except for her sweet, gentle nature.

During the next two years, I especially enjoyed exchanging baby stories via letter with my cousin Ashley. She would tell of visits to the Palisades, while I regaled her with tales of hikes into the mountains, Beth lashed securely to her daddy's back. We were two young mothers, thousands of miles apart, yet delightfully absorbed in the lives of our children and unaware of the forces of evil about to be unleashed on our pleasant little worlds.

It was only through my occasional visits to the mandarin that I noted the politics of the world around me.

Summer was filled with trips to the mountain villages and family outings along the banks of the Yellow River. The crisp winds of autumn focused our attention indoors, in preparation for the long winter evenings, when we would play Chinese checkers or Mah-jongg with the Gibsons or dream about the trip to Shanghai that Dr. Gibson promised us, come spring of 1930.

On December 1st of 1929, a merchant arrived at the clinic requesting treatment for a serious toe infection. During the examination, he asked, "Did you people hear about the big stock market crash in the United States?"

"Stock market crash?" I dabbed the antiseptic-soaked cotton ball between his toes.

"They say the country is in chaos, rich people killing themselves when they learn all their money is gone, riots in the streets—terrible things."

"Where did you hear such a story?" I chuckled to myself.

"It's true, ma'am."

Dr. Gibson grunted. "Sounds like Shanghai during the government purges of Communist sympathizers."

The merchant eyed the doctor nervously. Such talk from a foreign devil could result in trouble for the merchant if the foreigner happened to be a government informer.

I thought about my parents and my grandparents. *Have they lost all their money? Is the country in as much a turmoil as this man describes? Perhaps it's all fiction, anyway.* I'd long before learned that news was often embellished for audience appeal, and nothing appealed more to a Chinese audience than to hear of the distress or demise of foreign devils.

On the next trip through the area, the muleteers delivered letters and packages from home. After settling Beth in her crib that evening, I opened the first of my stack of letters, the one from Mama.

After reading the first few paragraphs, I called across the room to Thad, who sat reading by the fireplace. "It's true. It's all true what the merchant reported."

"Your parents? Are they OK?"

I nodded. "She says Daddy lost a small sum, but not being a risk taker, he will probably come out of this pretty well. Oh no!" I reread the words. "Charles lost everything!"

"Everything?"

"Worse yet, no one knows where he is. He took Ashley and the children to Aunt Drucilla's for the afternoon and never returned. That was almost two months ago."

Thad laid the letter from his father on the reading table. "What is she going to do?"

"Mama says that Ashley's been forced to leave her home and move in with her parents. The brownstone is to be sold at an auction. Uncle Phillip lost heavily, but Mama doesn't think he'll go under any time soon." I gestured toward Thad's letter. "What does your father say about the crash?"

"Nothing much. He says they've hardly felt it on the Cape. Probably they will see the difference next summer when the rich folk come up from the city." Thad read the next passage. "But as long as people need to eat, the fishing industry will survive."

On Christmas Day, after the morning services, Hsi Kim agreed to care for Beth while Thad and I accompanied Dr. and Mrs.

Gibson to the point where the Great Wall came the closest to the mission. As we jounced along in the wagon, we passed an old man scooping horse droppings into a straw basket to fertilize his spring garden, yet three months away. Maples, stripped of their autumn foliage, stood gaunt in the soft winter light. The tranquillity of the scene erased the world's turmoil from our minds.

When Yang brought the wagon to a stop beside one of the wall's watchtowers, we climbed the steps to the top of the tower. Breathless, I gazed out at the Great Wall, snaking across the mountains, wave after wave, disappearing behind one peak, only to reappear across another.

I breathed in the fresh winter air. "The wall seems to go on forever."

"From here, one can almost believe that the Chinese civilization will stand forever," Dr. Gibson mused.

"Almost," Eve remanded.

Thad folded his arms across his chest. "I can't see the Chinese Nationalists and the Communists ever coming to terms with each other or with the Japanese militants. Sooner or later, something has to blow."

"The people of China will weather it all, as they have since long before Genghis Khan or the Tartars attempted to rule this vast country." Dr. Gibson gestured toward the west. "What political leader is going to waste his time and resources by invading these little provinces hidden among the mountains, or worse yet, the villages of the Gobi Desert?"

Thad sighed. "I hope you're right. There's more unrest in those little villages than one might think, especially among the youth."

"The mandarin believes that it will be the Communists who eventually bring down the Chinese society as we know it," I added.

"Well, if anyone is in the know, he's the man," Dr. Gibson replied.

Over our picnic lunch, we discussed the problems at home in America and in Europe.

"It's a time like none other," Eve remarked. "Brings to mind the great trouble of Revelation, doesn't it?"

I shivered at the thought. "Oh, don't say that. If we're facing the time of the end, I'd prefer to be closer to my parents."

Eve looked thoughtful. "I know what you mean. Somehow, we never outgrow the feeling that our parents can make all things better."

Thad dug the heel of his shoe into the sandy soil. "Maybe that's why God calls Himself Father—and calls us His children."

I mulled over Thad's words during the ride back to the clinic and in the days that followed.

Surprises Come in Threes

"When the enemy advances, we retreat. When he camps, we harass. When he tires, we attack. And when he retreats, we pursue. Our weapons are supplied us by the enemy." Faces from my past flashed through my mind as I stared at the words printed on the cheap paper—Vaughn La Strada—André Zabinsky, Comrade Korsikoff—men willing to do anything in order to impose their own brand of politics on others.

"You might like to look at the pamphlet the mandarin gave me today."

"And how is Ho Feng?"

"Worried. He actually asked me to read the poetry of the Psalms to him today—Psalm 91, to be exact."

"So what does the note say?" Though he would never admit it, Thad didn't appreciate my friendship with the mandarin.

Thad's face blanched as he read the familiar words. "Who would have thought I would travel more than halfway around the world to confront my old comrades once again?"

"Do you think the Russian or Chinese Communists can connect you to the movement in France?" I worried the dish towel in my hands.

"I don't see how they could. But still, the idea of encountering those people again—"

"I know what you mean. When Ho Feng handed me this paper, I felt a sudden chill go through my body. He says that the Soviet government in Shaanxi is training what they call the Fourth Red Army in guerrilla warfare." I paused. "Shaanxi is not far from here. The circuit you and Dr. Gibson take each month actually crosses into their territory."

"I know, but so far we've not been harassed in any way."

I felt apprehensive in spite of Thad's reassurance. "I wish you and the doctor wouldn't resume your mountain trips."

"So many hurting people back in those hills need medical and spiritual attention. We have to go now that the snows have melted in the passes."

I tossed the dish towel I'd been twisting onto the kitchen table. "I know."

A whimper from the bedroom interrupted our conversation; two-year-old Beth had awakened from her afternoon nap.

"I'll get her," Thad volunteered, tossing the Communist pamphlet onto the mantel. "You finish preparing dinner."

As I reheated the bean casserole our cook had prepared earlier, I fussed to myself. *Thad's a family man now. He can't just up and head off into the mountains.*

I knew I wasn't being fair, but that didn't matter to me at the time. All I wanted was assurance that Thad would be safe if he and Dr. Gibson stumbled into the hands of the Communist guerrillas.

I glanced down at the envelope postmarked San Francisco, California—February 1930. It contained a letter from my mother describing the financial depression America and most of Europe were experiencing as a result of the October stock market crash. I removed the dinner plates from the cupboard next to the cookstove and placed them on the table. *I guess there's trouble everywhere. My faith wavers, Father, far more often than I'd prefer. Forgive me my weakness. You've brought us this far—I know You can continue to lead us.*

On April 1, Beth and I waved goodbye to Thad and Dr. Gibson when they left for the first medical circuit of the new year. My worries proved unfounded when the two men returned four days later, perfectly safe. This encouraged me to begin planning for our jaunt to Shanghai for necessary supplies.

I mentioned our plans to the mandarin on my next visit to the palace, when his number-one wife went into premature labor while Dr. Gibson was unavailable.

"Don't go."

I looked up into Ho Feng's face questioningly. He showed no emotion. "Don't go to Shanghai. There's much unrest about the country. And often foreigners are the target. Please, don't go."

When I told Thad and Dr. Gibson of the mandarin's warning, they took the warning seriously and decided to put off the trip until fall. All summer long I eagerly looked forward to the promised vacation. However, along about the third week of September, I grew increasingly suspicious that I would not be making the journey to Shanghai for supplies that year.

The logical part of my mind refused to believe my symptoms. "It's impossible, totally impossible," I told Eve.

She gazed at me through her silver-rimmed spectacles. "Have you and Thad taken a vow of celibacy?"

"No, of course not, but after I lost my last baby, the physicians said I would never be able to conceive a child again."

Eve threw back her head and laughed. "It's not the first time doctors have been wrong about such things."

To say Thad was delighted hardly described his reaction to the news. He picked me up and twirled me around the kitchen, singing, "For Unto Us a Child Is Born." Beth sat in her highchair, clapping her hands and laughing at her crazy parents.

I waited two more weeks before I wrote to my parents about the pregnancy, sharing my concerns regarding our unexpected good news. "To say that I'm not afraid that this pregnancy won't end much like my last would be a lie. Yet having admitted my fear, I feel good about this baby. If everything proceeds according to schedule, the newest member of our family will arrive toward the end of May." I refilled my fountain pen and resumed writing. "Mama, oh, how I wish you could be here when the baby arrives, but, alas, an ocean lies between us." I went on to tell her of Beth's latest antics. "Thad took her kite flying the other afternoon—which means Thad flew the kite, and Beth laughed and cheered."

When Dr. Gibson learned of my condition, he insisted I gradually turn over my heavier responsibilities to Jian Mei, training her to take over during my confinement. Personally, I think Eve had a talk with the doctor about my earlier miscarriages. The frequency of summons to the yamen decreased once my pregnancy became obvious. On my February visit to the women's quarters, the mandarin sent for me.

After we completed the formalities, he said, "I must warn you that conditions are worsening around the country. I can see the day coming when you and your family will be forced to flee the area. Remember, I will always be ready to help you." He studied my face for several seconds. "Don't wait to ask for my help until it is too late for me to protect you, my friend."

"But what about you? Neither of the warring parties will deal kindly with—" I couldn't bring myself to continue.

"Alas, if death be my fate, so be it." He opened his hands in acceptance. "I will not send for you again until after the birth of your child. Should there be a medical emergency beyond the palace doctor's expertise, I will call for Dr. Gibson." He smiled and bowed. "And I will be praying for you and your unborn child."

I returned his bow. "Thank you."

The mandarin's warning faded when I returned home and found a letter waiting for me from my mother.

"Dearest CeeCee, I have some great news, but you'd better sit down before you read any further. Your father and I are packing for a six-month trip to the Orient. The company has asked your father to supervise geologists searching for possible oil deposits in and around the South China Sea. If all goes according to plan, we will be with you by the end of May for the birth of your child. Your father will need to leave again the second week of June, but I'll be able to stay and help with Beth and the new baby. I hope this news pleases you as much as it does me."

Even though my parents had joked about "dropping in" on us sometime, I never dared hope for such a blessing. And that my mother could be with me when my child arrived had never once crossed my mind. Mama went on to write that they'd been working on the travel details since the previous fall but had hesitated to tell me until they were certain my father would be the executive the company chose to send. Mother's letter included still another surprise. "I would be glad to assist in the clinic until you're up and around again."

I laughed to myself. *Mama and Dr. Gibson working together?*

She continued, "I can hardly wait to get acquainted with my precious little Lisbet." In my last letter, I'd told my parents that Beth had begun talking, always referring to herself in the third person as "Lizbet."

"Tell her that Grandma Chloe is bringing her something special from America. If there's anything special you and Thad would like from home, let me know—anything! If you answer immediately, your letter might get here before we leave. We sail on March 30."

Oh, Mama, you're already giving me what I wanted the most, to have you here when I deliver.

With my responsibilities lightened at the clinic, the weeks that followed dragged by like centipedes on parade. Each day, Beth and I took walks in the garden, since leaving the compound was becoming more and more unsafe as detachments of northern provincial troops passed through the city. Side by side, we tilled the soil and planted vegetable seeds in our little garden space. Beside the veranda, I cultivated my tiny herb garden, eager to show it to my mother.

I missed my visits with the mandarin, but I understood the problem he'd have continuing them. Having a woman admitted to the official court was unusual enough, but to have a woman so obviously pregnant was more than even my broad-minded friend could handle.

Thad and Dr. Gibson offered to cancel their April excursion to the mountains, but I assured them that I was feeling fine. "Besides, there is no way I am going to deliver this baby before my mother gets here. Did I tell you that she's the best midwife in all of San Francisco?"

Dr. Gibson laughed. "Many times, my dear. Many times."

I did agree to keep my bedroom window open whenever Thad was away so that if I needed help, I could be heard in the clinic, next door. All in all, it was a pleasant time, those weeks preceding the arrival of my parents and the birth of our child.

On the calendar tacked to my kitchen door, I starred the day my parents' ship was scheduled to dock in Shanghai. *They're here, in China! Really, truly here!* I tried to imagine them disembarking in the busy seaport. *Most likely, they'll be met with a company rickshaw.*

I took a world atlas from the bookshelves, set it on the kitchen table, and opened it to the world map. "See, Beth. Grandma and Grandpa Chamberlain got on a ship here in San Francisco and traveled all the way across the Pacific Ocean and landed here today." I pointed to the port of Shanghai. Taking her finger, I traced the route they'd follow. "Next week Grandpa and Grandma will ride on a train, *chug-chug-chug*, to Peking, then, *chug-chug-chug*, to the end of the tracks."

She looked at me questioningly. She didn't remember the train ride she had taken as an infant to and from Peking. And she'd never seen a ship. I lumbered to the desk for a sheet of paper, which I folded into the shape of a sailboat. Then I filled the dishpan with water. Two pumpkin seeds in the craft represented my parents. Together, Beth and I played "coming to China," until the paper boat became too waterlogged to float.

We played "coming to China" each day for the next week. When I tried to explain to Beth about a train, Thad helped me by attaching a hook and eye to each of Beth's blocks, then linking them. We chugged Grandma and Grandpa—the two seeds— all over the living room. When I'd be working in the kitchen, I could hear Beth in the next room, saying, "Chug-chug-chug-chug."

The third week of May, my parents arrived at sunset. The gatekeepers had seen the mule train coming in the distance and had delayed locking the city gates. Thad, Beth, and I were sitting in the middle of the living-room floor, playing "choo-choo" for the last time before putting her to bed, when a knock sounded at the door.

"I'll get it." Thad leapt to his feet.

I groaned. "They must need an extra hand at the clinic," I muttered, struggling to my feet. Evening calls always meant an emergency shift.

He opened the door to a grinning Dr. Gibson. "Say, Pastor, I wonder if you and CeeCee can put up a few unexpected guests for the night?"

Thad glanced toward me. Even though my back was aching, and I'd put in a busy day at the clinic in spite of the lighter schedule, I nodded. He smiled and returned his attention to the doctor. "Sure we can. There's always room in the inn."

The doctor's grin widened as he waved to the unseen visitors. "Come on in. The pastor and his wife have agreed to house you folks for the night. I hope you'll find the accommodations pleasant."

I screamed as my mother and father walked through the open doorway. Mama rushed to me, laughing and reaching out to me. Overjoyed, all I could do was weep. My sobs triggered a similar reaction in Beth. While my mother led me to the sofa to sit down, Thad scooped up the child in his arms, and my father thanked Dr. Gibson and bade him good night.

Thad looked as stunned as I. "How did you folks get here so soon? We didn't expect you for at least another week."

"When we got to Peking, we found a mule team heading this way. So instead of waiting for a wagon train, we chose to ride." He rubbed his hip and groaned. "No one ever told me those beasts were so bony!"

"Two days can be torture," Thad admitted, "when you're not used to riding."

My mother laughed. "I'll say an amen to that!"

"On our way home, your mother wants to detour to Tientsin to visit Au Sam's family." My father draped his arm around my mother's shoulder. "We considered stopping on our way here, but your mother was too eager to see you folks."

"Oh?" My mother poked him in the ribs. "And who was up before dawn every single morning since we left Shanghai, making sure our travel plans for the day hadn't changed overnight?"

"What can I say?" We laughed at my father's little shrug. I squeezed my mother's hand. "I can't believe you're here, in China."

"When we stepped off the ship in Shanghai, I felt the same way. For so many years, China had been an elusive dream, a place I'd have loved to visit but knew there was little chance that I would. And here I am!"

Beth sidled up to my mother and won her heart instantly. "Gamma?"

"Oh, you precious little sweetheart. 'Gamma' has something

special for you." My mother opened her purse and handed Beth a picture book. The little girl's eyes brightened as Mama looked at me. "For you too, for that matter."

Beth played coy with my father, twisting her little body from side to side, inching toward her grandfather, then retreating to the familiar safety of her daddy's arms. The game ended when my father reached into his jacket and pulled out two strips of licorice. One he bit into, dramatically savoring the flavor. The other he offered to the shy little girl, who glanced at me for approval.

"Go ahead, honey."

In a flash, she scampered over to his extended hand, grabbed the licorice stick, and darted back to Thad. Five minutes after the candy touched her tongue, with her pajamas covered with licorice stains, Beth and her grandfather became friends. She fell asleep that night on his lap. His face glowed as he carried her into her crib and covered her with her blankets.

We talked late into the night, catching up on the news from home. "Rusty wanted to come with us," Mama explained, "but he's finishing his junior year in journalism at the university. He wants so badly to graduate next spring with his class."

They told me all the latest family news, especially about Ashley's troubles. "Here she's left with three children to raise. She'd be penniless if her parents hadn't taken her in."

"Doesn't anyone know where Charles disappeared to?"

"Not a trace. He could be dead, for all Ashley knows. She's spending the summer on Martha's Vineyard with Grandma McCall."

Sweet memories wafted through my brain as I remembered the idyllic summer I spent at the Cape. "Someday, I'd like to take Beth and her little brother or sister back there to see their Grandpa Adams and to visit their Grandma Adams's grave, and Au Sam's, of course."

Thad mentioned the recent political turmoil. "I'm surprised you chose to come to China during such unrest."

My father snorted. "Is there ever a time when China has been at peace?"

"Besides," my mother confided, "our lives aren't any more at risk than yours. So, tell me all about your mandarin."

"My mandarin? Hardly that. He's a very complex individual." I told about Ho Feng's request for a Bible and about his arrangement to purchase Beth for us. "I keep the official papers in the box—" I gestured toward the large wooden box on the mantel. "—beneath our family Bible. Granddaddy Spencer's twenty-dollar gold piece is in there too, along with our passports and the money order Uncle Phillip gave us before we sailed from home."

The subject returned to Au Sam's family. "I am looking forward to meeting them," my mother admitted. "I brought along her Bible to show them."

The men retired around 3:00 a.m., leaving my mother and me to continue talking until we greeted the sunrise by sipping a cup of hot chamomile tea on the veranda.

Beth awoke at her customary early hour. Groaning, I squinted at my watch lying on the bed stand; I had been in bed less than an hour. Thad rolled over. "I'll go get her, honey. Maybe she'll go back to sleep if we put her in bed between us."

Some mornings, that tactic worked. Not this day. "Gamma? Gamma?" Beth pointed toward our bedroom door. "Gamma?"

My parents devoted the entire day to her, playing with her, helping her put together the toys they brought with them from America. I cringed when I thought of how loaded down the mules must have been, transporting all the gifts over the mountains to our city. I couldn't complain too much, since Thad and I did equally as well. My favorite gifts were the three tins of cocoa powder, which enabled us to have hot chocolate again.

Beth's favorite toys were a baby doll with a porcelain head and its accompanying baby carriage, which Thad and my father spent most of the morning assembling. This freed Mama and me to take a tour of the clinic with Eve, ending in her parlor for tea and cookies. The two women liked each other instantly, though I had the feeling each was trying to outmother me.

That weekend, at the church services, I sat proudly between my parents, Daddy holding Beth while Thad preached. It was the first time they'd heard him preach, and did he ever shine.

Two weeks after my parents arrived from America, Thaddeus

James Adams arrived. He weighed in at seven pounds, four ounces. No baby was ever more welcomed and showered with love. I cried throughout the delivery, not so much from pain but from joy. Thad and my father paced on the clinic's veranda while my mother assisted Dr. Gibson in the remarkably short and easy delivery. I'd prepared myself for worse but was pleasantly surprised.

The next morning, the mandarin's head servant delivered a silver spoon for the baby and a poetry scroll from the Ming Dynasty, both gifts from the women of the mandarin's court.

"I can't believe it." My mother examined the priceless antique. Since she'd dedicated her life to working for the women of Chinese descent in San Francisco, she'd come to appreciate their country's art and literature. "This scroll deserves to be in a museum."

At the end of the week, Daddy left for Hong Kong, in order to meet the geologists his company had hired. Mama stayed behind, as planned, to help me with the children and to assist at the clinic. The big surprise for me was how well she and Dr. Gibson got along. From the first moment they met, it was easy to see they regarded one another with respect. And their admiration for one another only grew as the summer passed.

I enjoyed a summer of peace and happiness, with my mother helping me care for Beth and the baby. I remember lazy afternoons, lounging on the veranda, nursing Baby Thad, while Eve and Mama exchanged recipes for everything from lentil soup to corn bread. On the floor, with her doll clothes spread out around her, Beth would "nurse" her baby doll and put her to bed in the doll carriage.

With my mother working at the clinic in my place, Dr. Gibson and Thad resumed their monthly four-day journeys into the mountains. It was during their September trip that I received the first summons from the mandarin since the birth of our son. The messenger delivered the summons to Mama, who, in turn, brought it to me. I'd just put both children down for their afternoon naps.

Oh no, something is terribly wrong. For weeks, we'd been hearing the sound of rifle fire coming from the western mountains. The rumors reaching us all reported sporadic fighting between government troops and the Chinese Communist guerrillas.

I begged Thad not to go until the shooting stops! No! He and Dr. Gibson have to be heroes. What good is a dead hero to his wife and children? Hurriedly, I donned my favorite blue-and-white seersucker suit and brushed my hair. At the last minute, I placed Thad's book of sketches of the baby and the rest of the family in my pocketbook.

"The mandarin can command you to go to his court at any time? Doesn't Thad object to that arrangement?" my mother asked incredulously.

"We have an agreement, Mama. Ho Feng would call me like this only if there's some sort of emergency." All I could think of was that something terrible had happened to Thad or to Dr. Gibson.

"Emergency?" Mama's voice raised half an octave.

"Please stay with the children. I'll be back as quickly as I can." I slipped my pocketbook under my arm and dashed out of the house.

Throughout the ride in the sedan chair, I tried to calm myself, to reason away my fears.

Mu Tong led me straight into the mandarin's receiving room. This time, I highly resented taking the time to perform the proper protocol. I wanted to shout, "What is wrong? Has something happened to my husband?" Impatiently, I bowed and asked all the required questions.

"And your number-one son? He is healthy?"

"He is healthy." The mandarin bowed. "And your number-one son? He is thriving well?"

I bowed. "Yes, he is also healthy."

When we finished the routine, the mandarin stood. Two claps of his hands sent his servants and his administrators scurrying from the room. Only his personal servant remained. The mandarin turned to me. "We will speak on the balcony."

Once outside, he ordered his servant to leave and to close the doors between the balcony and the official chambers behind him.

My gaze darted nervously about the area. *This is very strange.*

Why all the precautionary measures to ensure our privacy? Another tremor of fear coursed through me. All the warnings I'd received about the man and all the rumors I'd heard of his desire to sire another son flashed through my mind. Other than his number-one son, his wives, concubines, and slave girls continued to produce daughters instead of sons.

After checking that the balcony doors were securely closed, Ho Feng stepped toward me, his eyes studying my face. Intimidated, I inched backward until I felt the balcony's cold metal railing against the middle of my back. I couldn't hide the fear.

"You act afraid of me, my friend." He touched my forearm. "You're trembling. What is wrong?"

I tried to reply, but my lips refused to move.

"Do you feel ill?"

I shook my head. "I'm fine," I gasped. "You called me here for a reason. Please, tell me the reason."

"You are right. I've truly missed our discussions during your confinement. You are the only person with whom I can be totally honest." He glanced down at his long, slender fingers for a moment. "I have received word—"

I don't like the sound of this!

"I have received word that the Japanese army is on the move south from Manchuria." His face remained passive. "They have already seized Mukden and are pressing south and west toward the Great Wall. It is only a matter of time before they sweep through this province. You and your family must leave quickly."

"I can't—"

"Please, don't argue. You know how the Japanese feel about white people. Their soldiers are merciless. They kill for the fun of killing."

As I listened to the voice of this tall, thin figure in his scarlet robes, I wrapped my arms about myself and shuddered. So many times throughout history, this scene had been enacted. Generation after generation, whether foreigners or greedy warlords, the invaders would sweep down from the north, bringing mayhem, murder, and destruction. And, as so often before, the people would flee to the mountains, then creep back after the invaders had left.

"There is a time for everything under the sun—a time to be born and a time to die." I shook my head and tried to concentrate on the mandarin's words.

"I have three wagons that will take you, your family, and Mrs. Gibson to the railhead on the other side of the mountain. From there, you will board the train for Tientsin, then a ship for Hong Kong."

"But Thad! Dr. Gibson! We can't leave without—"

"The two men are being detained by Communist troops."

"And Mr. Lin?"

Ho Feng's eyes told me what his lips did not.

"He's dead, isn't he?" Sadness filled my heart. *Oh, dear God, how? How?*

"My sources tell me that it could be weeks before your husband and Dr. Gibson will be freed. I am doing what I can to arrange for their release." The mandarin reached into the folds of his satin robe and extracted a rolled document. "Here, this will guarantee you and the others safe passage with the warlords in each area through which you will pass."

"But you don't understand—"

"No, *you* don't understand." A flash of irritation swept across his face. "You will take the children and go. If I have to make it an official edict, you will go, my friend."

My eyes filled with tears as I pleaded with him. "I am sorry for defying you, but I can't leave my husband. Don't you see?"

Tucking his hands inside the wide embroidered sleeves of his robe, Ho Feng said, "And don't you see what is happening here? I cannot protect my own people—let alone you and your family, CeeCee."

I inhaled sharply. He'd used my nickname for the first time.

"Go to Hong Kong. Once there, go immediately to the American consulate. I will direct your husband to you." He strode to the closed door, then turned. "One of the wagons is filled with food and objects that you can use for barter. Beneath the wagon seat, you will find a silk purse filled with a roll of bills to use at your discretion."

"I can't take—"

He waved my objections away. "Of course, you can. You can

and, as a mother, you will do whatever it takes to save your children." He gazed toward the mountains, then looked back at me. "I have one request, however. Take my son with you."

Clutching the purse and the scroll, I nodded my agreement. I closed my eyes and gulped several deep breaths to steady myself. *This is a nightmare. I will soon awake, and it will all go away.*

Yet when I opened my eyes, I found myself standing face to face with the mandarin. "We will not see one another again on this earth."

"You don't know that," I argued. "Once the government squelches the uprising, we'll return."

He shook his head sadly. "No, no, the China we know will soon disappear." Tears formed in his dark almond eyes. "Before you leave, I want to pray with you. I don't know how to accept Jesus Christ as my Saviour. Will you help me?"

Humbled by his request, I knelt on the polished wooden floor. Ho Feng fell to his knees beside me, a first for this man of power. I prayed first for his safety, then that of his family and his province. Following me, in the most beautiful traditional Chinese, the mandarin gave his heart to the Lord. As we rose to our feet, tears swam before my eyes.

"This is no time for tears." He gently wiped away one tear from my cheek, happiness radiating from his face. "This is a time for joy. I will never forget you, CeeCee, my friend." He bowed low. "One day, we will meet in the kingdom of glory."

Returning his bow of respect, I responded, "I also look forward to that day, my friend."

I turned and rushed down the palace stairs to the waiting sedan chair. Cowering inside, behind the silk curtains, Dao Lin looked up at me with frightened eyes.

Poor little boy. Where's your mama? How does she feel about sending you away with strangers? I ached to wrap my arms around the child and pull him close to me, but I knew he would feel that he'd lost face. In a short time, the carriers deposited the sedan chair back at the mission compound. When I stepped down and helped the boy from the chair, I noticed that the three wagons and their drivers were already waiting behind the clinic, along with the boy's loyal protector, Chin Shui.

I ordered his servant to hide the eight-year-old in the first wagon. *Oh, Lord, what do I do next? One step at a time; one step at time!* I ran across the compound to my house to sound the alarm.

Flee the Enemy

"Please hurry!" I shouted at Yang as he hefted my trunk onto his shoulder. Beth sat in the corner of our bedroom, clutching her doll and sucking on her two middle fingers. Baby Thad lay asleep in a dresser drawer I'd emptied and lined with flannel and my favorite quilt, undisturbed by the confusion. I could hear my mother in the kitchen slinging pots and pans into a barrel Jian Mei had brought over from the clinic.

"What will we do for diapers for the baby?" I called.

"We'll change and wash, change and wash," she replied. "Do you want me to pack your wedding china in your bath towels?"

"Forget the dishes. We'll worry about them later. For now, let's take only things that are absolutely necessary." I packed my personal Bible among my bedclothes. Turning, I gazed down at the turquoise wedding dress I'd discarded as unnecessary. *No! This is a necessary item! Thad would want—* Hastily, before I could change my mind, I wrapped the dress around my violin case and placed both on top the extra changes of clothing we'd need once we reached the ship. The lid of Thad's trunk slammed shut with an unsettling finality.

Trying to ignore my forebodings, I called to Yang as he strode past the open bedroom window. "Yang, the second trunk is ready to load onto the wagons." For Beth's sake, I struggled to keep the terror out of my voice. *The secret to overcoming fear is praise,* I reminded myself. I recalled Mandarin Ho Feng's conversion and rejoiced. *Praise God. Praise God! To You be all glory and honor and praise. How faithful You are to Your children. I love*

You, Lord. I truly love You.

But the praise didn't eliminate the cold chills of fear that prickled my spine whenever I thought of Thad and Dr. Gibson being held captive. *Father, I can't allow myself to worry about them. Preserving the lives of my children and the mandarin's son is all I can allow myself to think about today. You promised to be with us to the ends of the earth. Surely the insurgents' mountain hideout qualifies, Lord.*

Next door, in the Gibsons' house, I knew Eve also scrambled to pack her and her husband's belongings. When I had first alerted Eve to the mandarin's warning, she refused to leave. "My husband will return for me!"

"You'll meet him in Hong Kong, Eve."

"But these are my people," she argued. "I can't abandon them now, when they will most need medical attention."

"The mandarin didn't give us any options, Eve. He ordered all Westerners to leave the city. He's hoping that when the Japanese soldiers find no foreigners here, they will advance without wreaking havoc on the city and the people."

Her eyebrows shot up in skepticism. "And that is why he sends his only son with us?"

"That child will probably be our safe passage out of here! Now, start packing, and I'll send Yang to load your trunks on the wagons." The forcefulness in my voice surprised me. Obviously, it surprised Eve too. She stared at me for several seconds before she turned to begin packing.

"Plan to leave in thirty minutes."

The dreaded moment arrived when I took one last tour of our home, the bedroom where Thad and I conceived and I bore our son, the kitchen where Beth and I baked almond sugar cookies for her daddy, the living room where Thad and I spent so many hours enjoying one another. *Will I ever return, Father?* My gaze fell on the Chinese checker game box Thad had slid under his reading chair the last time we finished playing, and a tear trickled down my cheek. *Get control of yourself, CeeCee. It's only a game. You can buy a new one in Hong Kong!*

As I scanned the room for any mementos I wished to take with us, my eyes focused on the wooden box that contained our family Bible. I'd almost forgotten the importance of its contents. Hurriedly, I slid the mandarin's writ of safe passage under the Bible, then paused to run my fingers across the smooth hand-tooled insert on the cover.

Suddenly, I sensed my mother standing behind me. She held Beth in her arms. Both were dressed in peasant garb that the clinic staff members obtained for us.

Her eyes spoke the words her lips couldn't. She'd lost all her possessions, not once, but twice, first in a fire and then in a tornado. When my real father had died, she'd had to turn her back on her home and walk away. "I'll see to the baby while you change your clothing."

I set the treasured box on the sofa. "Please tell Yang to place this under my seat in the first wagon." After slipping into the faded and patched cotton garments of a peasant woman, I wound my hair into a tight bun and pinned it at the back of my neck, then covered my head with a faded blue scarf.

Hearing my mother talking baby talk with my son and my daughter spurred me to rush. *No more dawdling over things you must leave behind. The most important things you're taking with you—except for Thaddeus. Thaddeus, my life, my joy.* I gulped back a fresh wave of tears while stuffing my small velvet purse containing what little currency I possessed beneath a fabric band I'd tied around my waist as a money belt.

"Do you need any help with Taddy?" I asked as my mother scooped the gurgling child into her arms.

"No," she responded on her way to the door. "I think we have everything, don't you?"

I rolled my eyes. "And a whole lot more."

Grabbing my portmanteau with one hand and holding Beth's tiny hand with my other, I followed Mother out of the house and slammed the door shut behind me.

Storm clouds filled the sky above our heads, obscuring the mountains toward which we headed, as the clinic staff assembled by the back door. With hands linked together and tears flowing, we sang "Blest Be the Tie That Binds." I gazed about the circle of love, and for a moment, I wondered if the missionary families we had met aboard the rickety old side-wheeler that deposited us on Chinese shores were also fleeing for their lives.

After Eve offered a prayer for each person in the circle, I kissed Jian Mei on the cheek, wiping at a tear on her chin. "I will miss you, Jian Mei. Please help yourself to our possessions if we do not return after a few weeks."

Unable to speak, she vigorously shook her head.

"It would please me to know that you are enjoying them and that the Japanese hadn't stolen or destroyed them."

We kissed again as Yang lifted Beth into the back of the wagon. The child froze when she saw the mandarin's son sitting at the far end of the wagon. Her eyes round with fear, Beth whimpered and reached for me. I urged her forward. "It's all right, darling. This is Dao Lin. He will be traveling with us."

Cautiously, she inched to the front of the wagon, choosing to sit across from him on the wooden seat that ran along the right side of the wagon. I climbed into the wagon after my daughter and took my son from my mother's arms. After Yang handed me the dresser drawer that would hold Taddy during our journey over the mountains, I settled myself next to Beth and placed the drawer on the floor in front of me. Mama chose to sit beside Dao Lin because Chin Shui, his servant, would be riding on the wagon bench with the driver.

Eve handed a large black bag to my mother. "I thought it might be wise to pack a few medical supplies in case of emergency."

My mother nodded her approval as she took the bag and stashed it under her seat. Once Eve had settled herself near the back of the wagon, Yang called to the driver, who flicked the whip over the heads of the two shaggy horses—and we were on our way. Jian Mei and the other staff members followed our wagon to the front gate of the compound, waving and calling farewells.

Between the woven bamboo forming the roof of the wagon, I watched as our little entourage rolled through the narrow city streets. Word of our departure must have spread through the community, for the doorways and alleys were lined with patients we'd treated at the mission, bowing respectfully as we passed.

As our wagons rumbled past the palace walls, I noted that

the massive carved doors leading from the veranda were shut. *Behind those closed doors are a mother and father whose hearts are breaking.* I glanced down at my sleeping son and thought, *What an incredible love Ho Feng must have for his only son.*

My own heart ached as I darted a glance at Dao Lin. Except for one tear coursing his cheek, the boy sat stone faced, staring at a distant spot above Beth's head. My mother intercepted my look of compassion and quietly slipped her arms around his slight, rigid body, drawing him under the protection of her arm.

The tears I'd managed to control while leaving the compound now slid down my face. But through the tears, the promise in Isaiah 66:13 washed through me like an incoming tide. *"As one whom his mother comforteth, so will I comfort you."*

"Thank You, Lord," I whispered, "for reminding me again of Your faithfulness. You're so good at that, Father."

The rumble of the wagon lulled me into a stupor until Taddy's cries for food stirred me awake. Bouncing over bumps and ruts on the road while nursing my son, I gazed out at the passing countryside, ablaze with autumn color.

The rainstorm caught us in the high mountain pass, forcing us to take shelter in an abandoned hut. Throughout the night, I held my children close to me and listened to the rain beating on the tiles above our heads. The slick mud on the trail delayed our departure the next morning until the sun dried it enough to make the trail passable. By the time we arrived at the Wongs' village the next evening, my mother, Eve, and I had exhausted all the games we knew to entertain Dao Lin and Beth. The two children were tired and cranky. As for Taddy, he gurgled and cooed as if he were resting safely in his crib back at the mission.

Before we left the Wongs' home the next morning, I prayed with Mrs. Wong and her family. After my prayer, I drew her aside. "My friend, I want to give you something to remember me by." I placed in her hands two pieces of the paper money given me by the mandarin.

She stared down at it as if it were a poisonous insect. "No, no!" Her face paled.

"It is a gift from one friend to another, not a payment for your hospitality and friendship. Please, if the soldiers come upon us, they'll confiscate it anyway."

Reluctantly, she agreed.

After I climbed aboard the wagon, we waved to one another until the other two wagons blocked our sight. When we arrived at the river, I insisted that the other two wagons cross first. Then, as the horses pulling our wagon stepped into the current, I clutched my infant son and closed my eyes while Eve did the same with Beth and Mama held Dao Lin close to her side.

Oh, dear God, please keep us safe. Please make the horses sure-footed. By the time I finished my prayer, the horses were pulling the wagon up the bank on the other side. Laughing and crying with relief, I started to relate the story of my previous passage through the same river. In the middle of my story, Beth raised her dark eyes to meet mine. "Daddy, where is my daddy?"

"Oh, honey." I cupped her face in my hands. "Daddy is still with Dr. Gibson. He'll meet us later." Fear niggled my mind. *What if you can't keep that promise?*

"Come on, let's sing your daddy's favorite song." I broke into a cheerful rendition of "Joyful, Joyful, We Adore Thee."

Mama, Eve, and I sang so loudly that Chin Shui turned around and grinned at us, the only smile I'd ever seen on his face. I can only imagine what he thought of the three crazy white women singing for joy while fleeing their enemy.

We crossed the second range of mountains before nightfall. As we rode into the village where the railroad ended, we were dismayed to find armed soldiers patrolling every street corner. Graffiti on walls and buildings read "Go home, foreign devil!" and "Death to all traitors."

When I leaned forward to speak with Chin Shui, he waved me back with, "Be silent, woman!"

Before I could respond, I spotted two soldiers at a roadblock at the next intersection. The driver of our wagon slowed to a stop. Following a quick exchange between Chin Shui and the soldiers in a dialect I didn't recognize, we resumed our journey.

"They are looking for 'white devils' fleeing the city," he hissed. "Keep the children silent. And you be silent, as well, and pretend to be a good wife!"

Pretend to be his wife? How audacious! I glared at the man.

As he turned back around, I caught my mother shaking with silent laughter. So I shot her a glare for good measure.

Chin Shui ordered our driver to turn away from the main streets. As our wagons jounced over the rutted side streets, the sun disappeared behind the distant mountains over which we'd so recently trekked. Ahead of us lay darkness and uncertainty.

The driver led us to a small inn on the eastern side of town. We remained in the wagon, inhaling the uneasy atmosphere of a city under siege, while Chin Shui arranged for our overnight stay.

"I don't like this," Eve mumbled. "What do we know about this man? How can we trust him with our lives?"

"I don't see that we have much choice at this point. As to trusting him, he has taken a vow. He would lay down his life for Dao Lin." I gazed at the exhausted child, lying on the wagon bench, his head resting in my mother's lap. "Yes, as long as Dao Lin is safe, we can trust Chin Shui."

My mother peered out through the wagon's woven bamboo cover. "I thought our enemy was the Japanese."

"You certainly picked a delightful time to fulfill the dream of your youth, Mama." I grinned. "Apparently, the only uniform we'll be able to trust will be that of the Nationalist Republic Army."

Several minutes later, Chin Shui strode out of the inn and over to our wagon. "We will stay here for the night. We will be safe as long as no one discovers that you are not Chinese."

With jaundiced eye, Eve examined the exterior of the inn. "Chin Shui, what kind of place is this, anyway?"

He bowed toward the woman. "It is a place where muleteers stay, a place where no one asks questions."

Eve and I exchanged worried glances. Instantly, we both knew we could expect communal sleeping quarters and sleeping mats infested with bedbugs and other vermin.

"And food?" Eve asked. "We must feed the children."

"We will be served the standard fare for travelers like ourselves, a bowl of rice and a slice of wheat bread." He gazed unblinkingly at Mrs. Gibson.

I smiled at Chin Shui. "Thank you so much for taking charge

today at the roadblock and for finding a safe place where we can sleep tonight." Around me, the children were beginning to stir.

"Mommy," Beth whined, "I want to go home. I want to see my daddy."

"Sh-sh-sh, honey. Everything will be fine; you'll see." I gave my daughter a hug and smiled at the mandarin's servant. "Perhaps once the children are settled down for the night, we should discuss plans for tomorrow," I suggested.

Chin Shui bowed graciously. It was obvious that while extremely polite to all, the man balked at answering to any woman other than me. Sensing this, my mother picked up the fussing baby and handed him to Eve. "Mrs. Gibson and I will go inside and care for the children's needs while the two of you discuss our travel plans. Dao Lin, would you help me by carrying this portmanteau for Mrs. Gibson? I fear that little Taddy needs his diapers changed."

"Thank you, Mother. I'll be in to nurse him as soon as possible."

With Chin Shui's help, she climbed down out of the wagon. Taking Beth's and Dao Lin's hands, she led them into the inn. Eve followed with the baby.

"Take the wagons around back and stable the animals," he called to the drivers. When the last wagon disappeared, I asked, "What will we do about tomorrow? Obviously, we can't board the train, with the military scrutinizing every face for Occidentals."

"You are right, Adams Tai-tai [Madam Adams]. We will need to continue in the wagons until we are out of this province."

"But didn't the mandarin commission the wagons to go only as far as the railhead?"

The man's face remained impassive. "The drivers are loyal to the mandarin and to his son. They will do as they are told. Tonight, they will sleep in the wagons to avoid theft."

From the tone of Chin Shui's voice, I knew he was willing to forcibly persuade any driver who dared complain otherwise. From inside the inn, a baby squalled. I smiled and bowed. "I must hurry to my son. He's getting impatient with me."

Chin Shui's eyes softened. "Rest well, Adams Tai-tai. I will see to everything."

"I know you will. If my friend Ho Feng trusts you with his most prized possession, I know I can trust you with mine." I bowed and headed inside to join the other women.

Once inside, my eyes took a while to adjust to the dimly lighted, smoke-saturated room. I located my mother by Taddy's cries more than by sight. *Leave it to Mama, or maybe Taddy deserves the credit.* Somehow, she'd laid claim to an entire corner of one of the lower levels of the wooden sleeping platform. The two women and the two children sat eating rice from small porcelain bowls. On a quilt in the middle of the cordoned space, Taddy squirmed on his back, alternately sucking his fist and making insistent demands for food.

Cradling my son in my arms, I quietly slipped to the darkened corner where Mama had stashed the few possessions we'd carried inside the inn. I had nursed and changed the baby by the time Chin Shui staggered in from the stables. As he drew closer, I could see he'd been beaten: his eyes were blackened, his body was bruised and bleeding, and a front tooth was missing.

"What happened?" I ran to him and helped him limp to the platform we'd claimed.

"I am so ashamed. I have dishonored you, and I have dishonored my mandarin," he slurred through his cut lips.

"Oh, dear heavenly Father, what has happened?" My mother leapt to her feet. "I'll get some water to cleanse his wounds."

As we women treated his injuries, Chin Shui told us how two of our drivers and four other thugs hanging around the area had jumped him as he entered the stables. "They beat me. They also beat and bound our third driver, Bei Tsei, and tossed him into the first wagon before stealing two of the mandarin's wagons." He averted his eyes in shame. "They knew we couldn't report them to the authorities, under the circumstances."

I dabbed at an oozing cut above the man's left eyebrow. "You say Bei Tsei also needs medical attention?"

"Yes."

"Eve, will you finish caring for Chin Shui while I go to

Bei Tsei's aid?"

"You can't go out there alone!" The giant of a man struggled to sit up, but I gently pushed his shoulders back to the floor. The fact that he didn't resist indicated to me the severity of his injuries.

"I'll go with you, CeeCee." My mother, who'd been reassuring the children of their safety, stood to her feet.

"No." The man's voice weakened.

"I suppose they stole the two supply wagons?" I asked.

He nodded and closed his eyes.

"Everything's gone!" I made a mental list of the items that had been stolen—my violin, my wedding pictures, Au Sam's dress, Beth's new toys. Blinking back tears, I reminded myself, *Things, CeeCee, they're only things!*

Mama touched my arm. "A man needs our help."

"You're right. Of course, you're right." I shook myself out of my grief.

Eve closed the medicine bag. "Here, you'll need this." My mother snatched up the case and followed me through the maze of inn patrons sleeping or sitting on their rented mats. Moonlight illuminated the pathway to the open stable door. We found Bei Tsei where Chin Shui had left him, unconscious, with blood streaming from his head. While I located and lighted a kerosene lamp, my mother found water and bathed the cut on his head.

Kneeling opposite one another, our patient between us, I removed a roll of cotton bandaging from the case and handed it to her. "I am so sorry, Mama, for dragging you into all of this. Almost everything you brought with you from America is gone."

She smiled and gently touched my cheek. "Darling, I'm incredibly thankful that God arranged it so I could be with you through all of this. Imagine if you had to go through this experience alone! He's such a merciful God."

I nodded tearfully.

As she bandaged the man's head wound, Mother suggested, "Why don't you check whether the thieves missed anything."

Suddenly, I remembered—*Beth's adoption papers! The writ of passage beneath our family Bible!* I leapt to my feet and scrambled to the front of the wagon. *It's gone! The box is gone! What about the mandarin's money?* Fumbling beneath the canvas tarp that protected the toolbox, I breathed a sigh of relief when my fingers brushed against the smooth silkiness of the coin purse. Taking the bills from their hiding place, I slipped them beneath my tunic and stuffed them into my makeshift money belt.

A chill passed through me when I remembered the missing Bible box containing Beth's purchase papers. Without them, she would be taken away from me when I tried to leave the country. I jumped down from the wagon and felt my way along the side of the wagon. As I rounded the rear of the wagon, I stumbled over a soft object—Beth's baby doll. I picked up my daughter's precious toy and placed it in the wagon.

Mama looked at me questioningly.

"They didn't find the purse. But the Bible box that contained all our important papers is gone." My voice caught.

She looked at me in surprise and shook her head. "No! No, it isn't. It's right here. I'm sitting on it!"

"What?"

She stood and pushed the box toward me. "I don't think they touched anything in this wagon. Give God the glory!"

I opened the box and removed the Bible to find that all our papers and Granddaddy Spencer's twenty-dollar gold piece remained inside. *"Before they call, I will answer; and while they are yet speaking, I will hear."* I bowed my head and thanked God. *You're always ten steps ahead of me, Father.*

A groan from our patient reminded us we weren't alone. My mother touched his shoulder. "Bei Tsei. Bei Tsei, can you hear me?"

The driver groaned again.

My mother rinsed a rag in the basin of water, then wiped his forehead. "Bei Tsei?"

He opened his eyes slowly. A wave of terror swept across his face before he recognized her. "I am sorry—"

"It's all right. It's all right."

"My head hurts." The man rolled his head from side to side.

"There, there," my mother comforted. "You've been injured,

but it's not serious. Do you understand?"

He nodded and closed his eyes.

"We can't leave him here alone all night. And we can't stay out here with him. The children need us."

Hearing the word *children*, the man stirred. "Hurry! We must protect the children."

I patted the man's shoulder. "The children are safe inside the inn."

"No! No!" His eyes flew open. "We must get them and leave immediately."

My mother washed the man's face with cool water. "Sh-sh-sh, everything's all right, Bei Tsei."

"No!" He struggled to a sitting position. "Please, you must listen to me. One of the other drivers bragged about turning you over to the authorities for the reward."

My mother and I looked at each other, bewildered.

"We must leave at once. The soldiers will be here by dawn," he warned.

"But where can we go?"

For a moment, I thought Bei Tsei hadn't heard my question. I started to my feet. "Chin Shui! He'll know what we should do."

"Wait." The man stopped me. "We can go north to my village. My brother Fu Shan will hide us. He hates the Japanese and the provincial rowdies more than he does foreign devils from England and America."

Without waiting to hear more, I dashed out of the stable and across the yard to the inn. Chin Shui listened intently as I told him what Bei Tsei had overheard and what he now proposed.

He nodded solemnly. "He is right. We must leave here immediately. Is he in any condition to drive?"

I shook my head.

He glanced toward his left arm, hanging in a sling.

"Well, we can't stay here and be slaughtered either," I reminded. "One of us women will have to drive."

He snorted. "A female driver would be spotted and stopped within five kilometers."

"Hmm, I have an idea. Do you have any spare clothing? And a straw hat?"

A glint of humor entered his eyes. "You will find a change of clothing in the canvas bag under the driver's seat. Remember to attach a queue to the hat," he reminded. "I'll awaken Gibson Tai-tai, and we'll smuggle the children out of the inn without being noticed."

"I'll take the baby with me." I reached over the sleeping bodies of Beth and Dao Lin and collected the baby into my arms. He whimpered. "Sh-sh-sh, little one. Mama's here for you. Sh-sh-sh."

I slipped out of the inn unnoticed and rushed to the stable. "Mama," I whispered.

"Over here." Her voice came from the shadows behind me. I whirled about to find myself facing a glinting Mongolian dagger. I froze.

"Don't be afraid, woman. I will not harm your mother if you do as I say." When I didn't reply immediately, the stranger jabbed the knife toward me. I leapt back to protect my son. "So, will you agree?"

"My mother. Where is my mother?"

"I have her tied up behind me. Now, will you agree?"

"Will I agree to what?"

"I have a daughter, Ana. The soldiers killed her mother for being British. We were hiding in the stable when the drivers beat your servants and stole your wagons." He stepped out of the shadows. "And I heard the injured man tell you about fleeing to his brother's place. I want you to take Ana with you. I will come and get her once the trouble has passed."

"I can't—"

"But you must."

From the darkness, Mama spoke quietly. "I will be responsible for your child. All you needed to do was ask."

At the sound of feet scuffing across the courtyard, the man froze. "That's the rest of our party. Untie my mother and bring your daughter to me; then you'd better leave before Chin Shui finds you here," I hissed.

As Eve and Chin Shui hurried into the stable, each carrying a sleeping child, a beautiful girl of twelve or thirteen stepped out of the shadows and bowed before me. "I am Ana, your servant, Tai-tai. I owe my life to you."

I lifted her to her feet. "You can pay your debt by helping me with the children. And you, sir," I said to the stranger, "can help by hitching the horse to the wagon for me, since both of my servants are incapacitated."

The stranger sprang to action. In silence, he hitched the animals to the wagon and led them into the courtyard while I disappeared into the shadows to change into Chin Shui's clothing. Finding a black shirt among his belongings, I tore it into strips and braided myself a queue. Fastening the braid to my head scarf, I put on a hat I'd spotted near the doorway of the stable.

I stepped out of the shadows behind Eve. "Well, how do I look?"

She turned and gasped. My mother took in my disguise. "You'll do until it's time to feed your little one. Perhaps I should be the one in disguise. Besides, I've driven a number of wagons in my time."

"How did you know what I was up to?"

She grinned. "It was obvious that Chin Shui couldn't handle a team with his arm in a sling, and our driver is in no condition. Now, let's exchange clothing."

After Chin Shui helped Bei Tsei move to the rear of the wagon, Eve spread our quilts out on the wagon bed and settled the children down to sleep.

At the sight of my mother's disguise, a glimmer of a smile teased the corners of Chin Shui's mouth. "I will ride up front with Chamberlain Tai-tai in case we are stopped and must speak."

I climbed inside the wagon and crawled to the front, directly behind the driver's seat. My mother and Chin Shui climbed onto the driver's bench, and with a flick of the reins, we rolled out of the courtyard. With every rumble and creak, I prayed we wouldn't be heard by the innkeeper or his sleeping patrons.

We rode several blocks through the city and arrived at the North Gate at the same time as a cluster of mule trains and loaded wagon trains, all heading north. While we waited in line to exit, I removed the important papers from the Bible box and stuffed them into my homemade money belt, along with my grandfather's twenty-dollar gold piece. Chuckling to myself, I tried to smooth my tunic over my bulging middle but finally decided it was hopeless. Between the tummy I still had from giving birth to Taddy and all my hidden treasures, I appeared to be five months pregnant.

A sleepy guard peered into the back of our wagon while the second questioned Chin Shui as to our purpose and destination.

"We are taking our brother home to die." He gestured toward Bei Tsei resting in the back of the wagon. I breathed easier when the two guards waved us through the gates. Outside the gate, the road ran parallel to the swift-flowing Yellow River. There was a ford five hundred yards from the gate. To reach our driver's village, we had to cross the river and travel halfway up the steep mountain gorge beyond the great plain on the other side.

Kneeling, I peered out over my mother's shoulder as we crossed the river. Once safely across, I glanced down at my whitened knuckles and sighed. Another foe defeated.

Chin Shui watched anxiously as my mother maneuvered the wagon over the rocky path. I dragged the Bible box up to the front of the wagon to use as a seat. In the early-morning light, terraced fields of harvested grain cordoned our journey north. As we drew closer to the mountains, we watched soaring eagles search for a breakfast of field mouse, rabbit, or squirrel. At any other time, the ride would have been idyllic.

At the base of the mountain, we paused at a spring to water the animals, then proceeded up the narrow roadway past millet patches into the high country. Toward midmorning, the children awakened. Beth tugged at my tunic. "I'm hungry, Mama."

I caressed the side of her face. "I know, honey. I know."

"Why can't we eat?" she asked. She'd seen my mother filling the barrels with cans of preserved food and bread. "I want one of Gamma's cookies."

"They're all gone, I'm afraid. Some bad men stole Gamma's cookies."

She thought for a moment, then brightened. "Then Gamma will just have to make some more."

I smiled at my daughter's innocence. Before I could answer, Chin Shui, who'd overheard the conversation, turned to us. "I don't have any of your grandmother's cookies, but I do have three rice-and-honey cakes—one for each of you children." He reached into his tunic and pulled out a brown pouch.

My mother cast a quick glance at the man seated by her side. "Chin Shui, you are a man of many surprises."

The man bowed. "Compliments of the inn's private larder." He handed a rice cake to each of the three older children. This was the first time Beth had noticed Ana's presence. Curious, she sidled up to the older girl.

"Sorry, ladies," Chin Shui apologized, putting his hand back in his tunic. "The only other food I could grab on my way to the back door were these." He pulled out a handful of hard breadsticks.

My stomach growled as I eyed the food the man offered. Twenty-four hours earlier, I might have turned up my nose at his offering, especially considering he'd stored it unwrapped next to his body. But that was twenty-four hours ago. The rice I'd eaten less than twelve hours before had long since ceased to satisfy. After my mother accepted his offering, I took one, as did Eve, who graciously thanked him for his thievery.

He laughed. "This is the breakfast we paid for when we rented the sleeping space." We all laughed with him.

The narrow gorge through which we traveled most of the afternoon opened onto a high plateau and to Bei Tsei's village. At that altitude, the leaves on the deciduous trees already decorated the golden brown grass.

In Bei Tsei's house lived his aged mother, his brother, and his brother's wife. But because of the advancing armies in the valley below, others had also fled to the mountain cottage for safety. Among them were a pregnant woman, several grandmothers, a blind man, and five mothers with eleven small children between them. The other homes in the community housed as many and, in some cases, more.

Exhausted from running, we couldn't imagine traveling any farther. Our hostess prepared what food she had and shared it with all of us. We'd barely eaten, when a villager came to the door and whispered something to Bei Tsei's brother. The man turned and asked, "You women are nurses, yes?"

We nodded.

"There are several injured people who need medical attention. Would you—" Our host bowed, as if hesitant to ask.

My mother arose instantly. "Of course, we will help. Let me get the medicine bag from the wagon."

Eve and I joined her. "Is there someplace where we can set up a clinic? We could treat more people in a shorter amount of time."

Our host nodded and bowed. "The schoolhouse."

News spread from house to house about our improvised clinic. Our medical supplies were simple: castor oil, sulfur, potassium permanganate, first-aid ointment, hydrogen peroxide, and bandages. Our hostess cared for the children while we three women did what we could for the injured.

The bright spot of the evening was when one of the women gave birth. It was encouraging to see new life amid the destruction and chaos.

Later, a young teacher hobbled into the school with a bullet wound in his side. I removed the bullet and cleansed the wound as best I could in our primitive conditions. While I bandaged the wound, the faces from my past melded with his—the brave, unflinching faces of men injured on the battlefields of Europe; confused, bewildered faces of children from whom childhood had been snatched; and the resigned faces of weary nurses who fought their battles with death, one human being at a time. *Oh, dear God, be with this man. I can do no more for him.*

I rubbed my tired, burning eyes. My head ached, and I felt very, very old. *Will the carnage of war ever end, Lord? How long will the blood of Your children be spilled by ruthless men, intent on their own greed? When will they hammer their swords into plowshares?*

Press on to the Sea

I watched as the last patient limped out the schoolhouse door. My mother walked up behind me and massaged my neck and shoulders. "Is that it? Do I dare believe we're finished here?"

"I hope so." I rolled my head from side to side, responding to her ministrations. "When I left earlier to nurse Taddy, I thought I heard gunfire in the distance."

"I don't know about you, ladies—" Eve dumped a basin of used water onto the ground. "—but I'm going to get some sleep. The children will be awake before you know it, and they'll be needing attention."

"Leave everything." Mama gestured toward the clutter about the room. "We can take care of everything in the morning."

"Good idea." Eve snapped the medical kit closed and headed out the door.

Arm in arm, my mother and I strode out of the schoolhouse into the night. I gazed up at the rising moon. *Thad, where are you? Are you watching the moon rise too?*

At first light, I awakened to the sound of men riding into the village, shouting, "The Japanese are coming. The Japanese are coming!"

By the time I pulled myself together and raced from the house, a crowd had gathered in front of the school in the early-morning grayness.

I pushed my way through the crowd, where I found Chin Shui quizzing the riders for details. "You must join up with us," one of the strangers demanded of the mandarin's trusted servant.

"We're here to recruit men to fight the enemy."

"But where exactly is the Japanese army?" Chin Shui asked, his voice calm, yet intense. "How close are the soldiers to us, here in this village?"

The same rider gestured wildly in the air. "Oh, close! Very, very close!"

A rumble of fear passed through the crowd. First one man, then another volunteered to ride with the strangers.

"We will defend our families!"

"Death to the invading devils!"

Chin Shui drew me away from the confusion. "Adams Tai-tai, these men are bandits recruiting a guerrilla force to face the enemy. Their words may or may not be trusted."

I knew that these lawless gangs of men could be as ruthless with their own people as the Japanese.

"What should we do?" One look in his eyes, and I had my answer. "We need to leave, don't we?"

"We need to take to the mountains to avoid both the advancing Japanese army and the bandits. I will harness the horses to the wagon while you prepare the children. Chamberlain Tai-tai will need to once again dress—"

I placed my hand on his arm. "I understand. Give us thirty minutes, and we'll be ready to leave."

"Fifteen?"

"Fifteen." I bowed.

Seventeen minutes later, we bundled the sleeping children into the wagon and were ready to roll once more. Bei Tsei, choosing to join the guerrilla forces, gave Chin Shui directions to a valley where he believed we'd be safe. "Two miles farther up the road, you will come to a fork. Go left—"

"No," I wailed. "That will take us farther from our destination. We must travel east!"

Chin Shui bowed. "To retrace the miles we traveled yesterday will bring certain trouble."

With a sigh, I relented. As I climbed into the wagon, our hostess handed me a bundle and thanked us for all we'd done. Tears sprang into my eyes when I opened it to find three loaves of bread. I understood the sacrifice she'd made to share her food with us. *The bread won't go far to fill these little tummies*, I thought as I glanced down at the sleeping children, *but I am grateful, Lord*. I remembered the little boy who shared his lunch with Jesus. *But, then, if You made five loaves feed five thousand, You'll have no trouble stretching three loaves to satisfy the stomachs of seven.*

We'd ridden no more than half a mile from the village when I felt a strange uneasiness. I lifted my hand to tap my mother on the shoulder, when she glanced over her shoulder at me. "CeeCee, something's not right. I'm uncomfortable about this."

"Me too," I whispered.

I scanned the countryside, damp with morning dew. Despite the apparent calm, some instinctive sense made me apprehensive. As our eyes met, I knew that her intuition gave her the same message. Without a word, she pulled the reins to the left. I grabbed hold of the wagon bench for balance as we bounced over the rocks and bushes.

"What?" Chin Shui shouted in surprise as she halted the wagon behind a clump of bushes. "Why are you stopping?"

She stated candidly, "I don't really know."

He turned toward me. "We must not—"

A rifle shot split the morning air. Without another word, Chin Shui leapt from the wagon. I snatched the baby and whatever else I could carry while Eve hurried the three sleepy children from the wagon.

"Take everything you can," Chin Shui ordered as he scooped the mandarin's son into his uninjured arm and the closest bundle into the other. "Run for that large outcropping of rocks halfway up the hill."

Ana grabbed two cases and charged after Chin Shui. My mother cradled the sobbing Beth in her arms. "Come on, honey. Grandma and Beth are going to play hide-and-seek."

We half ran, half stumbled up the mountain after Chin Shui. My chest ached as I struggled to keep up with the others. When Taddy began to whimper, I soothed, "It's all right, darling. Mama has you. It's all right."

Suddenly, Chin Shui was back at my side and snatched the baby from my arms. Taking me by the elbow, he dragged me the rest of the way to the rocks. There, we huddled, listening to the thundering hooves of approaching horses. Wanting to know what was happening, I peered over the rocks.

As the lead horse and rider came into view, Chin Shui withdrew a dagger from his belt. "Bandits!" he hissed. I started to protest, but my mother grabbed my arm and shook her head.

The leader lifted his hand, signaling to the others to halt. While I couldn't hear his words, I saw the man point to the bushes where we'd hidden the wagon. Two of the bandits rode over to the wagon. One man leapt to the ground and ran his hand over the backs of our horses, then shouted to his leader. The other man rode around to the back and disappeared inside the wagon. He came out seconds later, laughing and holding up a piece of clothing.

"How dare he touch my undies!" Eve choked indignantly.

The rest of the riders, seven in number, laughed when he tossed the garment at one of his buddies, who, in turn, tossed it to another and another, until the garment landed on the top of a nearby bush. When the leader stood in his stirrups and scanned the hillside, obviously searching for the owners of the wagon, I ducked my head and pressed against the rock.

"Of all the indecent—" Eve started to stand. I pulled her back down beside me.

"Sh-sh-sh!" I ordered.

She huffed and sat back down on the ground, her hands tightly folded across her chest, her face filled with embarrassment and anger. Once certain that she'd calmed enough so as to not give us away, I arose to my knees and watched the men arguing and gesturing toward the hills.

"If you believe in your God as you say you do, Adams Tai-tai," Chin Shui whispered, "now is the time to ask Him for a miracle."

"That's all I've been doing since we heard the gunshot." I watched the leader gesture toward the town and start off in that direction while another man tied his horse to the back of the wagon, climbed into the driver's seat, and drove away with our only means of transportation and the rest of our belongings.

As the riders and the wagon disappeared from view, I sank to the ground. "Now what? Here we are, stranded on this mountain with four children and no wagon."

"We can't stay here," Eve groaned, "and we can't go back to the village now that the bandits have arrived."

My mother rose to her feet and brushed the dust from her trousers. "We walk. That's what!"

"Walk?" I stared at her in horror. "To the sea? Do you know how far that is?"

"No. Do you have a better idea? Come nightfall, it will be bitterly cold up here in these mountains." She knelt and opened the portmanteau she'd rescued from the wagon.

"And the children? How far can we expect them to walk over this rugged ground?"

Instead of answering, she pulled from the case a full-skirted linen dress. Chin Shui silently watched the drama without comment.

"Here!" Mama tossed the garment at me. "Rip out one of the side seams in the skirt; then separate the skirt from the top."

"A baby sling!" Chin Shui's face became animated with excitement.

"That's right." She smiled as she threw a second dress at Eve. "Here. We'll use this one for carrying Elizabeth on our backs."

"What about all this stuff?" Eve's hand swept over the pile of bundles we'd grabbed in haste.

"Not all of these are necessary to our survival." Chin Shui opened one of the bundles. "We need to find out what we have."

While the children ate chunks of dry bread, we adults sorted our remaining belongings. When I came to my diary, I couldn't abandon it, so I stuffed it under my bulging money belt. Chin Shui turned his back, giving my mother a chance to remove the men's clothing she'd worn while driving the wagon. She donned several layers of her own clothing, then topped it all with her Chinese peasant disguise. Eve and I did the same.

Once Taddy had finished nursing, Chin Shui helped me lash the baby to my back. Then he assisted my mother with Elizabeth. We tried to make a game of it for the little girl, but she wasn't to be humored. When her protests proved futile, Beth fell into a pout. I will always remember the sight of her riding on her grandmother's back, a furious little Buddha.

Chin Shui, carrying Dao Lin on his shoulders, set the pace. Picking our way through the wooded area behind the tiny village that had housed us hours earlier, we could hear the priests at the temple, blowing horns and pounding drums, begging their gods to protect them from both the Japanese and the bandits pillaging the village. The villagers' shouts of anger and cries of pain would haunt my sleep for years to come.

Eventually, the noise faded and was replaced by the sounds of bird calls and leaves crunching beneath our feet. Staying close to the rugged mountain terrain, we could see the golden valley we'd crossed on the previous day. On the opposite bank of the glistening river stood the walls of the city. Chin Shui pointed to the smoke rising from the city. "The provincial army has left its mark."

For a moment, I felt faint. I looked toward my mother for support. *Do something*, I silently cried. *Do something!* Unlike me, my mother always seemed to know what to do in an emergency.

Dry eyed, she gazed in the direction of the city for a moment. "Let's proceed, Chin Shui."

Mama and the others set off once more while I stood paralyzed at what I saw, reaching desperately for inner strength to continue. Then, in the confusion of my mind, I heard a clear, gentle voice reminding, "My grace is sufficient for thee: for my strength is made perfect in weakness."

I whirled about, afraid we'd been discovered. No one was there—I stood alone. My panic subsiding, I hunched the baby farther up on my back and hurried after the others.

We walked eastward, clinging to the edges of mountains and skirting fertile valleys, always keeping the slim silver line of the railroad tracks in view. Each evening, we women waited with the children while Chin Shui slipped into the nearest town to buy food and to determine the town's political temperament.

"I want to go home." Beth whimpered the sentiments of all of us for the first three days, then for some reason stopped. Dao Lin and Ana never complained. The baby jogged along on my back or on my chest, content and quiet.

Days later, after concealing us in an abandoned hut, Chin Shui left on his evening foray for food and information. As we awaited his return, I nursed Taddy while Eve did a foot check to treat any new blisters, and my mother entertained the children with stories of her past. It was a routine I'd come to enjoy. Hearing the familiar stories of home reminded me that the pain and inconvenience we were suffering were temporary, that an entire world awaited us beyond the shores of Asia.

This evening, my mother told of the time she and my real father went to a bandit's hideout to deliver a baby. While I'd heard the tale many times, I still found myself leaning forward so as not to miss one word.

Suddenly, she stopped speaking, putting her finger to her lips. "Sh-sh-sh, someone's coming," she hissed.

Women and children alike froze at the sound of feet crunching over the gravelly terrain outside the shack. We looked at one another in terror, knowing that it was too soon for Chin Shui to return.

Silently, Eve rose to her feet. From a little pile of discarded, broken furniture in the corner of the shack, she selected a table leg. Lifting it high above her head, she positioned herself behind the open doorway. As the giant shadow of a man filled the doorway, she screamed and swung the club at the intruder. Her scream triggered the children's screams, as well as my mother's and mine.

The man caught her wrist, suspending the table leg above their heads. Amid the chaos, the man shouted, "It's me, Chin Shui."

"Chin Shui?" Eve froze.

"Chin Shui! See?" He stepped back to allow the moonlight to illuminate his face.

"Oh! Chin Shui! I am so sorry. We thought—"

Gently, Chin Shui removed the table leg from her hands. "I always imagined you women to be defenseless out here, alone in the night!"

"How did you manage to return so soon, anyway?" my mother questioned. "Next time, you need to whistle or something so we'll know it's you."

"Perhaps there will not be a next time." He knelt and set a sack of food on the floor in the center of the room. "I think it will be safe for us to board the Tientsin train tonight. It leaves before dawn tomorrow morning."

"No more walking?" Ana spoke up for the first time.

Chin Shui glanced her way. "It looks that way, child."

"I have enough cash for tickets," I reminded, patting my money belt.

Chin Shui shook his head. "The town is overflowing with foreign refugees like yourself. The tickets are sold out."

Eve clicked her tongue impatiently. "Then how do you expect—"

Chin Shui glanced at my mother, a slight smile tugging the corners of his mouth. "Chamberlain Tai-tai, I think you know the answer to that, don't you?"

My mother groaned. "I suspect that I do. Even so, riding in a boxcar is better than walking the same distance, I assure you."

"But CeeCee and the children can't hop a moving train," Eve interrupted.

"I found a break in the fence surrounding the station where we can sneak through. Once inside the rail yard," he explained, "we'll have to avoid being seen by the local militia. I will distract the guard while you women climb on board with the children. That way, I'll be the only one hopping a moving train."

My mother eyed him suspiciously. "And what will we do if a yard man comes to check the car for illegal passengers?"

He glanced toward the table leg lying on the floor beside Eve. "Mrs. Gibson, you have an excellent swing."

"And if a guard detains you?" I asked.

Chin Shui turned to me, his face as inscrutable as ever. "You must pray to your God that it doesn't happen."

Ana touched the man's sleeve, her voice revealing her concern. "Would you kill him?"

"Anyone hungry?" Chin Shui opened the satchel and handed each of us a steamed bun and an apple.

After we finished eating, we carried out Chin Shui's scheme to steal aboard the train. The plan worked—we squeezed through the break in the fence and climbed aboard the nearest boxcar without one guard detecting our presence. Chin Shui stood guard beside the partially open door, the table-leg club in his hand.

At dawn, the massive wooden gates swung open. The soldiers watched helplessly as hundreds of desperate people, rich and poor, educated and illiterate, flooded into the station yard, filling every passenger car and boxcar—including ours—to overflowing. I grinned across the crowded car at my mother. "So much for subterfuge, huh?"

The train rolled past crowded railway stations without stopping, straight to Tientsin's main terminal. Again, soldiers, this time from the central government, looked the other way as the passengers, legal and otherwise, tumbled out of the train.

Despite the hordes of anxious customers, Chin Shui dickered with a man who owned a donkey and cart to take us to the docks. We rode while he walked alongside the cart. The closer we came to the wharf, the more pedestrians, bicycles, carts, wagons, sedan chairs, and automobiles clogged the roadway. Inch by inch we drew closer to our destination. Ana shouted and pointed when she saw the mast of the closest ship.

"Would it help if you ran ahead and purchased our tickets?" I shouted to Chin Shui.

"I think we should stay together." By the set of the man's jaw, I knew there was no dissuading him.

"He'd never be able to find us again in this crowd," my mother shouted over the deafening confusion.

After we had sat immobile in the blocked street for several hours, word filtered back through the crowd: "All passage on ships sold out for the next two weeks."

Pandemonium spread through the disappointed throng. They surged forward, throwing themselves against the wooden fences surrounding the docks.

"Hurry!" Chin Shui snatched Dao Lin from the cart, then grabbed my wrist. "There's going to be a riot."

I grabbed what belongings I could and leapt from the cart, as did the rest of our party. My mother hoisted Beth onto her shoulders, then handed the cart driver a couple bills for his time.

"Wait!" I shouted at Chin Shui, pointing back into the sea of humanity. "My mother! My daughter!"

He tugged on my wrist. "You can't stop now. They'll catch up!"

"But, I—" Ignoring my protests, Chin Shui plowed through the pressing throng, opening a pathway for Eve, Ana, and me.

Two blocks from the docks, we slowed to a walk. Chin Shui turned right at the next corner, then left, all the while ignoring my pleas to wait for my mother and daughter. Three blocks later, he stopped at the front gate of a Buddhist monastery and rang a tiny brass bell hidden in a recess behind some vines.

A man dressed in the garb of a monk opened the gate. After he and Chin Shui had exchanged a few words, the monk beckoned us to enter the garden.

Once Dao Lin had slid from his shoulders, Chin Shui turned to me. "So sorry to leave your mother and child behind. You stay here with Dao Lin while I go search for them." He bowed and slipped out of the gate and down the street.

The monk spoke a few words I couldn't understand and beckoned us to follow him under the stone arches into what appeared to be an annex to the temple. The high-ceilinged room was dark and empty except for two long trestle tables with matching benches running along each side. He gestured for us to be seated at the closest table. We obeyed.

Eve, sitting across from me, leaned forward and whispered, "Where do you suppose that man disappeared to?"

I shrugged and gazed about the silent, mysterious room. To speak out loud somehow seemed sacrilegious.

Dao Lin tugged at my sleeve. "I'm hungry," he whispered, his eyes wide with curiosity.

I smiled down into his solemn little face. "Me too."

We'd sat there several minutes before the monk returned, carrying a tray loaded with bowls of hot soup for us. I thanked him; then Eve offered a blessing over the food. By the time she whispered the Amen, the children had eaten half of their soup.

"Let me hold the baby while you eat your soup," Eve suggested. "Then I'll eat while you nurse him."

Not waiting for a second invitation, I attacked the hot soup as if I hadn't had a decent meal for days, which was very close to the truth. When I finished eating, I took Taddy and the portmanteau that held his diapers over to a corner, where I changed him and fed him undisturbed. Within a few minutes he was asleep on a flannel blanket on the tile floor.

The monk reappeared out of the shadows and removed our empty bowls. He returned immediately and led Eve and the children out into the courtyard. Exhausted myself, I lay down beside my son on the narrow bench. Awakened by a commotion in the courtyard, I sat up in time to have a tiny body fly into my arms. "Mommy! Mommy!" Beth wailed. "Gamma and me lost you and couldn't find you. Chin Shui found us." She snuggled up to my neck, her arms tightly wrapped about me. "Don't leave me again, OK?"

Tears filled my eyes as I patted her back and assured her that I'd never leave her again.

"And Daddy too?" she asked.

"I'm sure when we find Daddy, he'll never want to leave you again either."

The monk silently led my mother and Chin Shui into the dining room. "Are you all right?" I whispered. "I was so worried about you two."

"I was a little worried about us too, for a while." Her voice quivered as she laughed. "Chin Shui had to bully his way through a street brawl to reach us. I'd pressed myself and Beth up against a brick building to keep out of the fray."

"Excuse me." Chin Shui bowed. "We can stay here only until nightfall; then we must leave. Women are not allowed within the sacred gates of this monastic order after sunset."

"Where can we go?" Concern filled my mother's face. "Back into the streets?"

"Wait!" I stood to my feet. "We could go to the mission inn for the night."

Chin Shui shook his head. "No, Adams Tai-tai, the building is boarded up. We passed it earlier. Do you not remember?"

I'd been so frightened and agitated over my mother and child I hadn't even noticed.

"What about Au Sam's relatives?" Mama suggested. "Didn't you say they live near Tientsin?"

I thought about her suggestion before answering. "About ten

miles outside the city. We'd need transportation." I glanced toward Chin Shui. "It's worth a try—at least we'd be out of the city before nightfall."

"I will ask our host where we can get a cart and driver," he volunteered. After the two men conversed briefly, Chin Shui turned toward me. "He says he has a brother who owns a horse and cart, and the brother will take us to your friend for a price. I warn you that it's likely to be a high price under the circumstances."

"A price? Wonderful." I patted my money belt. "I still have most of the money Mandarin Ho Feng gave me."

The bodyguard shook his head, his face expressionless. "He says his brother won't take paper money because it will be worthless when the Japanese arrive. He wants silver."

"Silver? I don't have any." My hand rested on a hard circular object in my money belt. *Granddaddy Spencer's twenty-dollar gold piece!*

For an instant, I wavered, remembering my wedding day, when I vowed I would treasure his gift forever. Then I recalled my grandfather's prophetic words. "You'll treasure it until you need to trade it for food or for shelter."

And, now, the time has come. I reached inside my tunic and withdrew the shiny gold coin. My mother inhaled sharply as the gold piece glistened in the afternoon sunlight. Holding the coin out for the Buddhist monk to examine, I asked, "Will this do?"

The monk's eyes widened with greed before he bowed and babbled something in his dialect. Chin Shui eyed the coin with surprise and the monk with disgust. Our burly guide snarled a reply, and the monk was gone.

"He'll be back," Chin Shui informed us. "What other surprises do you have hidden in that garment of yours?"

A niggle of fear tugged at the recesses of my mind. *I trusted this man with my life and the lives of my loved ones. Would his loyalty have wavered if he'd known about the gold piece?*

"No more gold, if that's what you're asking." My apprehension must have shown, for a look of disappointment flickered across Chin Shui's face.

"Do not give the brother the coin until he delivers us to your friend's home." Chin Shui's face once again an inscrutable mask, he continued, "The brother is likely to abandon us, or worse yet, rob us, thinking there is more treasure to be had." He nodded toward my money belt.

My mother, observing the exchange between Chin Shui and me, cleared her throat. "There is another little matter my daughter failed to mention that I think you should know." She glanced my way, then at our guide. "We are going to the house of Au, the warlord of the province. His sister was my dearest friend before she died."

"The house of Au? The house of Au?" He mouthed rather than spoke the words. Folding his hands behind his back, Chin Shui turned on his heel and strode into the garden, where Eve was tending the three children. I put my son into the sling I'd made for carrying him while my mother collected the rest of our belongings; then we walked out into the garden to join the others.

Minutes later, a small cart, just big enough for us women and the children, pulled up behind the temple grounds. The driver demanded I give him the gold coin. Immediately, Chin Shui stepped in between us. While I couldn't make out his words in the unfamiliar dialect, I did understand the phrase *house of Au*.

The driver and the monk, who had hung back in the shadows, suddenly grew agitated. With choppy motions, the driver gestured for us to climb into the cart. Quickly, he and Chin Shui hopped onto the seat while we women settled ourselves and the children in the back. The sway-backed mare lumbered forward at the flick of the reins. Because multitudes of refugees fleeing China's interior still clogged the main arteries into the city, the driver remained on the back roads. The late-September sun hung low in the western sky before I recognized the stone walls and the massive carved wooden gates guarding the home of the much-feared warlord.

Chin Shui announced us at the gate. After several minutes, the wooden gates swung open, but our driver refused to drive the cart onto the grounds. He and Chin Shui spat words back and forth.

Then Chin Shui turned to me. "He says that for reasons he refuses to explain, he will not enter the warlord's courtyard. You may give him the coin now, if you wish. Though since he has broken his promise to take us to the door, you have the right to refuse payment."

I shook my head and reached into the folds of my garment. "No, I will keep my part of the bargain. Here." I handed the gold piece to Chin Shui. "Please give this to the driver, and tell him that his services were greatly appreciated."

Chin Shui took the coin and bowed. After a short exchange between the two men, the driver cracked the whip over the tired little horse's back and lumbered away toward Tientsin. I took Beth's hand and led the way toward the palace doors. As we neared the building, Chin Shui drew Dao Lin protectively close to his side and hung back.

I studied my mother's face and wondered what thoughts were going through her mind. *Is she surprised at the elaborate surroundings in which Au Sam was raised? Or is she reliving the scene through her memories of Au Sam?*

The arched doors at the top of the staircase swung open, and the warlord's head servant stepped out of the building and waited for us to ascend the staircase. He bowed and invited us to follow him inside the palace.

As Chin Shui and the warlord exchanged the mandatory bows and greetings, the warlord's attention kept wandering to me and my peasant garb. Impatient with protocol, he brushed Chin Shui aside and motioned for me to step forward. He spoke to me slowly, as one would a young child. "It is good to see you, once again, friend of my mother and my sister."

"And you, Honored Brother."

A smile spread across his face. "You speak excellent Mandarin, Adams Tai-tai."

"It has been many months since I arrived in your beautiful country. I have had time to appreciate the beauty of your language and your culture." I bowed.

He smiled again. "And these clothes that you wear help you to better appreciate my country and my language?"

"Hardly, Au Wan. These clothes hide us from our enemies." I

proceeded to tell him of the events leading to our abandoning the mission compound and our trek eastward. "When we arrived in Tientsin to find all the passages sold on ships leaving for Hong Kong, I remembered my friend, Au Sam's favorite brother."

"We will talk of this later." His eyes flickered toward my mother.

"May I present my mother, Mrs. Chloe Chamberlain." As I mentioned her name, Mama bowed. "She was your sister's best friend in America."

The warlord returned Mama's bow, then clapped his hands. Immediately, a servant stepped out of the shadows. The warlord gestured toward my mother. "My mother has not been well," Au Wan explained to my mother. "Swee Joo will take you to her chambers. She wishes to hear all that you can tell her about her daughter."

I introduced each of the rest of our party. The warlord frowned slightly when I pointed out the mandarin's son, Dao Lin; and Chin Shui drew the boy close.

Our audience with the warlord ended when he took my hand. "You will dine with me tonight, Adams Tai-tai, while our mothers dine together. They have much to share."

I glanced down at my clothes. "I'm afraid that I brought nothing approp—"

"Chen Ho will take care of everything." At the snap of the warlord's fingers, two female servants came forward. The girl, Chen Ho, took the baby from my shoulders and handed him to the other woman. Then the second woman gestured to Eve and the children to follow her.

Au Wan intercepted my worried glance. "The children will be bathed and fed, then brought to you for your inspection, Aa." He used the Chinese term of endearment for *mother*.

As Chen Ho led me from the room, I glanced over my shoulder at the stoic-faced Chin Shui. "Do not worry," Chen Ho soothed as she led me into the guest room. "Au Wan will extend to the son of his neighboring peer all the proper courtesies afforded his father's position."

I smiled when I caught sight of the bathing pool recessed in the pink marble floor. *It's been so long*— I sighed, eager to submerge my tired body in the hot water.

"I will bring an appropriate garment for you to wear—" She glanced down at my heavy walking shoes. "—as well as whatever else will be necessary for your comfort." Chen Ho then held out her arm. "If you will shed your clothing, I will see that it is cleaned and pressed for your departure."

I stifled the urge to laugh as the gentle creature, a vision in delicate blues and lavenders, gathered my soiled and smelly clothing and exited the room.

After a bath and a shampoo, I felt like a new woman. I took time to nurse Taddy and comfort Beth before I slipped the royal blue satin dress over my still damp curls. Once I had pinned my hair into a chignon, Chen Ho fastened a lavender orchid along one side of it. "Ah, that is lovely?" She beamed with happiness.

"Yes, thank you." I slipped my feet into the satin-cord sandals and took a deep breath. "There, I think I'm ready to dine with the warlord."

Chen Ho giggled and handed me a fan with a mother-of-pearl handle. "You will need this. You are the first woman to dine at Au Wan's table. It is indeed an honor."

"The first?" My breath caught in my throat.

The woman bowed. "Au Wan is deeply grateful for all that you and your family did for his sister. He thinks you are a brave woman for saving the life of his compatriot's son, Dao Lin."

"I've done so little, really. Chin Shui is the one to be credited for leading us to safety."

"He will be rewarded." She gestured toward the door. "Come, Au Wan awaits you."

A Circle Within a Circle of Love

Dressed in our freshly laundered peasant clothes, Eve, Chin Shui, my mother, and I, along with the children, huddled beside the warlord's east gate in the early-morning chill. The night before, as we had dined on exotic dishes whose names I couldn't pronounce and whose contents I preferred not to identify, Au Wan had assured me, on the name of his beloved sister, that we would be granted safe passage to Hong Kong.

A moment after we heard the scuff of sandaled feet, twelve men carrying three sedan chairs emerged from the morning shadows. I laughed to myself. *Is this how we'll get to Hong Kong?*

Au Wan called to us from the balcony above our heads, "Travel in peace, my friend. May your God, Adams Tai-tai, deliver you safely to the arms of your husband. And, please, give him my regards. He is a learned and wise man."

"Thank you for your hospitality. I will remember you always, Au Wan, as a brother and a friend." I bowed.

He returned the bow. "My junk awaits you in the harbor. It is a seaworthy craft."

I thanked him again and bade him farewell before stepping into the sedan chair beside Beth and my mother, who held Taddy in her arms. The curtains dropped in place, hiding us from the outside world.

"That was an interesting encounter," Mama commented. "Au Sam's mother and I talked until almost dawn." My mother paused to swallow. "I saw Au Sam in her mother's every move. Before we said goodbye, she gave me this in exchange for two

243

photographs I brought with me and for her daughter's Bible." My mother handed me Au Sam's brooch. "Who knows what influence Au Sam's Bible will have on the lives of these people?"

Through misty eyes, I stared at the brooch in my hand. "When I gave it to the old woman, I never imagined seeing it again."

"You impressed her with your generosity. That's why she wants you to keep it, to remember her and her daughter fondly."

I slipped the brooch into the folds of my money belt.

"Now, how did your evening go with Au Wan?"

After I told Mama about my dinner with Au Sam's brother, we slipped into a pleasant silence as we jounced along on the shoulders of the carriers. Somewhere beyond the sedan chair's curtains, I could hear a rooster crowing.

At the harbor, we boarded the warlord's junk as quickly and inconspicuously as possible. A crew of four burly sailors set the sails as we settled ourselves in the trading vessel for the long journey to Shanghai, where we would board an oceangoing vessel to Hong Kong, passage paid for and guaranteed by Au Wan.

When we finally reached Hong Kong several days later, we found my father anxiously awaiting us. In Hong Kong I said goodbye to Dao Lin and to Chin Shui, who'd become my friend and my savior. They would stay with a friend of the mandarin until it was safe for them to return to northern China. I wondered whether any of the prayers the man and the child had heard us pray would one day bear fruit. And I praised God for people like Chin Shui and Au Wan, who, regardless of their religious beliefs, try to do what is right and good and honest.

Eve arranged for herself and Ana to stay at the mission board's regional headquarters. The president of the mission board offered to house me and my children, as well. I thanked him but declined. "Until I hear from Thaddeus, I'd prefer to stay with my parents." As a courtesy to my father, a former embassy employee, the American ambassador arranged for us to stay in one of the guest suites at the embassy. The ambassador, a tall man of slender build and thinning hair, leaned forward in his leather-upholstered desk chair. "I know your children need your attention at this time."

We could hear Taddy outside the office in the waiting room,

demanding his next meal.

The ambassador continued, "I would appreciate it, Mrs. Adams, if, in the morning, you could answer a few questions about the political situation in the northern provinces."

Then one of his aides took us up the polished wooden staircase to a second-floor suite. I paused in the doorway of the room furnished in European style and took a deep breath to inhale the fragrance from the bouquet on the table.

"A tray of food will be sent up to your suite in about half an hour." The aide tipped his head toward my father, a blend of the Western nod and the Eastern bow.

"That would be greatly appreciated, sir. Thank you."

While my parents bathed Beth, I bathed and changed the baby. Soon after Beth's bath, the food arrived. From the bedroom where I was nursing Taddy, I could hear Beth entertaining my father in the next room with her perspective of our hair-raising journey. I cringed at her description of being lost in the crowd with Gamma. "Mommy just kept walking. I called for her to come and get me, but she couldn't hear me."

Once Beth fell asleep, my father joined Mama and me in the parlor. "When I first learned of the Japanese invasion of the northern provinces, I immediately sailed north from Saigon and landed in Hong Kong. Here, I was told that travel north to Tientsin or Shanghai was restricted to all Americans." My mother put her head on his shoulder. "Well, I badgered every American and British official who had any contact with China for news."

Every few sentences, my father would reach out and touch Mama's hand, as if assuring himself she was safe. Watching that sweet gesture made me miss Thad all the more.

"But Thaddeus and Dr. Gibson." I tried to conceal my distress. "Have you heard anything from them? Anything at all?"

My father's eyes were filled with compassion. "Sorry, CeeCee. As of yesterday morning, none of the embassies knew much of anything about their fleeing countrymen in the north. Communication has been virtually cut off between here and there." His voice was edged with frustration. "I hated throwing the company's weight around, but sometimes, it's the only thing that works with government bureaucracies."

"It's surprising what one can do," my mother confessed, "when the lives of those you love might be at stake."

In a quiet voice, my father asked, "We've avoided the subject all evening, sweetheart, but have you thought about what you will do if—" He paused. "—if Thad never returns?"

I clenched and unclenched the muscles in my jaw. "He will be here. You'll see. He'll make it back safely."

"Your mother and I are booked to sail for the United States in a week." He glanced toward my mother.

She turned to face him. "I won't leave CeeCee alone in a foreign country with two children to care for!"

"I didn't mean to suggest— Perhaps she should—" he started.

"Daddy, don't even suggest that the children and I return to the States without Thad. Now, if you two will excuse me, with Taddy around, my day will begin much too early." I yawned and rose to my feet, kissed my parents good night, then padded to the bedroom the children and I would use.

Quietly, I turned on the small desk lamp and closed the bedroom door. Overwhelming love flooded through me as I gazed at Beth snuggled beneath the bedcovers. I peered over the edge of the bed at Taddy, who lay on a quilt in the space between the bed and the wall that I'd blocked off with pillows.

Before joining my daughter beneath the warm bedcovers, I found a Bible in the desk drawer and read a few passages of praise. Then I fell to my knees beside the bed and buried my face in the quilt. *I will praise You, Lord. You know where Thaddeus is at this very moment. I trust You to care for him and to magnify Your name through him.*

Although tired, I crossed the room to the small mahogany secretary, where I'd placed the journal I'd carried next to my body all the way from northern China. I seemed compelled to record our experience. Several pages later, I wrote, *And now, I must wait for Thad. In many ways, I think waiting will be more difficult than running.*

Finally, I put down my pen and padded over to the bed to get some sleep. When I awoke to nurse the baby, I found a continental-style breakfast with juice, pastries, and fruit waiting for us in the parlor. I bit into a cream-filled croissant and savored the filling. I thought of how many times I'd tasted the pastry and barely appreciated the flavor. *I'll never take food for granted again!*

During the previous few weeks, I'd experienced going to sleep hungry. I now knew what it was like to sacrifice one's own rations to ease the hunger pangs of one's child. I'd dreamed of tables abundant with food, only to awaken and find myself huddled in a hut, usually with only a little bread for the children.

By the time my parents awakened, the children and I had eaten and dressed in the new clothing my father had ordered for us the night before. *What embassy personnel spent the early morning shopping for this light gray silk dress?* I crossed the parlor's midnight blue carpet and knocked at my parents' bedroom door.

"Come in," my mother called.

I opened the door slowly.

She sat before the dressing table brushing her hair. "Don't worry. Your father's taking a bath."

"I need to report to the ambassador in a few minutes," I reminded. "Would you mind if I left the children with you?"

"Of course not!" My mother stood and tugged at the belt of her robe. "I love being with my grandchildren."

I turned to go. "Mama, please pray for Thad and for me."

She hurried to my side and gathered me into her arms. "I haven't stopped praying for either of you since this entire tragedy began. God is a good God who loves you very much. Remember, God's 'strength is made perfect in weakness.'"

"Thanks, Mama. I love you so much." Eyes brimming with tears, I slipped out of her arms and headed for the parlor door. *I won't cry. I won't cry.*

At the door I blew Beth a kiss, then hurried down the stairs to the ambassador's office. There, I chose a chair that faced the floor-to-ceiling window behind his desk. The ambassador, along with two aides who joined him for the debriefing, questioned me for more than two hours. Besides the military unrest in northern China, they found my relationship with Mandarin Ho Feng most interesting. When I mentioned that Ho Feng converted to Christianity, they exchanged looks of cynical disbelief.

Finally, at the bottom of their list of questions, the ambassador asked what my plans were now that I'd made it safely to Hong Kong.

I looked at him in surprise. "Find my husband."

"And if you don't find him right away?" The man pursed his lips thoughtfully.

"I'll search until I do."

The ambassador stood and began to pace behind his desk. Gravely, he expressed his doubts for Thad's and Dr. Gibson's safety. "I don't need to tell you that the news out of the north hasn't been good. Reports have told of severe fighting throughout the region and of many Occidentals being taken prisoner, with all that entails."

My attention wandered to the limousine that had just pulled up in front of the embassy.

"And who knows how many— Mrs. Adams?"

"Oh, excuse me, sir." I craned my neck to watch a chauffeur get out of the car, open the rear door, and assist a man on crutches from the back seat.

"Thad! That's Thad!" I leapt to my feet. The ambassador and his aides stared as I dashed from the room. As I crossed the lobby's polished parquet floor toward the entrance, the doorman jumped from behind his desk to open the door.

The door swung open just as the chauffeur pressed the doorbell. I skidded to a stop less than six inches from Thad's startled face. Sobbing with joy, I hurled myself into his arms, causing him to lose his balance. Fortunately, the chauffeur grabbed Thad's arm in time to keep us from tumbling down the steps.

"Oh, darling, it's you. It's really you! What happened? Are you all right? I was afraid you had been killed." I stopped babbling long enough to plant an enthusiastic kiss on his lips, then resumed my flood of questions.

"Wait, wait." Thad struggled to hug me while maintaining his balance on crutches. I was oblivious to the ambassador and a large number of embassy staff standing behind me. All I could see was my husband—and he was alive!

"You've been hurt. Is your leg broken? Dr. Gibson, is he all right? I've been so worried," I hiccuped through my tears.

"Honey, sh. I'm all right. Yes, my leg was broken during an interrogation session. Yes, I missed you and the children terribly. And, yes, Dr. Gibson is fine. He has a lot of bruises plus a couple of broken ribs, but he's all right."

"Thank God. I've been so worried. I didn't want to leave the mission without you, but Ho Feng insisted." My words came rapidly. "Ho Feng said you'd been captured."

"Dr. Gibson and I escaped with the help of two of the mandarin's men, whom he sent to infiltrate the camp. We didn't learn of Mr. Lin's death until we got back to the clinic. Mr. Lin refused to deny that he was a Christian." Thad's voice broke. "God's people are suffering severely for their faith. I predict that it's going to be a long and bloody struggle for them. Ho Feng sent his family and servants away to his mountain retreat, but he himself stayed behind to help maintain order in the region."

Thad laughed gently as he brushed one hand over my hair. "Now, I refuse to answer another question until you allow me to enter the building, woman. Besides, I have hundreds of questions for you, like, How are the children? Are they safe?"

"Yes, dear, they're upstairs with my parents. Beth asked for her daddy at least fifty times a day throughout the entire journey."

"Oh, that must have been pleasant." Thad laughed.

The ambassador stepped forward, extending his hand. "Mr. Adams, it is so good to see you. Your wife refused to believe you might not make it. When you are rested, I would appreciate a full report on your ordeal and any information on the unrest in northern China that you can give."

Thad balanced on his crutches in order to shake the man's hand. "I will be glad to tell you everything I know. My friend, Dr. Gibson, is reporting to the British Embassy as we speak." He gestured toward the uniformed chauffeur. "They kindly supplied me with a car and chauffeur. Thank you, Carlton. I'm in good hands now."

The chauffeur snapped off a proper bow before returning to his limousine.

Thad stepped forward and winced, favoring his injured leg.

"Johnson!" the ambassador called, to one of the aides lingering nearby. "Please call the embassy physician. I want a full examination and report of this man's injuries."

The man named Johnson clicked his heels together. "Yes, sir."

"Phinney! Direct Mr. and Mrs. Adams to the elevator. Maneuvering up the staircase on crutches is difficult."

Another eager young man stepped forward. "Yes, sir. Right this way, ma'am, sir."

Thad's reunion with my parents and the children, especially Beth, brought tears to my eyes. Once the little girl lodged herself on his lap, she refused to budge. While the adults talked, catching up on the events, Beth continued to run her tiny hand over his jacket and purr, "Daddy, nice Daddy."

When the staff physician arrived to examine Thad, I slipped into my parents' room to nurse Taddy. My mother came in by herself while he was nursing. "Where's Beth?"

"Playing giddyap with her grandpa."

I smiled, remembering how much I'd enjoyed riding my father's foot when I was her age. Mama offered to take the children to a nearby park to play so Thad and I could spend a few minutes alone.

"If you think you can convince Beth to leave her father."

"Oh, she's already excited about the ice-cream cone your father has promised her." Mama changed into a pair of walking shoes. "Have you spoken to the ambassador regarding her adoption?"

"No!" I inhaled sharply. "I can't believe I forgot such an important thing!"

"I wouldn't wait too long, if I were you."

"You're right. I'll have Thad take care of it immediately."

Over the next few days, I learned that nothing is immediate when it comes to government red tape. If it hadn't been for my father's connections in Washington, Elizabeth's adoption would have taken us months to complete.

Before too many weeks, it became obvious that none of us would be returning to the mountain clinic in the near future, because the political situation remained too unstable. The mission board assigned the Gibsons to a clinic in Malaysia. Saying goodbye to Eve was difficult. "Write often," she pleaded as we clung together.

"I will. And if you ever come to the States for your furlough, you have a home in San Francisco, do you understand?"

She nodded, slowly releasing me.

Thad and the doctor shook hands, their eyes glassy with tears. I turned awkwardly toward the doctor. We'd never fully worked out our differences.

"Nurse Adams—" He cleared his throat, and his eyes softened. "CeeCee, you are the best head nurse with whom I ever worked."

"But I thought you didn't—"

"I know I didn't make it easy for you." He grinned. "If the truth be known, you were a threat to me, especially after you established a friendship with the mandarin. I resented that, and I apologize." He swallowed. "It was your friendship with Ho Feng that saved my life—and I am grateful. By the way, tell that mother of yours that she can work in my clinic any day."

In the week that followed, Thad and I talked for hours regarding our future as missionaries. We prayed together and asked for God's guidance. A part of me wanted to stay in the Far East. There were so many people and so much to do. Yet I refused to think of the day I would say goodbye to my parents and watch them sail away for America. The embassy doctor solved our dilemma. He discovered that Thad had contracted a lung infection while in the prison camp. The mission board conferred with the doctor. We would sail home with my parents on the HMS *Westchester*.

We boarded the ship in the late afternoon. Our accommodations aboard the *Westchester* proved far more luxurious than those on the *City of Tokyo*. The dinner dresses and the other clothing my mother and I bought before leaving Hong Kong would be needed for the type of life we could expect aboard the sleek luxury liner.

Thad and I huddled together at the railing to share our last glimpses of Asia as the tugboats eased the graceful ship out of the harbor. My parents stood apart from us, holding our children in their arms. Considered to be one of the most beautiful harbors in the world, the Hong Kong harbor contained the paradox of the Orient for me that day—traditional values conflicting with the modern. Our ship glided past Chinese junks with their picturesque sails, past spick-and-span British navy vessels, past fragile sampans, and past chunky freighters.

"What will happen, Thad, to all our friends? Were our efforts to share God's love with them all in vain?" I rested my head against his shoulder.

"Oh no. God will bring the seed we've sown to fruition one day. You'll see." I glanced over Thad's shoulder at my mother, holding her grandson in her arms and gazing across the bay at the Kowloon hills, the "nine dragons" of Hong Kong.

"Who would have thought that you and I would be the means God would use to fulfill the desires of Mama's heart?"

"A desire that could have cost her life," Thad added.

"But a dream she would never have sacrificed for all the comforts of Russian Hill."

Thad looked down at me with love-filled eyes. "And what about you? If you'd known all the risks you were taking when you followed me to China, would you have come?"

"Followed? I didn't follow you! We stood side by side all the way."

He chuckled. "That's not what I asked. Do you have any regrets?"

"No! No regrets. If anything, I feel an overwhelming gratitude for the way God used us to touch so many lives and for the rich memories I will always cherish." I took a deep breath of tangy sea air. "Another gift China gave me, besides Elizabeth, of course, is my mother. You know, I never before truly appreciated her for the delightful and resourceful woman she is."

Thad laughed and kissed the tip of my nose. "How did you become such an incredible woman?"

I glanced over his shoulder at my mother and winked. "It's in the genes."

Thad's face darkened. "The doctor said this lung infection could worsen."

"I know."

Thad shuddered and tightened his hold on me. "I wish I knew where God was leading us from here."

"What?" I smiled up into his questioning eyes. "And spoil life's greatest adventures?"

"You are incorrigible, woman."

I snuggled against his chest. "Just the kind of woman you deserve."

That evening as I prepared for bed, I wrote in my journal. *Today, I left a piece of my heart in the highlands of China. All along the way, I can see God's hand guiding Thad and me. Like the brass rings the circus magician links with other hoops, then miraculously separates, the circles of love that have filled my life repeatedly intertwine with the lives of those around me—circle with circle, loop with loop. I gazed across the room at my snoring husband. Putting my pen to the paper once more, I continued. Who would imagine that a grandfather's twenty-dollar gold piece and a Pennsylvania teenager's dream could lead to the conversion of an Asian despot's heart? Who would guess that a girl stolen from her family could, after her death, unite all the people she loved? Truly, "All things work together for good to them that love God, to them who are the called according to his purpose."*

Taddy whimpered in his sleep. I reached over the bars of the crib and patted him gently. As he settled back to sleep, I studied the shape of his tiny head and the gentle wisps of red hair curling at the base of his neck. *Lord, with all the traits we pass on to our children, why must each generation have to learn for themselves to trust You and to follow Your leading? How I wish I could see where You will lead my precious son. How much better I could guide him, if only I knew.*

A playful voice from deep within my heart spoke. I could almost see the mischievous twinkle in my grandfather's eyes. *What? And spoil life's greatest adventures?*